[ERROR] TITLE NOT FOUND

Ellen Taylor

Contents

Map   VI

                                             VII

1. Chapter Title Not Found   1

2. Chapter Title Not Found   11

3. Chapter Title Not Found   18

4. Chapter Title Not Found   27

5. Chapter Title Not Found   35

6. Chapter Title Not Found   43

7. Chapter Title Not Found   50

8. Chapter Title Not Found   57

9. Chapter Title Not Found   63

10. Chapter Title Not Found   70

11. Chapter Title Not Found   78

12. Chapter Title Not Found   86

13. Chapter Title Not Found   92

14. Chapter Title Not Found — 100

15. Chapter Title Not Found — 108

16. Chapter Title Not Found — 116

17. Rebooting Chapter Title Function, Please Hold — 124

18. In Which I Use Flashbacks to Further Pad My Story, Keeping it Out of Reach of the Stupid Rogue Narrator. Oh, Wait, Do Chapter Titles Count Toward the Overall Word Count? — 134

19. God in the Machine — 149

20. We Try at Peace — 158

21. The Device Summarizes Everything Too Masterfully — 168

22. Capturing the Essence of Childhood — 176

23. A Discussion Full of Words — 187

24. We Prep for a Wedding! — 196

25. Grace Keeps Going — 203

26. The Wedding — 212

27. Celebrations — 219

28. Professor Andrews Adds Party Crasher to His List of Crimes — 228

29. Tara Shows Off What She's Learned — 236

30. Professor Andrews Reveals He Has No Humanity Left — 244

31. Professor Andrews Keeps Threatening Me   252

32. Paldric and Alwin Revisit Aspects of the Original Outline   260

33. We Take Care of Roger   266

34. My Plan Is Revealed   273

35. The Shield Closes   280

36. We Wrap Up the Trilogy   286

Epilogue: Do Epilogues Have Chapter Titles?   289

Acknowledgements   296

About the Author   297

Also By   298

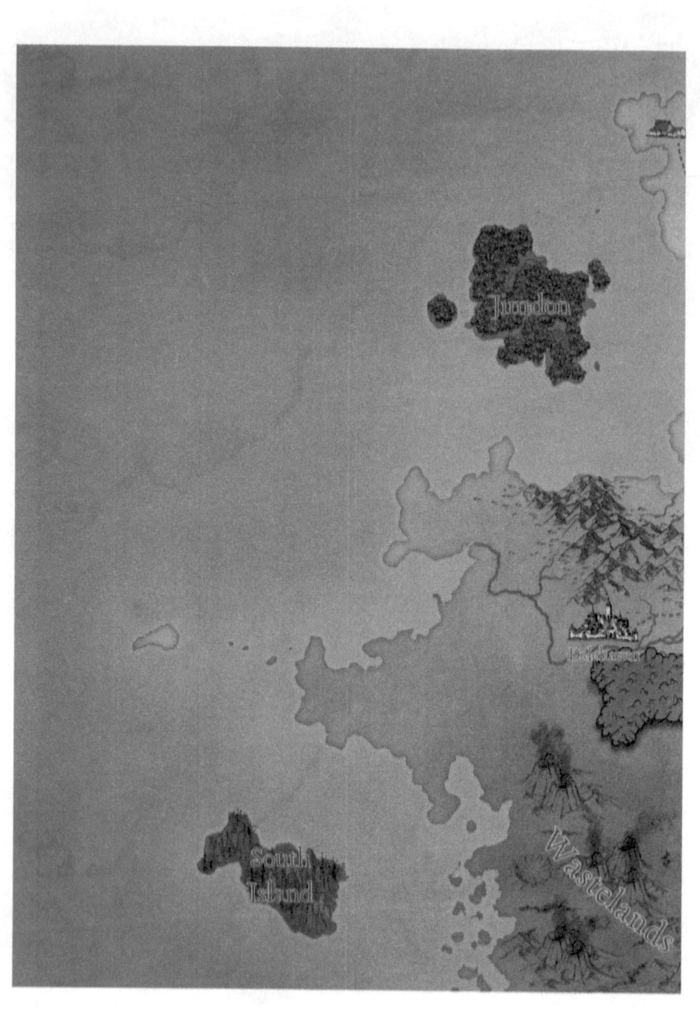

Jungleon
South Island
Wastelands

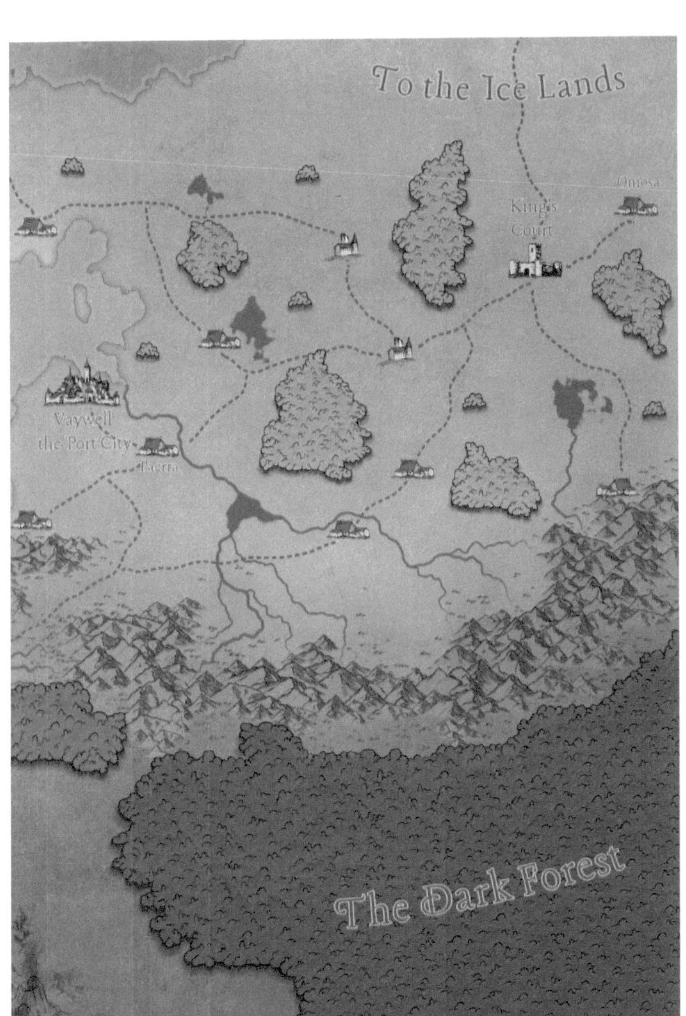

To the Ice Lands
Oniosa
King's Court
Vaywell
the Port City
Faerra
The Dark Forest

Chapter One

CHAPTER TITLE NOT FOUND

The early sunlight hit my face, enticing me to wake up. I took a deep breath of fresh air before opening my eyes to see a glorious sunrise full of reds and golds. My hand slid underneath my sack of feathers that I used as a makeshift pillow, blinking as my eyes got used to the light while also marveling at the sunrise before me. Despite the long list of chores that demanded my attention, I spent a good minute or two appreciating a beautiful sky.

However, I couldn't ignore my to-do list for long. My feet slid off the bed as I straightened and rubbed my face. I got up and left the small hut that was already here when I arrived, but I ignored that fact just as quickly as when it came. Don't think about before, my brain seemed to tell me as I took another deep breath. Don't think about when you arrived, it said as I grabbed the lantern hanging near the firepit. There is only here and now.

It wouldn't rain today. I didn't understand how I was so certain. Possibly because I was never wrong before. My knees groaned as I eased myself down toward the burnt out firepit. What did I do to my knees? Probably age, except I didn't know how old I was. No fear came at this revelation. It was simply how things were, and I accepted it.

Once I stocked the fire with new wood, I used a stick and lit it on the edge of my lantern before setting it near some kindling. I breathed life into the flames, watching them burn through the kindling on its way to igniting the logs.

The morning sun started its daily climb when I walked over to my little chicken coop. There were four chickens in there. I grabbed the bucket and dumped some corn husks on the ground. The four chickens were likely to eat each other if I didn't give them enough. I also dumped out the scrap bucket from my soup I made last night, and they pecked away as I walked into their small, makeshift coop I built for them. I learned to gather eggs while the chickens were distracted with their own food.

They all laid an egg, which was nice. For a while, I was only getting three. I didn't want to figure out if they were just taking turns not laying. Eventually, they would get old enough to stop producing eggs. That meant I could kill them for their meat, but I would wait until they died of old age. I wasn't in the mood to kill. I may not remember anything since appearing on this island, but the disgust at killing remained.

I walked over again to my hut to grab the shield leaning against it and the kettle hanging from a hook. The shield had a blue-gray mist I didn't understand, but it was the best instrument I've ever cooked on. Whatever that mist was, it must be magical because it cooked the best omelets. I placed the shield on the wooden sticks to keep it from going straight into the fire before filling the kettle with water from the stream near my hut. I situated the kettle on the shield so the water inside could start heating.

Once the shield and the kettle were in place, I picked up my eggs again and walked carefully to the running stream. The eggs weren't too messy today, but I still cleaned them off as best I could before delicately placing them near the fire. I straightened, checking on the sleeping girl in my hut before going out to my garden. The onion was stubborn this morning, but I managed to pull it up. I brushed it off, monitoring the fire before picking a bell pepper and a huge tomato. I rinsed them all off before returning to my hut, grabbing the sword that also had the blue-gray mist coming from it. If the shield was magical, the sword definitely was. I never cut myself once on this thing, and that was even after a deliberate experiment.

Resting on my small stool, I chopped the vegetables on my little table as best I could, leaving the onion for last. Cutting onions is the worst.

I grabbed a clay bowl and plate, piling my diced vegetables in the bowl before walking back outside and sitting beside the fire. It had died down, but still incredibly hot. The water was already bubbling, but I needed it to be boiling. I broke open the eggs, mixing them into the veggies. I took my container of avocado oil, spreading it over the shield before pouring the egg mixture on it, listening to it sizzle. My grinder and roasted coffee beans were just inside the hut, so I didn't have to take my eyes off the fire once. I'd have to roast more tonight, which meant I'd have to pick more today, but that was alright. It was the perfect day for it. It wouldn't rain, so I'd leave the pits out to dry.

A nutty aroma filled the tiny space as I grounded up the last of the roasted coffee beans. The granules spilled into my mug before I flipped my omelet over. I used a crocheted hot pad and picked up the kettle, carefully pouring the now boiling liquid into my mug before setting it aside.

I ran my hand through my brown hair, waiting for the other side of the omelet to cook, mentally going through the list of things I needed to do today. Pick coffee cherries, check on the sheep and goats, go over my garden to make sure nothing is getting too ripe. Roast some of my already dried coffee beans to keep up my supply. Wait for the moon to rise before gathering plants and herbs to help the little girl in my hut.

My omelet slid onto my clay plate before I grabbed my mug. I poured the coffee into another mug, straining the bigger bits out with a thin cloth before taking a sip. Still hot, but coffee existed here.

Using sand, I put out my fire before inhaling my breakfast, listening to the birds and other animals. This island wasn't too big. It took me three hours to walk the entire length of it. No one else lives here but me and the animals. And, of course, the little girl sleeping in my hut. The island was beautiful, and I didn't mind living the simple life.

It was a little past lunch when I returned to my hut with a large sack of coffee cherries. I spent longer than I thought picking them. When I checked my unroasted supply, it was frightfully low. Getting low on supplies always made me anxious. I grabbed my large pestle and mortar, grinding up the cherries before fishing out the pits and placing them on a large sheet. The chickens were going to enjoy the cherry skins.

I popped a few of the pitted cherries in my mouth to keep me fed. The hottest part of the day was ahead, and I wanted the pits to dry soon. I didn't have an issue skipping lunch. A four-egg omelet kept me full for a while.

Once my fingers brushed the bottom of my basket, the cherries were already quite squished from the weight of the ones on top. Pulling out the pits was easier as I finished filling the rest of the sheet.

My body groaned as I stood up and did some stretches before checking on my garden. On the way, I scattered a couple handfuls of cherries to my chickens. I worked on the weeds, making sure they were gone. Yesterday it rained, so I wasn't too worried about watering my garden.

I checked on the little girl in my hut one last time before taking a trip to the small pond. The heat was oppressive today, and I needed to wash off.

Once my clothes were off, I slipped into the pool. The lukewarm water was pleasant. I spent a little longer relaxing, mentally going through my to-do list again as I scrubbed my feet. I didn't have any shoes. Not that I needed them. My soles had tough callouses, and I couldn't see a reason to wear them even if I had them. I gave my clothes a good wash, too. They were starting to smell.

I dried off by walking down to see the sheep and goats happily munching on the grass on the other side of the island. I recently shaved the sheep. The makeshift fence I put up was enough for them not to come to my side and destroy my garden, so I was happy.

The next on the list was visiting my small orchard. I plucked a few avocados before getting two healthy mangos from another tree. Honestly, this place was paradise. There couldn't be a better island to appear on, especially with no memories.

Back at the pond, I gathered my still wet clothes before returning to my hut. The little girl was still fast asleep, but I wrapped my blanket around my lower waist before checking on her. I stepped out to check the pits of the coffee cherries. They'd be dry enough to store away. I'd have to roast my other supply. It wouldn't rain tonight.

Another fire flickered to life as I prepared for dinner. I draped my wet clothes over a few sticks near the fire, but not too nearby. Once again, I pulled out the shield, placing it on the sticks over the fire before turning to my large sack of corn flour. I made a lot the other day, and it would last me a while. Which was fine by me. It took over two days to grind all that dried corn with my coffee grinder, and my arms still felt a slight pinch of soreness. But now I wouldn't have to worry about making flour for months.

I grabbed my clay bowl and scooped in some corn flour and a pinch of salt. Gradually I poured in some of my now cold but sanitized water to make a dough. The fire warmed me and dried my clothes while I kneaded the dough. The sun dipped below the horizon. Once I finished kneading the dough, I placed it near the fire to pick some more vegetables from my garden. A lot of the bell peppers were getting ripe, and I needed to use as many as I could handle.

Dicing the bell peppers, tomatoes, and carrots was easy. The onion was tougher, but I managed. I tossed them all on one side of the shield and pushed them around using my wooden spoon. They sizzled in the avocado oil. I placed the spoon in my mouth while I grabbed the dough, broke it in half, and flattened them into round disks. I tried making them even. It was a skill I'd gotten pretty good at.

Both tortillas sizzled as they landed on the shield, and I barely gave it time to brown before turning them over. My spoon was back to mixing the veggies again.

The huge avocado squelched open beneath the sword. I eased both tortillas on my plate, spreading a healthy amount of avocado on them before scooping the sauteed veggies on there. By now, the sun had set, and the moon and stars were the only light from the heavens hitting my island. I walked around to my herb garden, grabbing some lavender and aloe that had been baking in the moonlight the past few days before once again grabbing my mortar and pestle. I mashed the herbs together, making a fine paste before spreading it over one tortilla.

I folded my blanket up before climbing into my now drier clothes. I ran a hand through my hair before picking up the plate of two tortillas and the mortar and pestle, entering the hut toward the sleeping little girl.

The makeshift bed groaned as I sat down next to her, placing the plate of tortillas on my lap before taking some of the lavender and aloe goo and spreading it across her bottom lip. It only took a moment, but her brown eyes fluttered open. She reached out, and I helped her sit up. Her hands immediately found the tortilla with the added herbs, and she wolfed it down. I couldn't predict if she wanted mine as well, but it looked as though tonight she was ravenous for another. I didn't stop her when she reached for mine, and she ate it at a slower pace. She wasn't entirely conscious of herself being here. I didn't know how I understood her thoughts, but I did. She drained the huge mug of water, her eyes glazed over. Once she finished, she wiped her mouth with the back of her hand and eased herself to the bed, pulling the blanket I made for her closer. Her sandy blonde hair fell across her cheek.

"Three hundred and sixty-four percent." She said it like she was talking in her sleep.

I smiled to myself, relieved as I made another notch on the wall over her bed to mark the end of another day. I, of course, didn't know what the number meant. However, something in the recesses of my forgotten mind told me that if I could get lower than one hundred, my memories would return. More importantly, I would know what to do. The first month on the island, this little girl kept saying nine hundred and ninety-nine percent before falling asleep. I didn't know what to think. But now, a good six months later, it's gotten more manageable. Just this past week alone, I dropped five percent.

The two mangos tasted delicious, but after cooking those tortillas, I craved one. I went through the process of making a small dinner for myself again. I didn't mind. That little girl needed to be fed. This little girl's life was everything to me, even though I didn't remember why.

My fingers found the last of the fried veggies, and I licked them off. It was getting late. However, I still stuck another log on the fire before getting my dried coffee beans. I wanted to do a couple of days' worth, just to be prepared.

The greenish beans tumbled onto the shield, and I smelled the smoke coming off. Not nearly as pleasant as the drink itself. I grabbed my spoon and stirred them constantly, listening for a cracking sound. I glanced up at the star covered sky, allowing myself just a moment to wonder how I got here. To probe my brain about how I woke up on an island, clutching a little girl and sobbing like she was dead. Vague clues flickered in and out. I saved her life multiple times. I am the reason she's an orphan. All of this seemed so important for me to remember, but even recalling my violent sobs six months ago, a soothing part of my brain told me not to worry about it.

So I didn't. There was no point worrying about it, anyway. Once I got below one hundred percent, I would remember.

It didn't take long for the beans to crack. Once I heard another crack, I scooped the shield up with a hot pad, which instantly turned cold once it was away from the fire. Honestly, it was magical. I moved the beans around to help them cool down before spreading them out again on the sheet.

It had been a long day, and I was exhausted, but I got a lot of things done. I doused the fire with water before entering my hut again. I was getting low on firewood. That would have to be on tomorrow's to-do list. I couldn't last long without firewood.

I tried to do the math in my head, but I wasn't the best at it. The percentage drop was erratic at times. Sometimes I'd drop five percent in a week like this week, and sometimes I wouldn't drop at all. The first few months were rough, but once I gave in to a more simplistic lifestyle, the numbers dropped like crazy, so that must have been the secret. I honestly didn't mind it. Even if I got my memories back, I could see myself staying here for a very long time.

Chapter Two

CHAPTER TITLE NOT FOUND

T he morning wind picked up as the sun peeked over the horizon. I opened my eyes. It would rain later today, I could tell. I needed to get some chores done before the rain came.

My crocheted blanket fell off as I climbed out of bed. I settled into my routine, making my breakfast, running through my mental chore list. Once the rain hit, there was plenty to do in my hut. I drank my coffee as I glanced up at the sky, watching the dark clouds on the horizon. It would be a downpour.

I gathered up the dried coffee pits and brought them inside the hut. There were plenty of projects to work on while inside, but the rain was still hours away. There were more projects outside the hut than inside. I double checked that the chickens, sheep, and goats were fine. I kept track of the felled trees for potential firewood later. They'd be soaking with rain, but I had enough logs to last until they dried. Besides, already felled tree logs were easier to burn.

Light rain pattered on the leaves by the time my hut came into view. The light rain turned harder, and I ran inside, slicking my hair back. I used my blanket to dry off a little before gathering the wool I sheared from the sheep. Through the entire process of sheering, washing, and carding, I got a little adventurous and tried dying some. The yellow came off too bright, but I was proud of myself for trying.

As the rain beat against the roof, I took my drop spindle and grabbed a small bundle of fiber, placing it on the hook. I spun it, watching as the fibers turned into thread. It was methodical. The rain pounded on my hut and the little girl slept on as I spun the wool into yarn.

The work was monotonous, and even though I slept well, something about the rhythmic rainfall tempted me to sleep. Having someone else asleep in the hut didn't help, either. I fought it, as I hoped to get the rest of the wool spun into a ball. It would free up a lot of space in my hut. As my eyes closed, I realized this was a losing battle.

She paced the room, wringing her hands as she tried not to cry. They had taken Roger ages ago upstairs, and not knowing when he would return was driving her out of her mind. He might be upstairs, but she couldn't tell.

The cell house having a basement was a new discovery when the cursed creatures dragged them here a few weeks ago. They threw her and Roger into the basement because the cells above were full. Now the cells were empty, as one by one, the Dark Wizard dragged her friends away. Tortured, altered, changed so that those who believed the strongest in Veniloria's freedom were now the loudest to sing praises to the Dark Wizard. Despite the empty cells above, she and Roger remained below. She played with a lock of her brown hair, her blue eyes searching, waiting.

The cellar door was pulled back. Men who once sat in this cell now dragged Roger down the stairs. They didn't get far before pushing him the rest of the way. He landed with a thud, softly groaning as he untangled himself, his long black hair matted. Her heart hammered as she rushed over to him.

"Are you..."

"Fine." He glanced at the men walking out of the basement. "I'm fine."

The door slid back into place, and she allowed herself a moment of relief. Then she scanned Roger with her healer's gaze. Her dear friend was the one to hide injuries from her.

Though he didn't look at her, he clearly felt the gaze. "I'm fine," he said again.

"No, you're not." She reached over, touching his cheek. "Your eye is swollen."

The crushing weight of realization burned her soul, making relief flee. Everyone, eventually, had been tortured to serve the Dark Wizard. She didn't know what that evil man said to the people, but it convinced them. Once Roger turned, she would be next.

"Did you see Paldric at all? Did you find evidence he's truly dead?" she asked.

He shook his head. "They only took me upstairs."

She placed her frozen fingers against her burning cheeks. "What if... what if he's..."

"Don't. Don't go there."

She nodded, her chilly hands not enough to stop the tears from forming. He wrapped his arms around her as she kept the sob inside. There was still hope. There had to be.

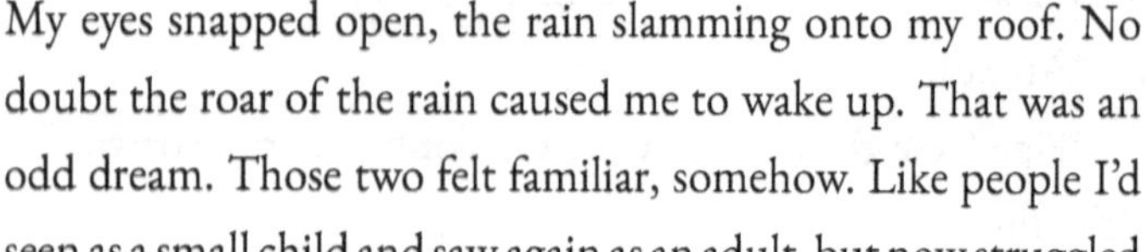

My eyes snapped open, the rain slamming onto my roof. No doubt the roar of the rain caused me to wake up. That was an odd dream. Those two felt familiar, somehow. Like people I'd seen as a small child and saw again as an adult, but now struggled to place their names. But they meant something to me.

The calming part of my brain returned, assuring me to not worry about it. Despite the distress the two of them were in, it probably wasn't real. It was a dream, after all. When have dreams been real?

The rainfall lasted a while, enough for me to go through and spin the rest of my wool, completing my task of making a nice ball of yarn from it. It freed up a lot of space in my hut, just as I hoped.

The downpour turned into a trickle as I ventured outside. It was a little past lunch, and the rain made it more humid. I grabbed the sword, heading toward the felled trees. I chopped a tree into manageable logs as the sun came out from behind rain clouds. There was never relief to the humidity. It felt muggy, like a shower. Though I wasn't entirely positive I knew what a shower was.

The logs were heavy in my arms as I returned to my hut. I spread them out to optimize the sunlight tomorrow morning. It was a no-fire dinner tonight. My knees didn't groan as much as I gathered some lettuce, tomatoes, and a few more bell peppers than usual from my garden. I then walked out to the avocado tree to pick another for my salad.

Dinner was peaceful as I waited for the sun to set before I got my report from the little girl. True, the moon was already in the sky, but it made the herbs more potent when I picked them after the sun was gone.

Darkness filled the sky, and I got my herbs, mashing the goo and placing it on the lips of the little girl. She ate her salad and reported I was still the same. Three hundred and sixty-four. That was fine. As long as it never went up.

I gathered my freshly made ball of yarn and pulled out my crochet needle before going to work, starting another blanket. Maybe I should've crocheted something useful, because I barely needed the blankets I have now. However, I enjoyed this time to create something, even if it was pointless. Maybe next year I'd try an equally pointless sweater when I cut the wool off the sheep again. Would I still be here?

The distress in the woman's face returned, enough for my heart to skitter. They were in danger.

No, they weren't. It was just a dream.

It was fully dark, but I continued to crochet my blanket. I stuck the needle in the hole, looping the wool over it before threading it through, repeating the process. After measuring the long strip against my body, I put in another line. A few hours of crocheting always caused a nice dip in the numbers.

Despite the nap, my eyes grew heavy, and I needed sleep. I placed my project to the side before making the final preparations. I double checked my fire, even though I had only lit it at breakfast before the downfall. One could never be too careful with fire. Insects chirped as I checked on the chickens nestled in their boxes for the night.

I settled on my makeshift bed, pulling blankets around me, hearing the girl sleeping on the other side of the hut. A part of me knew this situation was impossible. The little girl was in a coma, and shouldn't wake up and move like she did, limited as it was. Being like this should've deteriorated her muscles to where she couldn't move. And yet she was alive. Some mystical thing must be at play here. Was it something I did? Maybe it was. All I knew was the little girl shouldn't be alive after doing this for six months.

The other part of me knew it made sense. There were two pieces of me, both with different logic systems. Something about this place had its own logic, therefore the little girl would survive.

The other place? I didn't know. My brain refused to let me remember.

"Milla. Your name is Milla."

How did I know that? Oh, well. It doesn't matter. At least one of us knew their name now.

Chapter Three

CHAPTER TITLE NOT FOUND

As I hoped, my crochet project helped get me down to three hundred and sixty-three percent. Nothing interesting happened the next few days, even though my mind kept returning to that strange dream during my nap. Dreams usually melded into my subconscious and I forgot about them not long after. This one lingered.

I used the afternoon to cut huge logs into manageable firewood. The sword was thinner than an axe, but it worked exceptionally well.

Despite my brain begging me to give it up, I thought about the dream. Dreams were supposed to have pointless plots with ridiculous motivation. This one didn't have either. Sure, the one guy had a black eye, and they talked about the imminent doom of brainwashing, but that was the plot. Good thing dreams aren't real. It was from the view of the girl. I understood her internal thoughts, which should've been odd, but it seemed familiar.

I grabbed another large log, bringing it to my cutting stump. The log took a minute to situate, then I got the sword ready. Before I could swing, something whacked my shoulder. It didn't hurt, but it was a nuisance. I frowned, turning to see an arrow rolling on the ground. I crouched, reaching for it, when another whacked me between the eyes.

"Ow!"

My fingers rubbed the place the second arrow hit as I looked up, only to see another arrow whack my eye. I let out a scream, certain the arrow was sticking out of my face. I tried to scramble to my feet. An intruder was on this island, and I needed to save Milla.

But I wasn't quick enough. Or the man was insanely fast. Possibly a combination of both. The intruder tackled me to the ground and my face hit the dirt. The man tied my hands behind me.

"Who are you! What is this? Stop it, I mean you no harm!" I said.

"There is no way I believe that. Not after what you did," the man said.

I struggled with the bonds to make it difficult for him to tie, but he had already finished. "What do you mean? What are you talking about? Who are you?"

The man grabbed a fistful of my hair, pulling me up enough to place the blue-gray sword against my throat. His voice was seething. "Believe me, I would not come to you unless it was necessary."

I tried to remain calm, but also made sure this crazy man didn't realize there was a defenseless little girl in the hut. "I don't want to dampen your spirits, good sir, but the sword is magical. It doesn't cut flesh. It only works on things like trees and vegetables."

The man paused, then slowly stood up. I remained on the ground, studying his green eyes. They were the color of a forest, but how could that be possible? His brown hair was longer than usual. "Do you know who I am?" the man asked.

A frown crossed my face as I looked at him. "Should I?"

The man raised an eyebrow, studying me. "Don't lie, Gunther."

His words confused me. "Gunther? Is that me? Is that my name?"

The man pointed the sword at me, not as menacingly but still weary. "What did you do to yourself?" I tried to get up, but he took another step forward with the sword. "Answer the question, and if I like the answer, I'll untie you."

I sighed. "I told you, it's pointless. The sword doesn't hurt me."

The man narrowed his eyes, then kicked my face. I let out a surprised grunt that caused dirt to get in my mouth. I sputtered, terrified of what this insane person could do. He couldn't find out about Milla.

"Just checking," the man said, like he wasn't a psychopath.

"Checking what?" I asked, trying to keep him distracted. He waited, expecting me to do something, but I didn't know what. "Please, just take whatever you want on my island. I won't fight back. Take it and leave." Hopefully, he could untie me, and then I'd hide Milla.

Blood trickled down my face from where he kicked me. I frowned as the man continued to watch me with a level of mistrust I'd never seen in him. Wait, *had* I seen him before? My eyes narrowed, saw his forest green eyes and brown hair. "Alwin." I said it slowly and deliberate. "Your name is Alwin."

The man continued to hold the sword steady, the anger unnaturally clear on his face. "Yes, that's my name. Do you remember what you did to Veniloria? To Paldric?"

My frown deepened. "Paldric?" It was odd to hear this man say the name of someone I had only heard in my dream. My brain once again soothed me into believing it was just a dream, but this was odd, contradicting evidence. "How do you know Paldric?"

"Tell me what *you* know of him," Alwin ordered.

Although the sword was harmless, his feet were not to be messed with. "I don't. I just had a dream about him the other night."

A flicker of hope crossed Alwin's face. "You saw Paldric? Is he alive?"

"Alive? I don't... there were two people in my dream. One was a woman, I don't know her name, the other was... Roger? I think she called him Roger. They talked about Paldric."

Alwin held impossibly still, the blade pointed right at my face. "You saw Tara and Roger? Where are they?"

"Below the cell house somewhere. That's all I could decipher. I don't... I don't know where. It was just a dream, I swear. It's not even real."

The emotions that were clear on his face now disappeared. Yet he was feeling everything. Despair, hope, fear, and worry, mostly.

Alwin sheathed the sword, though I realized that was my sword he put in there, and yet he had the sheath for it. He was going to take the sword with him. Which meant I'd have to find another way to cut things. It should be fine. Another more laborious endeavor, but I would do anything to make sure he got off my island without Milla.

"Listen, Gunther, I need your help," Alwin said.

"And why should I help you?"

Alwin looked confused, then finally noticed the blood dripping down my face. He sighed. "I'm sorry. I had to check how much invulnerability you had."

"Invulnerability? What?" I felt confused. Alwin winced, almost embarrassed... no, terrified about bringing it up. Like I would figure out...

The sword. It never cut my flesh. I thought it was magical, but I never checked it on Milla. Of course I wouldn't check it on her.

The arrows. The ones I was certain should've been sticking out of my eye. And yet, here I was. On the ground. Whole. Except for my eye swelling up and the cut on my cheek.

Alwin pulled out the sword again, watching me carefully. His actions confused me. After all, I was still on the ground, tied. What was he afraid of? And why could I understand every emotion he felt? "I have no desire to hurt anyone. Just leave this island. Leave me in peace and go your way."

He sighed, looking at his sword again. "I want to, Gunther. Truly, I do. But it wasn't a dream, it's real. They captured Roger and Tara, along with the rest of Vaywell. The Dark Wizard is torturing everyone, turning them to his side. We've tried fighting back, but our numbers have dwindled, and the Dark Wizard's final defense captured the last of my fighters. For all I know, I'm the only one left." He glanced away, overcome with emotion. "Again."

I stared at Alwin, frowning. Despite this revelation that the dream I had was real, my mind seemed to shift. They got captured, but I couldn't worry about it. The most important thing was to make sure my numbers dropped. "I don't want to sound like an insensitive jerk, but I didn't understand many of the words you just used."

Alwin looked at me again, resigned to his fate. "You remember nothing." I stayed quiet, still watching him with a curious air. He walked over, untying me and helping me to my feet. "Perhaps it's better this way."

"What do you mean?" I asked, rubbing my wrists.

He didn't look at me. "Maybe it's better you don't remember what you did." My mind told me to drop the conversation. After all, Alwin was right. I shouldn't remember what I did. It was better for everyone to forget. "Roger has your glasses. Will you be fine without them?"

Once again, I wondered what Alwin was talking about. "I don't need glasses. I see just fine."

He paused, as though realizing he stumbled on a land mine, though I vaguely knew what those were. "Tell me more about this dream," he asked.

He was now purposefully changing the subject, but I allowed him to. I grabbed my sleeve to wipe the blood. True, Alwin had almost broken my cheekbone, so I couldn't trust him, yet I did. It was almost like hanging around an old friend. Except 'old friend' was the wrong word. It was like being with Milla. Alwin felt like my child, but none of that made any sense whatsoever because he was a grown man.

"In the dream, she had thoughts about how the dungeon was once crowded, but now it's just the two of them. I got the impression they were trapped, waiting to get tortured. Roger already had a swollen eye."

Alwin winced. "I lost contact with them weeks ago. They must be holding on, but I don't know for how much longer. And Milla? Did they say if the Dark Wizard said anything about Milla?"

I frowned, trying not to make a defensive stance, but still folded my arms. "How do you know about Milla?"

"She's the one that started this entire war. The Dark Wizard has her, and none of us will rest until we have her back."

Two sides of me argued. I should tell Alwin the truth so the war could end. But a stronger part forbid me from getting involved with anything Alwin needed to do.

It turns out I didn't have to say anything. Alwin studied me, and once again, hope filled him. I tried to hold back a wince. He spun toward the hut. "Milla?"

He had a strange sprint, moving like someone far lighter than a full-grown man. I caught up. "Alwin, wait!" He froze at the door, his eyes widening as he stared at the little girl on the makeshift bed.

"What did you do?" He dropped to one knee, taking her hand. "Milla? Can you hear me?"

"This is how she's been. Ever since I got here six months ago," I said.

Alwin listened to her breathing. "Why do you have her in a perpetual sleep?" He didn't sound angry, but he was.

"I don't understand."

Alwin stood up, glaring at me. "Why do you keep feeding her things to put her in a perpetual sleep?"

A trickle of blood slid down the side of my face, and I wiped it away. "Look, I may not remember a lot, but I wouldn't hurt a little girl. That's not who I am."

"How much do you want to wager on that?" There was no emotion in Alwin's voice.

I was so surprised, my train of thought stopped. Alwin was angry. In fact, he showed a lot of emotions which might have been normal for a regular human, but not him, since he was a different species. A species who shouldn't show this level of emotion.

"Alwin? What happened?"

"A lot of things happened. Understand that me tracking you down has shown the depth of desperation I feel."

"How did you find me?"

He gave me a look. "I followed the pull I have with..." He narrowed his eyes, then changed the subject. "I want to believe you wouldn't hurt a little girl, but we all saw too much six months ago."

I stared at him, unease filling my gut. Bitter. Angry. Hurt. This man—different species creature—shouldn't be like this. He was loyal. Trustful. Maybe a loner, but not this. Was his character altering? Is that even a thing? Why did I think that was a thing? And why did an alarming spike of panic hit me when I thought about it?

Chapter Four

Chapter Title Not Found

Alwin shook his head, turning again to Milla. "Just tell me what you did to her. She needs to wake up."

"I don't know how to wake her up. But I crush some aloe and lavender in the moonlight to get her up enough to eat and drink something, and then, before she goes back to sleep, she tells me some numbers."

Alwin's head twisted around when I said numbers. "What percentage are you?"

"How do you know about percentages?"

He waved my question away. "What's the number Milla tells you?"

I sighed. "Three hundred and sixty-three."

Alwin's eyes widened. "Gunther, that's bad."

"It used to be a lot higher." Why I needed to defend myself, I'll never know. "I've been spending the last six months lowering it, and it's worked."

Alwin watched me closely again before returning his focus to Milla. "We need to wake her up, that much is certain. And then we need to return to Vaywell."

"I'm not leaving."

At first there was no reaction, then Alwin stood up, facing me again. "I realize what I'm asking of you. Truly, I am, but I desperately need your help. All of us do. Tara. Roger. And if Paldric's still alive, then he needs your help, too."

"Who's Paldric?" I asked.

"The man you murdered."

I stared at Alwin, saw the truth of it in his eyes, but I couldn't believe it. A nervous chuckle came out of me. "I'm sorry, what? I don't... I have never murdered anyone."

Alwin gave me an annoyed look. "How can you be so certain of it when you don't even remember anything that happened?"

"Because I don't kill." I folded my arms, leaning against the doorframe. "I can't even bring myself to kill one of these animals. No way I murdered a person." Alwin said nothing, staring at me as though waiting for me to realize the truth. My nervous chuckle returned, but he didn't share it. "Alwin, come on."

"Roger saw it, Gunther. He saw you snap his neck."

"No," I said, because what he accused me of was absurd.

"He *saw* it."

"Then he must be mistaken." My voice rose in volume.

"I saw Paldric's body afterwards."

"Stop, Alwin."

"We all saw him, Gunther. He's dead."

My chest heaved, and I felt nauseous. "If he's dead, then why do you think he's alive?"

Alwin hesitated, studying me long enough before returning his attention to Milla. "I don't. Everyone else does. They all think you reconsidered and…"

I said nothing, my hands shaking, waiting for Alwin to finish the thought. There was no way this was true. I couldn't believe the word of one man. And a firm part of me refused to even toy with the idea. It was like my brain trained itself to not even go there. I wasn't a murderer. I could never be one. Alwin was mistaken.

Alwin stood, heading out the door again. I followed, because a part of me still wanted to know if I could make him not as bitter.

"We have little time. I can spare a day or two, but we've got to leave Jimdon and get back to Vaywell. It's a day's travel, if the weather's good," Alwin said.

"I'm not leaving."

He slowed to a stop before turning. "You have to."

"I'm not leaving my island. I've got to stay until I'm below one hundred. Then my memories will return, and I'll know what to do," I said.

Alwin frowned once again, his eyes narrowing. "You mean you'll leave these lands?"

"Sorry?"

"As soon as you get your memories back, you'll leave."

I gave a half smile, not sure I liked how certain he sounded. "I'll know what to do. That's all I know."

He turned back around, heading toward a patch of ivy by the chicken coop. "And if you're smart, you'd leave. So, it's better if I use you now while you don't realize how dangerous you are."

"And what makes you think I want to help you?" He was far enough away I called after him.

"Because it's Tara and Roger," Alwin called back.

I frowned, following him. "What's that supposed to mean?"

He sighed, rubbing his temples before turning around again. "You went to great lengths to make sure we were safe. And now you don't even remember. I'm far too exhausted to help you remember to care. If you weren't my last hope, I'd leave already." He carried on, and I remained standing, feeling unsettled about this entire thing. For the first time since coming here, I seriously considered who I was before this memory lapse happened. According to Alwin, I was someone who cared way too much, and yet also a murderer. None of it made any sense.

I caught up to Alwin, who crouched to look at some ivy, inspecting it before picking off a few of the leaves. "What are you doing?" I asked.

"Waking up Milla."

"It only works if you pick them when the sun is down."

"Yes, if you're not an elf," Alwin said.

I stared at him. "Wait, are you..." Alwin picked another one, straightening before giving me another annoyed look. "Like in the stories."

"Yes, like in the myths and legends," Alwin said, annoyed that he had to repeat himself. "The race of elves that abandoned men because they were too evil."

I rubbed my upper arm, frowning. "Well, I mean, there are the other stories. Like how they're blonde. Take out large armies. Usually there for some eye candy."

He frowned, scrutinizing me. "What's eye candy?"

"It's..." I froze, frowning. To be honest, I didn't know what I was talking about. Once again, my brain was divided into two sections. Trying to understand the logic of this world, and yet a deeper understanding of a different one.

"Eye candy. As in super hot," I said instead. That still didn't work. Alwin was deeply confused. Both phrases were ones that made more sense in the other logic system, and not in this one, so I cleared my throat. "Never mind."

Alwin's frown didn't let up. To counteract it, I smiled brightly. "I'm so desperate," he mumbled before entering a field of flowers, searching for a specific one. I followed behind.

"Let me help you not be so bitter," I said.

He saw the lily he needed and headed for it. "You think *you* can help me feel better when I remember surrounding Paldric's body with his neck—"

My soothing brain panicked. "Can we please not—just stop bringing that up. You must have been mistaken."

Alwin gave a loud, sarcastic laugh, and something deep inside me felt unsettled. Elves weren't supposed to make that kind of sound. "I wish I was, Gunther. I truly wish my eyes had failed me that night." Alwin picked the lily before making the short trek back to my hut. "Do you have something to crush this and mix it into a tea?"

"Yes."

"Good." I watched him again, frowning. "Stop looking at me like that."

"Like what?"

"Like you care. Because I know you don't," Alwin said.

I rubbed my arms, feeling uncomfortable. "You just said I cared an abnormal amount." Alwin gave me a scathing look. "You're just... different. Different from what I vaguely remember."

"Yeah, well, you are the second race that has walked out on men in my lifetime, leaving me alone. Everyone had such hope in you. Paldric, too."

I frowned. Race? What was Alwin talking about? I was a man. My thoughts didn't get far before they soothed away.

We got back to the camp. I handed Alwin the mortar and pestle, and he went to work as I started a fire. I placed the shield over it, and Alwin noticed.

"Do you have the armor, too?"

I glanced up at him, confused. "Is that the pants Milla's wearing under her dress? I guess if it's pants, there's a top part, too."

Alwin's face dropped, and he again glanced at the hut. "You... you have all three artifacts? Here?"

I stood to grab my kettle. "I guess so."

The shock on his face was more muted than the deep emotion he felt. "We might actually break their defenses with just the three of us."

"Whose defenses?" I asked.

"The Dark Wizard. Remember? He took over Vaywell when you left and has been manipulating the people to do his will.

He's already branching out from Vaywell to other cities and towns in Veniloria."

"But…" There was something deep in the recesses of my brain that went off. Something about this wasn't right, but I couldn't put my finger on it. "The Dark Wizard… he's the bad guy."

Alwin continued to mash the ivy and lilies as he observed me. "Yeah. He is."

I rubbed my head, trying to get the answer out of me. "Shouldn't he be dead? I feel like he should be dead."

The elf shook his head. "He's not."

"No, I could have sworn…" I stared at the fire, watching it burn the log. "Did I kill him too?"

The ivy and lilies were officially a pulp, but Alwin kept mashing. "You tried. But it didn't work."

An uneasy breath escaped me. I didn't like this conversation. A powerful part of me resisted all of this. A mountain of memories were locked up in my head. I couldn't discover them until I fell below one hundred. It was my only responsibility. And yet some people I once knew were in danger.

I grabbed the kettle from the hook, gathering some water from the stream into it before setting it on the shield. Alwin watched the whole thing, amused, even if his face didn't show it. "You use the shield of my ancestors to boil your water?"

"It's one of the best things for cooking I've ever seen. It's almost like it knows it's being used as a cooking device. The heat retention and distribution is crazy."

Alwin shook his head. "I guess they won't be too offended. Perhaps it's what they hoped men would use it for."

I sighed, watching Alwin finish his mashing. His eyes wandered back to Milla's sleeping form. The worry was undoubtedly clear on his face, even though it shouldn't. Something rattled Alwin to his core, even without the Dark Wizard trying to alter his character. Somehow, his alteration was my fault.

<u>Chapter Five</u>

CHAPTER TITLE NOT FOUND

Once the water bubbled, Alwin dumped the crushed herbs into the pot, and I stirred them around. "If I knew there was a way to wake her up, I would have. I hope you know that."

Alwin said nothing. He simply leaned against the hut, his eyes traveling over my living space for the past six months. I kept stirring, focusing on the kettle.

It was a few minutes before he spoke again. "Do you need me to hunt for dinner? I saw some sheep on the other side of the—"

"I need those sheep to make my blankets."

"Blankets?" He glanced into the hut, noticing the small pile by Milla's bed. "Does it get cold here at nights?"

"No."

My words always surprised Alwin, so after a while they shouldn't catch him off guard anymore. Yet Alwin found himself once again confused. "Then why do you need blankets?"

"Because I can often go down a percentage, sometimes even two, if I'm crocheting."

Alwin raised an eyebrow. "You've finally picked up crocheting?"

"What?"

"Nothing."

I didn't push it. For some reason, I felt awkward around Alwin. It was mainly because he disliked me, and I didn't enjoy being around people who thought ill of me. Though maybe I just didn't like being around people.

Using the same process of straining my coffee, I poured the tea into a cup. I hardly finished when Alwin swiped it from my hands and entered the hut. My heart pounded as I followed at a distance. Alwin grabbed one of my stools and placed it next to Milla's makeshift bed before rubbing the liquid on her bottom lip. Milla, as always, reached out with her tongue to taste it, but kept her eyes closed. He eased her into a sitting position. I moved to help, but he froze me with a look. "I'll do it myself."

The distrust was clear. True, if I heard someone murdered another person, I'd also have trust issues, but I'm pretty sure I'd remember if I did something like that.

Milla's eyes fluttered open and noticed the mug in front of her. She lifted her hands as Alwin supported her back to keep her upright. She drained the entire mug before dropping it, gasping for air. Her vision was cloudy, and she blinked it away. I remained by the door as she studied Alwin, her understanding and vision sharpening.

"Alwin!" She threw her arms around him. Alwin hugged her back, closing his eyes to allow himself a celebratory moment about this one victory. Milla was alive and safe. For now, it would buoy him among his sea of failures from the past six months.

How did I know what they were thinking? This was a strange power I had. Did the others know I had this too?

Milla broke away from the hug, smiling at Alwin before noticing me. All the joviality disappeared from her face and she screamed loud enough for the sheep to hear. I jumped in surprise. She scrambled out of bed and hid behind the elf.

"It's alright, Milla." He tried to touch her arm in comfort, but Milla refused to be comforted.

"Get him away from me. Get him away!"

I stayed where I was, watching as Alwin let her hide behind his back. "It's alright. I think he forced himself to forget everything."

She buried her head into his back, not wanting to see me, her legs trembling in fear. I didn't know how to comfort her. Alwin struggled to stand up as Milla clung to him, whimpering.

My thumb jerked over my shoulder. "I'll just... be outside."

I walked over to the small fire, sitting down and breaking some sticks to see if it would settle the unease in my stomach. For six months, I took care of that little girl the best way I knew how. Kept her safe and secure. But she screamed the moment she saw me. That, more than anything, confirmed Alwin might be right, even as my soothing brain assured me it couldn't be true. I needed to stop thinking about all this.

The soil in my garden was soft on my knees as I gathered more veggies. I'd make a large soup with mostly bell peppers. With Alwin here and Milla awake, I could finally finish the ripe veggies.

I finished washing them and placed a cloth against my bleeding cheek. My fingers gripped the bell pepper as I reached for the sword, but it was nowhere in sight. Oh, right. It was still with Alwin. I was about to go ask for it back when he appeared next to me. He had my mortar and pestle, crushing something before gesturing for my cloth. I was confused, but handed it to him.

"Might as well right one of my wrongs." He placed the cloth, the crushed herbs, and some water into a bowl. I watched, curious, as he soaked the cloth before wringing it out and handed it back to me. "It should help the swelling go down."

There was a tingling on my skin where I placed the cloth. It felt cool, somehow. I poked the fire with a stick to keep it burning. "So, you know who I am. From before."

Alwin watched the fire, holding still. "Yes, in a way. I'd only known you for two, maybe three weeks before..."

I watched him, trying not to look too desperate for information. "Before I murdered Paldric?"

"Among other things." Other things? Other things *besides* murder? I blinked as he glanced behind him, and I followed his gaze to see Milla still looking terrified, but observing me. "Now that we have her, we need to rescue Tara and Roger, then regroup somewhere. Form another plan." The fire crackled between us, my brain trying to convince me to stay on this island. "Thank you." The words were difficult for Alwin to get out, but they were sincere. "For keeping her safe."

"I wouldn't..." I trailed off. My desire was to make sure he understood that I'd never harm, let alone kill, a child. Apparently, I already killed someone. Even as I pondered it, part of me wanted to emphasize how I wasn't that person. "Could I borrow the sword to cut the vegetables?" I asked instead.

Alwin studied me before unsheathing his sword. I took it before grabbing my vegetables and moving to a small table. Dicing the veggies was a great task to keep me busy. I glanced at the elf, understanding his thoughts as he studied me. Despite his bitterness, it fascinated him to watch how I used a deadly sword to cut up vegetables for a soup. Then there was a part of his memories I couldn't understand. No, wait, that wasn't it. My mind simply refused to acknowledge what he thought about, and it had to do with his accusations of murder. My mind still refused to acknowledge what I'd done, which meant I must have done it.

I focused on cutting the carrots, slicing them into small disks.

"Just so I understand better. You have... forgotten everything except for the past six months?"

"Yes." I prepared to cut the onion, wondering if holding my breath would keep me from crying.

"And yet you purposefully kept Milla asleep?" Alwin asked.

The onion turned into tiny cubes before my watery eyes. "I didn't know how to wake her up."

"Sorry," Alwin whispered.

Blinking caused the tears to run down my cheeks, and I closed one eye to focus on him. "What?"

"I didn't... I didn't mean to offend."

The desire to rub my eyes was strong, but I refused. That would absolutely make it worse. "I don't know what you're talking about."

"You're clearly crying," Alwin said, almost with a deadpan voice. "Don't lie to me."

The last of the onion was diced, and I used my shirt to rub my eyes. "I'm cutting an onion!" I stumbled to my feet, moving to the stream to rinse out my eyes.

"What does that have to do with anything?" Alwin asked.

I groaned, grabbing handfuls of water and splashed my face. "Ugh. Elves."

"You mean the onion made you cry?" Alwin asked.

"The fumes or whatever mess with my eyes, yes." I dried my face with my shirt before sitting back down near the fire.

Alwin stared at the onion, frowning, before giving a slight shake of his head. Milla approached carefully. "Gunther, is it true you don't remember that you're a G—"

"Good Wizard," Alwin said, giving Milla the barest of glances before focusing on me, trying to smile.

Here's the thing. I knew Alwin was hiding something, and the more I looked at him, the more certain I was of that fact. And when I instead focused on Milla, I knew she was going to say something else. However, she realized Alwin was right to correct her, so she stopped thinking about her question.

"Good Wizard?" I asked, seeing if I could figure out what they meant.

"Yes." Alwin wracked his brain for some sort of lie. I narrowed my eyes, and he knew I knew he was lying. How I knew he knew I knew, I didn't know.

Well, that thought was confusing.

My fingers dragged themselves across my forehead before I grabbed my kettle and gathered more water from the stream. "This probably makes no sense to you, but I feel compelled to stay here. Stay until I'm below one hundred."

"I understand." Alwin glanced around the island. "If I have all three artifacts, I could go alone."

Milla frowned, looking at the elf as I scooped up the vegetables and dropped them in the pot. "But... but what about me?" she asked.

"Stay here with Gunther."

"No." Milla overlapped his words with her own. "No, no Alwin. Please no. I don't want to stay here with him."

Alwin wrapped an arm around her. "Hey, it'll be alright. He's forgotten what happened."

She was crying. "Are you really going to leave me here with him?" This little girl put on every charm in her collective toolbox. She widened her already large brown eyes. She made her lower lip tremble. Her voice wavered just enough to pierce through Alwin's soul.

He sighed, glancing at me. I narrowed my eyes as I picked up my spoon and started stirring the soup. "You're going to take a little girl with you on a dangerous mission?"

"The Dark Wizard took over Vaywell, capturing the men and turning him to his side. They just barely got Roger and Tara, and we need to stop him before they turn those two to his side," Alwin said.

This time Milla's whimper was more genuine.

"And, again, you're going to take a child with you?" I asked.

"You've had her go on more dangerous adventures."

It was enough to make me pause my stirring to glance at him. "That doesn't sound like me."

Alwin gave me a look, then I turned toward Milla, who nodded. I rubbed my forehead, frowning before grabbing some herbs, breaking them and tossing them into the soup.

"And on top of that, I still believe her coming with me to rescue Roger and Tara is safer than leaving her here with you," Alwin said.

More herbs snapped beneath my grip as I tossed them into my kettle. I didn't have a pot, so this would have to do. I sprinkled in the herbs as no one spoke. Milla watched me, afraid of how I would react. She, too, noticed the change in Alwin.

"What exactly do you think I'll do to her?" I asked.

He narrowed his eyes. "I don't even want to imagine."

"Go ahead, then." I got up, handing the spoon over to him. "Take her. Something tells me I'll know when I've dropped below one hundred percent. Soups almost ready. You can be on your way after you've both eaten."

I turned around, heading back toward my hut to gather some materials. I had some work to do.

Chapter Six

CHAPTER TITLE NOT FOUND

I knelt by the stream, picking up a few rocks and hitting them together to listen for the ringing sound. Alwin would leave and take the sword and shield with him. My only regret was the disappointment at losing that shield. I'd never find a better cooking instrument.

Maybe I should have fought for them, but once again, something in the recesses of my memory almost begged me to let him take them. Which meant I had to make my own knife. I'd also have to gather some clay and make a nice big pot, but the knife needed to be first. Luckily, I had a piece of wood back at my hut that'd make a great handle. I also needed to make some sturdy twine to keep the sharpened rocks tied together. It shouldn't be too hard.

Once I found the correct rocks, I whacked them with a third one to sharpen them. Footsteps came behind me and I glanced up in time to see Alwin. He watched me with narrow eyes, genuinely surprised I knew so much about survival since I never revealed these skills before.

"You're taking the sword and shield, I assume." I returned to my sharpening. "I'm making a substitute one for me."

Alwin folded his arms. "Milla's almost done cooking the soup. As much as I'd like to leave now, it's a full day's travel on my small boat. I'd rather set off in the morning than at night."

"Sleep on my bed, if you prefer. I don't mind sleeping on the ground." I honestly don't know why I said that. Alwin had been nothing but obnoxious to me since he arrived. And a bit of a bully. They would leave soon, though. Once they left, I could return to my hermit ways.

"You honestly don't care Tara and Roger are sitting in a dungeon right now in Vaywell, possibly changing their allegiances?"

"Their allegiances to who, exactly?" I asked.

The sound of sharpening rocks was the only noise for a few seconds. "I guess to you."

"Do you want me on this mission?"

"No."

"Then why do you keep asking me this?"

Alwin studied me carefully as the rocks slowly turned into a blade. "Perhaps because you are so wildly different from what I remember."

"So are you."

Alwin made a face, muted, but there. "You don't remember who I was before."

"I remember enough." I picked up the rock blades and returned to the stream. "You were never overly optimistic, but you were loyal. You may not have fit in, but no one doubted your validity. Your skeptical side was strong, but never outright pessimistic." I inspected the rock before glancing at Alwin. "Isn't that right?"

Alwin kept his arms folded, almost glaring at the stream. "And all that got me was the eventual disappearance of my friends. I mean, they would eventually. Everyone dies while I remain. But there's only so much loss a person can take, right?"

"Are you excusing your desire to go on this suicide mission with a young girl?" I asked.

"It's not completely hopeless," Alwin said.

"But you are taking a small child with you."

"Better than—"

"Leaving her here with me. I know." I stood up, brushing myself off. "That's the crux of your anger, isn't it? It's me you've poured all your hatred for."

The bitterness was strong, but even now he felt the need to brush it off with a joke. "Never really saw you as the 'sit down and talk about the complexities of human nature' type."

"Never really saw myself as someone who would talk to another person, to be honest." I did some stretches for my aching body. "I don't mind this hermit life."

"What's a hermit?" Alwin asked.

"It means I like to be left alone." I headed toward my hut, and Alwin reluctantly followed. "Honestly, the only way I'm getting off this island is if it burns."

Alwin, for whatever reason, was concerned by this. "What was that?"

I glanced over my shoulder. "I like to be left alone."

The elf instead glanced around, frowning. "Do you feel like the island is going to burn?" I frowned, and he hurried toward me. "Is it going to burn?"

"I hope not."

Which is when an arrow flew out of nowhere, hitting me right in the chest before harmlessly bouncing off. I frowned, staring at the arrow. It was different. Completely black, with a far more jagged arrowhead. The thought that crossed my mind was *dramatic irony*, but I didn't know why.

Alwin's eyes widened.

"Did you…?" I started to ask.

He shook his head. Which meant everyone coming to my island so far has wanted to kill me. Is anyone surprised I embraced the hermit lifestyle?

Alwin pulled out the sword, and I watched it glow. He filled it with some sort of magical powers.

We then heard screaming and jeering from far off. Somehow, I knew it was goblins. Alwin and I locked eyes again before I dropped the blades in my hands and sprinted toward my hut. We both had the same thought.

Milla.

We weren't too far, but the screaming got frightfully close. A goblin jumped out of nowhere, tearing after us with his sword. Alwin blocked it before stabbing him through the heart.

I paused long enough to check if Alwin was alright as three other goblins shrieked and raced after us.

"Go! Protect her!" Alwin shouted.

I nodded before dodging the swords too close to my flesh. Sure, maybe I could have survived it, but it still didn't stop me from feeling certain I would die.

Alwin killed the one trying to get me before distracting the others. The goblins seemed more interested in that sword. I sprinted to the hut when I heard Milla screaming from within. A goblin headed straight for her. She had the door closed, but it didn't help, considering the window had no glass. The goblin scratched and clawed, the wall bending dangerously as Milla cried.

I cursed myself for dropping my sharpened blades, so I did the next best thing. I grabbed the kettle of half-filled soup and whacked the goblin on the back of the head. On a positive note, it meant the thing was no longer focused on Milla. But as the creature turned toward me and started to scream and froth, I *really* cursed myself for dropping my only weapon.

The goblin was in a mad fury, trying to stab me in every way possible. I dodged the blade, feeling something in the recesses of my mind screaming at me to stop. Fighting was dangerous. My number was too high. Bad things happened when I was in a fight that could tempt me to use... something.

The jagged goblin sword snagged my attention as the thing lifted it over its head before throwing it down, aiming for my skull. I leapt out of the way as it buried into the ground with sickening force. Using the distraction, I kicked the sword out of its hands. It didn't deter the creature at all. In fact, the goblin ran right for me, tackling me to the ground. Air left my lungs on impact as the creature clawed at me. I tried to shout, but it was difficult with no air. It ripped my shirt, but my skin remained untouched. Every single logical thought told me I should be dead.

I grabbed for anything to get this goblin off me. My fingers closed around a log, beautifully thick as I smashed it in the creature's face. Once again it shrieked and I scrambled to my feet, whacking it with my log over and over until I was certain it was dead.

The thing stopped moving, and through the fog of my memory I remembered a goblin wasn't smart enough to pretend like it was dead, especially in the sunlight. I breathed deeply. The shrieks of goblins in the air indicated many more were headed straight for us. Milla opened the now broken door, peeking outside with her large, frightened brown eyes. Alwin came running but stopped short when he saw the dead goblin on the ground.

"I guess I better leave with you two. As much as I hate the idea, it's no longer safe here," I said.

Neither one of them replied. They still stared at me with shock. At first, I wondered if it was the destroyed state of my shirt. Yet me underneath was fine. But then I noticed my desperate weapon choice. It was a log from the fire, and I held it by the burning end. My hand was flat against the glowing ember part. I should have dropped it. Now that I saw the charred bits, my mind started screaming. My hand should bubble in blisters and start smoking, but there was none of that. I couldn't help but lift the log, circling it around as my hand remained perfectly fine.

"Three hundred and sixty-four," Milla said.

I glanced at her, frowning, then dropped the log like... well, like it was burning.

Chapter Seven

CHAPTER TITLE NOT FOUND

"We leave now. I don't know how many goblins there are, but we must get to my boat. It's the only way we're getting off this island," Alwin said.

I nodded before sprinting into my hut. I grabbed a sack before stuffing all the yarn and crochet needles into it.

"Gunther?" Milla asked, trying to be polite.

"What are you doing?" Alwin asked, not polite at all.

"Crocheting is a surefire way to get my number to drop. I'm bringing it with me." I grabbed the shield and tossed it to him. He caught it and I continued stuffing the yarn into my bag. "Go on, I'll catch up!"

Alwin nodded, motioning for Milla to follow. The elf allowed the smallest of thoughts to enter his mind that I would get so distracted I'd be overrun with goblins, but it was a small thought, so I tried not to glare at his retreating form.

Besides, I needed to pack. I was proud of myself for making the wool into yarn, because stuffing a ball into my pack was a lot easier than stuffing wool in there. My coffee grinder and a good-sized sack of green coffee beans were next, as well as a smaller sack of cornmeal. I ran outside to grab my kettle when I saw an army of goblins heading right for me, the trees already smoking. Once again, I thought of dramatic irony, and I couldn't for the life of me figure out why.

I stuffed my dirty kettle in my bag as I ran. My pack was heavy, but I still moved through the tall weeds until I, unfortunately, saw Alwin and Milla. They were moving fast, but not running.

"Alwin! Milla! Run!"

Milla turned around, her eyes widening as an entire army of goblins appeared just in her eyesight. Alwin trusted Milla's screams were genuine and picked her up, sprinting toward the beach on the other side of the island.

Adrenaline coursed through me, boosting the strength of my legs as I got faster. The goblins' shrieks were a fine motivation for sprinting as fast as my bare feet could take me.

The beach came into sight, complete with a makeshift raft. Alwin already placed Milla down and they both pushed it. It began, achingly slow, to move into the ocean.

I caught up, and the goblins wouldn't be far behind me. I dropped my pack on the raft and helped push. The three of us grunted, the raft inching along the sandy beach.

"Almost there," Alwin said.

The goblins screamed in a way that sounded like delight. They were too close for comfort.

"Milla, get on and untie the sails," Alwin shouted.

She obeyed. I tried to ignore the added weight as I kept pushing. It got easier as my feet got wetter.

Alwin let out a groan. I cracked an eye open to see an arrow sticking out of his shoulder and winced in sympathy.

The raft made it into the water, and I scrambled on it, helping Milla with the finishing touches. There wasn't much wind. Alwin handed me a large stick, ordering me to row. Goblins were already in the water, headed straight for us.

"Milla!" I handed her the shield. "Cover yourself!"

She did, crouching down and looking like a turtle. I kept feeding the large stick into the ocean, pushing the raft farther and farther away from the goblins.

They were undeterred by the ocean getting deeper. Alwin had his sword out, slicing anything that got too close. The raft wobbled dangerously as a group of goblins tried to get on. I smacked them with the long stick as Alwin continued to slice them. The sword was magical. Tiny slices in the goblin's flesh seemed to grow and infect until they could no longer use the limb.

Alwin shouted, slicing the goblins holding onto the raft, but the entire horde still swam for us. They were relentless in the sunlight. Something told me they would keep swimming as long as the sun was in the sky. We might fight off these creatures for the entire trip.

There was a lull as some of the dead goblins sunk to the ocean floor and more headed for us. Alwin was taking deep breaths, tenderly holding his shoulder that still had the arrow sticking out of it.

"Alwin?" I lifted the large stick and set it on the raft. It hadn't touched the sandy bottom for a while now.

He said nothing, simply prepared to fight through the pain again as more goblins got closer.

I watched his blood pool together before it trickled down his arm. Dread washed over me. Something told me to not let blood hit the water. A droplet dripped off his elbow, and I dove for it, catching it in my palm. The elf glanced down, frowning, before the ocean rocked with a wave from beneath.

The three of us watched the Siludontia appear from below, snapping his jaws on a bunch of shrieking goblins frightfully near our raft. We should have used the distraction to get away, but the chaotic display of the animal kingdom filled us with a sense of awe. And honestly, I should have wet myself, but I didn't.

The shark continued to thrash as he ate his favorite snack, and the goblins returned the favor by trying to kill him. Milla's whimpering brought me to my senses, and I noticed her still huddled under the shield, trembling with fright. Alwin eased himself to his knees, trying to hold the blood in. The arrow went completely through his shoulder, which could not feel good.

"Ready?" I asked.

Alwin nodded. I snapped the arrow near the fletching before pulling the rest of it through, and he clenched his jaw, groaning. "I have my pack. At my feet there." He unbuttoned the top of his shirt with one hand before peeling it off his shoulder.

Rifling through his bottles rewarded me with a container of ground burdock root. I kept an eye on the Siludontia as I eased some powder into the wound. My shirt was practically rags anyway, so I used it to wrap his wound as best I could. Alwin took a moment to ease himself into this new predicament. He had a bleeding wound while there was a shark not that far away, chowing down on some goblins. We would have to keep it as tightly bound as possible, and to make sure not one drop of blood touched the ocean.

I threw the pieces of arrow as close to the Siludontia as possible, who sensed the small drops of new blood, but was more focused on the feast at hand.

"Are you going to be okay until we get to Vaywell?" I asked.

"I need to be." Alwin said it more to himself, holding his arm because he wouldn't hold his shoulder.

We sailed on from the battle. The goblins were so focused on the shark that they didn't bother coming for us anymore.

To distract himself from his throbbing shoulder, Alwin started up a conversation. "That thing is like your protector."

The snapping shark drew my attention. "You think so?"

"At least from goblins."

The entire time I was on the island, I didn't realize an unnaturally large shark was circling around trying to protect me. "I don't think he's my protector. I think he'd eat me if I was in the water right now. It's more a matter of choice. He's got some quality beef in there, and I'm just a veggie stick."

Alwin frowned, shaking his head. "You have never made any sense."

A wave of pain hit the elf, and he tightened his grip over his arm, trying to focus on something other than the burdock root searching for the infection and the miles of ocean in front of us. He tried not to think about how we were going to sit here for a day, and how there were no trees to distract him with, or herbs to help this heal quicker. Though an idea struck him. "There's a bottle in my pack. It's got a red label on it."

I searched his bag again before finding the red labeled bottle. Once it was in my hands, I knew it was for numbing pain. Except it was for numbing a large amount of pain in humans. For elves, it was more to put them to sleep.

It was out of my hands before I could finish understanding what it could do. I glanced up to see Alwin uncorking the bottle with his teeth before he drained half the liquid. I lifted a hand. "Alwin, wait."

He brought it down, shivering as he swallowed. "Don't worry. I'll wake up in the morning."

I grabbed the bottle, trying to take it from him, understanding more of what it was. "And... you'll be drunk." This concoction he made had the opposite effect of heavy alcohol for humans. It would put him to sleep immediately, then when he woke up, he'd be in a drunken stupor. "We don't need a drunk and wounded elf while in the middle of the ocean with a huge Siludontia following us. You'll put us all in danger."

"Not if I drink enough of it. I should sleep until we arrive in Vaywell," Alwin said, lifting the bottle again. I grabbed it with both hands, but the elf was surprisingly strong.

"Stop it," I said.

He struggled to get the bottle back. "You stop it."

"You're acting like a child," I said.

"At least I'm not a murderer." He said it in such pain, so... human. It surprised me enough that my grip loosened on the bottle. Alwin drained the last of it before shoving it back at me. I was not looking forward to this elf waking up drunk with me in the vicinity and nowhere to escape.

Alwin kept a hand on his arm, resting on his good shoulder, with his back toward me. "I'll be awake by the time we get to Vaywell. Just make sure you keep us pointed south. Hopefully, you don't mess this up either."

I glanced at Milla, who still gripped the shield, her eyes wide as the elf fell asleep. I looked down at the bottle still in my hands. This confirmed that Alwin was a drastically different person than before, and the Dark Wizard hadn't even touched him. The dread I felt was sharp, the need to do whatever I could to please him. The battle of my soothing brain returned, telling me to stop worrying about it. It was his choice. But another part of me simply couldn't come to terms with the fact that Alwin hated me.

Chapter Eight

CHAPTER TITLE NOT FOUND

Milla, despite sleeping the entire six months I had known her, curled up once the sun fully set and drifted off to sleep. I stayed alone, sensing the shark. He swam lazily not that far from us with a full belly. He didn't know where we were, but I could only hope he ate enough to not be a threat.

I pulled out my crocheting to settle down and use the moonlight to craft my blanket. Though as I started, I decided this should be a bandage for Alwin instead. The wool was clean, as I'd checked it myself.

It was quiet, the lapping of the waves against the raft almost hypnotic. The wind was enough that it filled the sails, propelling us toward Vaywell. Toward these people I don't remember. To make sure I wasn't successful in murdering one of them.

With my crochet needle in one hand, I rubbed my forehead with the other. So much of me resisted this entire thing, but I couldn't stay on my island. Not anymore.

There was still a light on the horizon, most likely my beautiful island in flames. My heart sank as I paused my crocheting. That island, the only home I'd known, was gone. The little paradise, the chickens, the sheep, they were gone. It was the only place I felt at peace, even after probing my murky memories.

The bandage got longer as I kept crocheting. Hopefully, this would bring me back after the accidental rise in my percentage. My desire to reach lower grew the more I stayed around Alwin. I needed to understand why he hated me so much. And there was another part of me that needed to help him get "better", whatever "better" meant.

A bump in the raft woke me up. I partially sat up, frowning. Had I fallen asleep? I rubbed my eyes, sitting up straighter, feeling the chill of the morning air. No, wait. More than a chill. A thick fog surrounded us, and it was barely dawn.

I didn't intend to doze off. This fog was crazy thick, and I barely saw past the raft. I gathered my crocheting and stuffed it in the bag, trying to look for a landmark. Not even the stars dying in the glow of the promising sun could be seen.

Something bumped the raft again, and my heart leapt to my throat. Somehow, I sensed him just below us, curious about this contraption above him.

My hands and knees were near silent as I crawled over to Alwin, still asleep. If he was human, he would have been snoring, but his deep, heavy breathing was enough to know he wouldn't wake up soon.

Milla opened her eyes, looking around and frowning. "Gunther?"

I put my finger to my lips. The Siludontia might be smart enough to hear talking above water, but maybe not. I didn't sense he could, but I wouldn't risk it.

The little girl looked around again, shivering in the fog. It was still cold, and none of us knew where we were. Vaywell City could pass us by, and I'd be none the wiser.

No, actually, the more I concentrated, the more I realized where we were. I didn't know how I knew this, but we were only a little off course. If we kept going straight, which is what we were on track to do, we'd end up a few miles... a few miles to the... left? To the... I honestly wasn't sure about cardinal directions. Once we landed, a few hours of walking would get us to Vaywell. It was still doable. As long as we made it there in one piece.

The Siludontia's dorsal fin peeked over the water, and Milla stiffened next to me. I put an arm around her.

"We'll be alright." My eyes fell on Alwin's wound, and I released Milla so I could crawl over to the elf. Perhaps the Siludontia would keep thinking this was just a random bit of wood from a broken ship and wouldn't think twice about what was on it.

I moved Alwin enough to check his shoulder, but the instant there was a tremor of pain, he pulled out his sword with inhumanly fast reflexes. Next thing I knew, it clanged against my neck.

"Ouch!" It didn't actually hurt. It more startled me than anything. "Alwin, you almost decapitated me!"

"Can't be too careful." His loud and slurring voice split the quiet morning air.

"Shh!" I forced his fingers open to grab the sword hilt, wrestling it from his hands.

"Itsssmine," Alwin said. "Ssmine. Not yoursss."

"There is a humongous shark near us, and you're wounded. If you drop blood into the ocean, we'll have a shark chasing us. So please, just… don't be nearly as drunk as I fear you are," I said.

Alwin staggered to his feet, still clinging to the sword. "I'll get him. I'll get that monstrous devil of the deep!" He swung his sword back and forth, getting closer to the ocean.

Nope. He really was that drunk.

I grabbed him around the waist, pulling him back before succeeding at wrestling the sword out of his hands.

"You know what? It's on me for letting you keep a pointy object when you're crazy drunk," I said.

"I'm not drunk. You are. Drunk on power." He snorted at his own joke.

Milla gripped the shield, looking terrified. I tried to give her a calming smile, but she didn't find anything I did comforting. It wasn't a pleasant thing to realize.

"Alright, well, just give me the sheath, and please don't do anything stupid." Somehow, I knew I'd regret that phrase.

"I'm not giving you anything." Alwin tried to walk straight, but we were on a raft, and it weaved up and down. Although Alwin was an elf, he was also drunk. I ended up untying the sheath from around his waist as he kept shoving insults in my face.

It was only when I buckled the sheath around my waist that he almost returned to his sober self. "No, no. You don't get it. You're not allowed."

"I'm not giving it to Milla. She's a child."

"I trust her with it more than I trust you." Alwin tried again to get the sheath back.

"Just stay down, Alwin. There's no way this feels great while drunk," I said, trying to be as calm as possible. The shark bumped the raft again, knowing it was more than flotsam.

"I won't stay down. I stayed quiet for too long. Paldric trusted you. Everyone trusted you. Stupid humans with their stupid brief lives making stupid decisions. My ancestors were right to abandon them just so it wouldn't hurt them so much." Alwin still struggled to his feet. I grabbed his arms because he was now stubborn enough to not listen to me. If there was a pile of garbage in the middle of the road and I told him not to eat it, he would eat it simply because it was me that asked him not to.

He swayed dangerously around, looking like he was going to be sick. "I'm not listening to you." His words slurred dangerously. "I'm not. I refuse. Why am I so desperate?"

The Siludontia came around for a closer look. My heart pounded as Alwin struggled to break my grip.

"Stop. For your own safety, stop," I hissed. The raft rocked enough. There was no way I would let him go now.

"I'm not doing anything you say!" Alwin said, like the drunken teenager he had become.

My jaw clenched, my words barely audible. "Then do it for Milla's safety, you obnoxious elf teen."

It finally pierced through Alwin's drunken brain that Milla was in grave danger, and therefore the rest of us, too. Alwin blinked a few times before looking over at Milla, who watched the entire exchange with wide brown eyes. She was uncomfortable about two grown men having a verbal spat, and the elf she came to respect was acting worse than a child.

It was a long enough pause before the dorsal fin appeared out of the fog, hitting the raft and causing it to spin. Milla screamed in surprise as the raft jerked around. Alwin, who never tripped while sober, lost his footing. Since I had a tight grip over him, I fell with him. I hit my leg hard against the side of the raft. It was enough to make me gasp in surprise until we submerged in the ocean.

Which is when the Siludontia turned, pleasantly surprised to sense elf blood in the water.

Chapter Nine

CHAPTER TITLE NOT FOUND

I didn't know how I saw so clearly in the water. Once again, it was back to the division of my brain. In one place and time, I couldn't. But for some reason, being underwater gave me a clearer vision than what was above it. Which meant I saw in perfect clarity the Siludontia headed right toward us, his gaping mouth open with a thousand teeth.

Alwin tried to break out of my grip, and I was afraid to let him go. With me being heavier than him, we were sinking further into the depths and it made him squirm. He elbowed me in the face, which I should have expected since I can read people's thoughts and emotions, but it surprised me. I should be glad he only elbowed me in the face. All the air bubbles escaped me, and I gave into the impulse to breathe in from desperation. My chest heaved for a few seconds before I glanced around, once again adjusting myself to the reality that I could see *and* breathe underwater. Even though my brain didn't scream at me before about seeing, it screamed at me now. Even the logic in this place dictated I shouldn't be breathing.

Because he was lighter, Alwin rose to the surface, right in the Siludontia's path. I grabbed his foot and forced him farther into the depths of the ocean with me right as the shark sailed overhead, whacking Alwin pretty good. Air bubbles escaped him too, followed by the panicked intake of breath. But Alwin didn't have my ability. With the way my subconscious screamed at me, I shouldn't be using this.

I seized Alwin's waist, pulling him toward the surface as the shark turned around, the elf blood something new, something only his parents tried before, and he was curious.

We broke the surface, Alwin gasping for air. Milla sobbed farther to our left, so I started swimming. Alwin followed, his shoulder alive with pain after being submerged in salty water, but he wasn't about to reveal how much it hurt.

The dorsal fin was far away, but then it dipped into the water and I got a sick feeling in the pit of my stomach. "Go, go!" The Siludontia would do the same thing to us as he did with the goblins. Alwin and I swam toward the raft. We reached it, with Milla struggling to get Alwin aboard. He was light enough for her to help him on, even in his weaker state. He coughed, gripping his arm as waves of pain rocked him before he collapsed on the raft.

I struggled to get on. Milla tugged on my arm in a not super helpful fashion. I could've done it on my own, and would've told her, but another thing distracted me.

"Alwin. Grab Milla. Do not let her go. Keep her safe! Hold on to the sail!"

The urgency in my voice, coupled with the humbling experience of falling into an ocean, caused Alwin to snap out of his drunken and grief filled stupor enough to obey me. He scrambled to his feet and grabbed Milla, holding onto the shaft... the railing... the stick connecting the sail right as the raft lifted into the air. Milla screamed, gripping Alwin tighter as the Siludontia tried to eat the raft in one bite.

I was uncomfortably close to all those teeth. The shark tried to snap his jaws against the raft, tried to shake it to get Milla and Alwin into the ocean. Get them thrashing around so he could sense them and eat them since all his eyes were gorged out somehow.

The raft cracked, the wood splintering. Alwin and Milla were right there in the middle of his jaws, about to tumble in. I grabbed the shark's head, trying to force him away from the raft.

"The sword, Gunther! Kill it!" Alwin shouted.

The sword hung heavy on my hip, but I couldn't do it. I understood this creature, as terrifying as it was. Curiosity drove it. It wanted to taste elf. It wouldn't mind having the "veggie sticks" Milla and I would be.

Instead of pulling out the sword, I wrapped my arms around the shark's head as best I could and closed my eyes.

"You don't want to be near me. I'm too powerful. If you swallowed me and my friends, I would cut you open from the inside, killing you."

Something told me I did that before, and this shark wasn't about to push his luck. The creature shook his head to dislodge the raft between his jaws before dipping deeper into the water.

"What was that?" Alwin asked.

I waited long enough in the water to know the Siludontia was swimming away. "I changed his mind."

Milla shivered in the middle of the raft, hugging her legs. When she spoke, she directed it toward her knees. "It spiked you to three hundred and seventy-seven percent."

Once I got to the edge of the raft, Alwin helped me onto it. This barely put together floating device would last the next hour, which was plenty of time to hit land. I breathed deeply, pushing my hair from my eyes as I tried to process what had happened. I had powers. Milla and Alwin talked of me being a Good Wizard, but all of us knew they were hiding something. I used the excuse to get my breathing back to normal, but I was just nauseous. My subconscious screamed at me, wreaking havoc against my body.

"Why?" I asked Milla through gritted teeth. The nausea got to a danger point. "Why is this happening to me?" Somehow, she had the answer.

Milla closed her eyes, thinking. "You used too much. And if you keep using too much, you're going to forget everything again. Your brain is warning you to stop."

I nodded, waiting for the nausea to pass. "Forget everything? Has it happened before?"

"Just six months ago."

Alwin collapsed on his back, struggling with his own nausea and pain. If he was a human, he would've vomited already. "Why didn't you just kill it?" he asked, hardly a whisper.

"I don't kill."

Alwin cracked an eye open, almost glaring. "Yes, yo—"

"Whoever I was before doesn't exist anymore!" The anger took over. I just spent the morning struggling with a drunken elf, fell into the ocean, and then convinced a shark not to eat us all. "You're going through a hard time. The past six months have shattered you. And I'm sorry. Really sorry. You came to me for help, but are still pushing me away, and that kind of attitude will get us all killed."

The elf said nothing, partially sitting up. He looked ready to say something, but turned to the side of the raft and vomited instead. I hung my head, sighing. I wasn't in the mood to watch an elf vomit. Somehow, I imagined it still would have been model worthy. Whatever that meant.

Milla crawled over and hugged me, whimpering. I hugged her back; the nausea receding. The sun was fully up now, and the fog dissipated. We could see land in the distance. It made the state of our barely held together raft easier to handle.

Alwin finished vomiting and collapsed on the raft with a splitting headache. This numbing stuff sure traveled fast through the elf. Which reminded me...

I gave Milla a final squeeze before crawling carefully over the raft. I grabbed the pack now around my waist, searching through the healing balms he had there. The bottles were fine, but the ones in flimsier sacks were no good, which meant no more burdock root. I snatched a bottle of cleansing liquid, which wouldn't feel good, but I didn't care. The wound in his shoulder burned from the salt water, and with whatever else was floating in the ocean. He needed this cleansing liquid to get everything out of his shoulder.

Being in pain from his wound and from rethinking his life choices, Alwin kept his eyes shut tight as I unbuttoned his shirt. I peeled back the part around his shoulder to expose the wound. He clamped his teeth together, sucking in air as I tore off my shirt bandage. It was soaking wet with ocean water now, anyway. He cracked one eye open, but opened both in horror when he saw the bottle I was uncorking.

"Wait, Gunther—"

I didn't let him continue as I emptied the contents of the bottle into the wound. Alwin grabbed his arm, trying to muffle his scream, but he did a poor job of it. With all my talk of peace and harmony, I couldn't help but remember the guy never apologized for acting like an idiot this morning. Or for trying to decapitate me. Or for sliding insults at me, both subtly and not. It was one of those things where I knew this bottle would help with the wound, and the added pain was the cherry on top.

Once the bottle was empty, Alwin had the energy to sit up, groaning as he kept gripping his arm. "I guess I deserved that?"

My fingers were already unbuckling the sheath as I said nothing. I didn't need to. Once the sheath was free, I dropped it and the wet sack at his feet. "I don't need this anymore. You can have it back."

I would have walked away, made it dramatic, but we were still on a broken raft, and one wrong step would have made it snap in half. Getting back to Vaywell while clinging to pieces of wood wasn't a good idea.

Chapter Ten

CHAPTER TITLE NOT FOUND

T he sun finally fried the fog, or whatever caused it to disappear. I knew little about nautical traveling. I vaguely remember reading the sun burned fog, but... come to think of it, that might have come from a poetry book.

None of us spoke as the raft drifted toward land. Alwin kept his back unusually straight, considering he was sitting on some wooden logs tied together by shredded rope. Despite him drowning in grief, his elf nature revealed a grace in his movements. Maybe I'd been harsh, but I was also sick of his snide comments and bringing up a past I didn't remember. In elf years, he was a teenager, so it made sense.

I glanced at Alwin, who still gripped his arm, too afraid to button his ocean-soaked shirt in case the salt got his wound again. He stewed in an anger that never touched his face. Within his emotions, I sensed him trying to figure out the best way to apologize.

"Once we're closer, I'll get this raft onto the beach and cover it with something. We're a few hours from Vaywell, but we can't take any chances," I said.

Neither Milla nor Alwin said anything. Milla was still scared at Alwin's outburst from before, and she fell back into her most familiar role. The one where she felt like a burden to everyone. So she remained quiet and obedient and ignorable. In her mind, if no one noticed her, no one would ask her to go away.

Alwin simply didn't want to talk to me.

My heart felt heavy at these realizations, but I wasn't sure what I could do. Once we got close enough, I grabbed the ropes that barely held the raft together and pulled it toward the beach. Alwin went to help, but I told him no. He had his wound to think of.

Once the raft was in shallower waters, Milla hopped off and swam to the beach. Alwin got off once it was knee deep before grabbing the back of the raft with his good arm to help me pull it onto the sand. We covered it with leaves and other sticks, not because we would use it later, but because we needed it to not float down to Vaywell and alert the Dark Wizard's army.

Alwin headed up the beach, still holding his arm.

"You okay?" I asked.

"I need to be among the trees for a moment." Alwin almost perfected the teenage dialogue of needing to go to his room.

"I'll start a fire and get some things to eat," I said.

"Fine."

Milla glanced up at me, and I didn't need to understand her thoughts to know how nervous she was. Six months changed

Alwin. He was more bitter. More angry. More resentful. And he sometimes showed his emotions like a human. He reacted to hurt the human way, because he wasn't sure how to react like an elf. His solitude brought its own sort of hurt.

"He's got some things to work out. Are you hungry?" I asked.

She nodded, and I made sure she was safe on the beach before I foraged in the trees for anything we could eat.

We had a good fire going, eating off the shield again. Despite Alwin being gone for a long time, he was fine. He'd found an abandoned town and went through their supplies. Time alone was what he needed.

It wasn't until lunchtime when Alwin returned with a deer slung over his shoulder and a sack of supplies. He wore a fresh shirt, and I could tell he shoved every single pain killing herb into his shoulder. He wrapped it with supplies he found. His arm wouldn't be back to normal function for another week, though it was still a miraculous, inhuman healing quality of the elves. The brunt of the pain was at least gone for him.

He eased the deer on the ground far away from us before delivering the sack of supplies, glancing at me. "Do you still eat meat?"

I shrugged. "I think so."

He nodded as he moved toward the deer, unsheathing his dagger. "There's a shirt at the top for you." Milla didn't hear, but he knew I would.

The shirt was right on top, just as he said, and I was happy to throw something back on. Deeper in the pack were a few balls of yarn. Alwin's consideration strangely touched me. Even in his teenage angst, he at least thought to help.

We ate our lunch quietly. So quietly, in fact, that once we finished, there was a good, long awkward silence before I picked up a stick. "Can I borrow your dagger?"

Alwin glanced at me, then unsheathed it and handed it over. It didn't take long to whittle away at the stick. I'd lost my crochet hook and supplies. Alwin was kind enough to find some yarn, but I'd have to make a needle again.

The crackling fire stole most of Alwin's attention as he folded his arms delicately in front of him. "Do you have a plan?" He didn't want to ask me this, but felt the need to.

I blew the shavings from the stick. "Don't you have one?"

He kept looking at the fire. "Just... get in there and kill anyone who stands in my way."

"Charge in there, guns blazin', taking names, ready to burn in a ball of glory?"

Alwin frowned, glancing at me. "What?"

I shook my head, still stripping the bark from the stick. Those phrases were for a different portion of my brain. "Nothing."

We were quiet again before Alwin tore his gaze from the fire to look at his hands. "I guess... I guess I could make a plan. If I had enough time."

"How much time do we have?" I asked.

"I don't know. I never know. The Dark Wizard used to always know what you were thinking, so I'm honestly surprised he doesn't have his army here waiting for us."

"Or he's just waiting for us to come to him," Milla said. Alwin ran a hand through his hair. It almost looked human. The hopelessness I felt from him was certainly real.

The knife slid over the stick as I stared at the elf. "Alwin?"

"I don't like this." His gaze finally fell on me. "Any of this. It's pointless. It's hopeless. We're going up against impossible odds, and we should fail. We're going to die, but..."

"But we're stupid enough to do it, anyway?" I guessed.

Alwin buried his head in his hands. Something resonated with me about what he said. This entire predicament was hopeless. I shouldn't survive, yet I was stupid enough to try. At least, that was the personality of my old self. My mind still screamed at me for using power.

"You called me a Good Wizard." Alwin glanced at me through the gaps of his fingers. Milla's look was nervous. "I know you're lying about that. Something stopped me from understanding what I truly am. But another part of me is content with not knowing." Alwin dropped his hands as I continued to whittle the stick down until it was the length of my hand. I blew on it to get the fine dust away. "So tell me my limitations. What can I do? And not do? Describe to me in whatever detail you need so I can help you not feel like you're going in guns blazin'."

His confusion at this phrase never let up, but he glanced at Milla. He wasn't sure how this would help, but figured he needed whatever help he could. "Milla might know more than I. You're... you're usually a good person, but you can't use your powers much. If you do..." He was trying to find the right word for it.

"If you do, you turn into a Dark Wizard. Corrupt. Evil. You want to... to burn the world," Milla said.

From the depths of my soul, I knew she was right, but it still made my stomach twist. "That's what I almost did. Didn't I?" Alwin bowed his head, returning his gaze to the fire, his eyes hardening ever so slightly. Milla's nod was small and careful. "Did I set up this failsafe where I forgot everything?"

The word failsafe confused Milla, but then she closed her eyes, thinking about it. "Yes. You did. And it's impossible for you to change it. You set up an entire plan no one knows about, but once you dip below one hundred percent, you'll remember it, and—"

"And I'll know what to do." It felt like the right thing to say. "So even though I want to use my powers, I shouldn't. Ever. Because it's way more important that I drop below one hundred percent."

Milla nodded with more confidence. Alwin watched me carefully, trying to figure out my thoughts. To him, I acted far stranger than who he remembered. I was almost a completely different person now.

"So, it would have been better if I just stayed on my island crocheting." My brows furrowed as I worked on making a small head onto my already small stick.

"Except for whatever reason, the Dark Wizard now knows where you are. He found you on the island, and he will find you wherever you go. You're never going to be a hermit again."

I sighed, knowing Alwin was right. I lowered my handmade needle, staring at the fire. "Why does he want me?"

Alwin folded his arms. "Because through you he can make the world burn. Because you are strong enough to do it. You already tried it once."

I glanced at the elf, wincing. "That doesn't..." *sound like me.* I returned my focus to the fire. "I just need an army, then. An army to beat off the forces of darkness so I can... crochet."

Alwin gave me a look. "Paldric could have helped you gather that army."

I sighed, then picked up the newly discovered yarn. "But the two others? Roger and Tara? Can they help?"

"Possibly," he said.

"Can we think of a plan where we infiltrate their defenses without me needing to use my powers?" I asked.

Alwin looked at me, then at Milla. "We're a small enough number. We could sneak in. I'd just have to scout ahead, find their weak points."

I nodded. "Like a heist. We're going to pull off a heist."

"A what?" Milla asked.

An idea struck me as I sorted through the yarn. "Actually, you know what? This would be a really cool story. It's got all the parts it needs. Stakes, action, intrigue. Bitter character who's lost so much, lovable little girl, and a hermit mentor figure all on the last push to bring some hope in the world." I started my chain stitch, aware that Milla and Alwin were both staring at me like I was insane. I met their gaze as my newly crafted needle weaved yarn together. "What? I would totally read something like that."

"One thing never changed. You make no sense." Alwin grabbed a bucket to get some water for the fire. "Let's travel to Vaywell."

I placed the yarn in the pack before slinging it over my shoulders. "I can do this while we walk."

Chapter Eleven

CHAPTER TITLE NOT FOUND

The shadow soldiers slammed Roger against the table, and he let out a gasp. They bound him to the table with leather straps, and despite the gasp he let out, his face remained stoic. It was difficult to understand his thoughts.

He was in a cell with the door open. Being bound to a table would make it difficult to escape, let alone the dozens of shadow soldiers surging into the darkened cell.

The Dark Wizard walked through the front door, holding a torch which made the shadow soldiers shriek and slink away. A goblin was at his side as he stroked his black beard, his black hair falling around his shoulders. "Hello again, Roger."

His hands turned to fists. "You cannot make me kill her. I get a choice, and my choice is no."

The Dark Wizard smiled, then placed the torch in the bracket. "We'll see about that."

"There is nothing you can do. Absolutely nothing." He produced a deep, primal noise in the back of his throat.

The Dark Wizard moved toward him unnaturally, placing his crooked fingers against his forehead. "I have you forever, Roger. No one's coming to save you. I can torture you for as long as I'd like until you feel a deep desire to kill her. Until you feel like it's your one true mission."

"I will never harm a hair on her head," Roger sneered.

The Dark Wizard's fingers glowed purple. "We have the rest of your existence to figure out if that's true."

Roger's breathing turned shallow. Thin beads of sweat formed on his hairline. The heels of his bare feet dug into the table as he tried to get away from the glowing dark purple fingers, but his restraints kept him bound to the table, digging into his wrists as the Dark Wizard brought his fingers near his throat. Roger grunted as his eyes rolled up into his head.

"Feel it, Roger. Feel the rightness of it all. This is what you were created to do. There is something about killing her that just feels right. You want this. You want this desperately."

"I... will... not... kill... her," Roger said through gritted teeth. "I... have... a... choice."

The purple around the Dark Wizard's fingers disappeared, and he straightened. "Your will is unusually strong. But even the best will break, eventually. You are trapped here. Forever."

Roger panted, keeping his eyes closed. "You will never win."

"And who do you think is going to stop me? Gunther?" the Dark Wizard asked. The stoic man didn't reply, which didn't necessarily mean he agreed with the Dark Wizard, but he wasn't giving another option, either. "Doesn't matter. There's still a way I can get you to kill Tara. And it's in the same vein as what Gunther thought right before he killed Paldric."

Roger opened his eyes, glaring at the Dark Wizard. "What are you talking about?"

"Let me go!" Tara shouted from the basement of the cell-house.

He tried to sit up, but his bonds kept him from moving all the way. "No. No, don't hurt her."

"Gunther once believed murder was fine, as long as those under his care were in a state so horrible that it would be considered a mercy," the Dark Wizard said.

Roger's eyes widened. The basement door flung open, and shadow soldiers dragged Tara up the stairs. She struggled against their grip. Their fingers were cool and damp, causing goose-bumps to rise on her arms.

"Leave her alone! Let her go!" Roger shouted.

The Dark Wizard turned to the goblin at his side. "Punch her." His voice was far calmer than Roger's screams. The goblin obeyed, punching her in the gut.

Tara gasped in surprise, crumpling in on herself as Roger strained against his bonds. "Let! Her! Go!"

"Again, please," the Dark Wizard said.

The goblin obeyed, and Tara was on her knees, her stomach reeling from the impact.

"Tara!" Roger shouted.

"Once more."

The goblin obeyed, snarling and hissing. Tara was in the light enough that the shadow soldiers let her go. It wasn't like she was going anywhere. She curled in a fetal position, her cries coming out even as she tried to stifle them. This would break Roger, just as it would have broken Paldric. She tried to pretend it didn't hurt nearly as bad as it did.

The Dark Wizard grabbed her hair, forcing her to her feet. Her scalp felt like it was on fire.

"Leave her alone!" Roger shouted again.

The Dark Wizard pulled out a dagger before slicing through what she feared was her neck, but it was somewhere on her sternum. He pulled her closer, almost hissing. "Slicing through your neck is the job I'm giving to Roger."

Tara gasped, instinctively touching the cut, her healer's mind already deciphering if the evil man poisoned the dagger.

"Take them both below." The Dark Wizard undid the straps holding Roger to the table. Once his hands were free, Roger tried to punch the Dark Wizard in the face. A shadow soldier risked the light to grab his wrist and drag him off the table.

With unsteady feet, they dragged Tara down the stairs. She stumbled at the end, landing on the basement floor. Blood dripped from the wound and her stomach felt like it was trying to decide whether vomiting would somehow make it hurt less. There would be some nasty bruises on her stomach. The goblin cracked at least one of her ribs. Tara took a few moments to curl up again, trying to steady her breathing.

"Tara? Are you okay?" Roger's voice was full of panic. He placed a hand on her shoulder and she winced, which made him instantly take it off again. "Tara?"

The door above them slammed shut, and the tiny windows gave them hardly any light.

"How bad is it?" She slowly removed her hand from her sternum. It was covered in blood. Roger knelt next to her, easing her hair out of the way before wincing.

"Deep."

She nodded, still trying to get her breathing back to normal. Her brain still felt battered around. "It's got to be cleaned. Do you know how to wash wounds?"

"A little. Just tell me what to do. I'll try not to mess it up." Roger stood and went to their loose stone, where they kept their secret stash of healing ointments and herbs.

Tara tried to sit up. "Burdock root? Some of that. And... and do we have any more bandages?"

"Yes. We should have enough. No more clean rags, though."

Her breathing was back to normal as she rested against the wall. "Just put some of the dried root in some water and clean the wound with it." Her hands trembled as she touched the cut. Now faced with the situation of Roger cleaning it, the wound was a lot lower than she originally thought.

Tara felt every bump and bruise now forming on her body as she eased the sleeves off her shoulders to help expose the cut better as Roger knelt next to her, stirring the mixture in the small bowl.

"Are there any rags?" she asked.

"If you could call them rags. I wouldn't use them for cleaning, though," Roger said. Tara giggled, then instantly regretted it, moaning softly as she placed a hand over her belly. "Duly noted. I shall make no more jokes, no matter how lame."

"Pity. It will get so dismal here." She allowed this small moment of time to contort her face as an accurate reflection of the pain she felt in the guise of a joke. It did not fool Roger.

"How badly do we need rags?"

She didn't look at him. "Tear a piece off my dress."

"No, no. I won't do that." He handed her the bowl before taking off his shirt.

He shouldn't be doing that. It didn't matter that it was logical. Tara could never see him shirtless. It was a rule. Because... reasons.

Roger took the bowl back, dipping part of his shirt in the water before he glanced at her blood covered torso with his dark brown eyes. "Would... you feel more comfortable doing it?"

Tara took his shirt, wiping off the blood as best she could, wincing as the burdock root entered the cut, cleansing it.

"It's... lower than I remember." Roger was still on his knees.

Tara nodded. "Yeah, I thought so too. Do you want to prepare the bandages?"

Could they not see what this was? This was the Dark Wizard's plan the whole time. Like he wasn't using the oldest trick in the book.

Roger prepared the bandages as Tara dropped his shirt, wincing. He went to place the bandage, but took his shirt, dipping it in the water again, cleaning off some of the blood she missed that was stupidly near her cleavage. It was... the whole thing... come ON.

He oh so gently placed the bandages over the cut, and somewhere, I gagged in my sleep.

Didn't they see? It wasn't about getting Roger to kill her at all! The Dark Wizard only used that as a distraction. A red herring. To keep them from realizing his true intentions with them!

Tara moved the sleeves of her dress back onto her shoulder before handing his shirt back. Roger smoothed it out, making no move to put it back on, as it was still wet. That was most likely the reason. There was no way... he wasn't deliberately...

The Dark Wizard would never force Roger to kill her! He was forcing them to love each other! Bond over deeply traumatic encounters.

Get your stupid shirt back on your ridiculously ripped body! Stop looking at each other like that! The Dark Wizard was clearly doing everything in his power to make them fall in love because...

Because Paldric was still alive!

The scene instantly changed. I saw him on the ground, his brown hair ruffled, his neck at an odd angle, his brown eyes open and sightless. A man I didn't know, and yet did with every fiber of my being. All at once, his neck snapped back to place and his eyes regained sight. He gasped, taking in all the air he could as he looked around to see goblins. Everywhere. Sneering at him, laughing. They grabbed him, soon overpowering his weakened state as they dragged him away. That was six months ago. The enemy had him. They had my friend.

The scene changed back to the present. In the cell, with the two of them. Roger tenderly touched her chin, both of them way too close to each other.

"NO!" I shouted into the night sky, throwing myself to my feet. "DON'T KISS HER!" I stumbled and grabbed the tree to keep me standing as I felt myself fully waking up. I gasped for air like I had run a marathon. The dream remained in full clarity, but the more I woke up, the more confused I was. Why did I care whether those two kissed? And why did I get so worked up about the very thought of Paldric finding out? Shouldn't I have been more concerned about him being alive and dragged away by the enemy? But who was Paldric, really? I didn't even know him.

Chapter Twelve

CHAPTER TITLE NOT FOUND

Alwin placed a hand on my shoulder. It scared him to startle me, but I knew he was there. I still hugged the tree trunk, forcing my breath to come far steadier. "Gunther? Is everything alright?"

"Fine." It felt like I could only breathe through a straw, and I kept rubbing my head to make sure the headache was going away. "I'm fine. Nightmare. It felt strangely realistic."

As the dregs of sleep went away, I realized it was still quite dark.

"Gunther?" Milla asked.

"I'm fine," I said, straightening. "Go back to sleep."

She nodded, planning on pretending to sleep so no one would worry about her, except that I knew she wasn't asleep. This was a strange power. I wonder if it hurt my percentage.

"It doesn't," Milla said, pretending to act tired.

I frowned, but let it slide. My fingers dug into my forehead one last time before I dropped them. "I don't know what came over me, but I'm fine now." I meant it for both Alwin and the little girl who pretended to fall back to sleep.

Alwin didn't look convinced, but that was his general feeling ever since he saw me on my island. He couldn't trust me with anything, and I didn't blame him. Apparently, I couldn't even trust myself.

We spent all day yesterday walking. I got a good chunk done of the blanket I would never use. We set up camp a mile or so from Vaywell, and Alwin left to scout the town. I tried to stay awake, but nodded off. It was dangerous, and I could tell Alwin would lecture me about it once I woke up, but he didn't expect me to wake up screaming at someone.

"I've scouted out Vaywell. Both while the sun sets and during the night." Alwin folded his arms, hoping a change in topic would somehow help. It didn't, considering the topic was now the nearly impossible heist that would end in our capture or death. "We have to sneak into the city. If we wait until morning, there won't be as many goblins, but I'm not sure where he keeps them during the day. Which means there might be way more goblins in the dungeons."

My fingers rubbed my jaw. "So, if we leave during the night, we'd have to dodge more goblins in the city, but the cellhouse might not be nearly as guarded."

Alwin nodded, looking disheartened. "Yes. Essentially."

I rubbed my chin again, looking at the star filled sky. "What would you rather face? A crowded cellhouse of goblins who hate the sunlight and might go berserk on us? Or all those goblins spread out across the city and a lot more mellow?"

He didn't hesitate. "The goblins spread out."

I nodded. "Me too. Honestly, we should go now. I still can't predict what the Dark Wizard might hear."

"What are you talking about?"

"I have no idea," I said, and meant it, too.

"Shouldn't Milla get her rest?"

"Oh, she's not asleep."

"How do you—" Alwin started to say when Milla sat up, giving a small sigh. He glanced at her, then shrugged. "Alright. I guess we move out."

Milla got up, brushing herself off, and I shook my head. "No, not you Milla."

"What?" Alwin and Milla both asked.

"It's too dangerous for a child to do this kind of heist."

Alwin seemed genuinely confused. "But you always bring her along."

I shook my head again, grabbing my yarn and partially made blanket. "And I'm a changed man. There's no way she's coming."

The little girl defiantly placed her hands on her hips. "I've got the armor. I'll be fine."

"You will be fine waiting here for Alwin and I to return with Tara and Roger," I said.

Her eyes narrowed, and as an almost nine-year-old, she could be surprisingly stubborn. Though... maybe that shouldn't be such a surprise. "I'm coming with you."

"No, you are not." She didn't like my answer, and I lifted my finger to point at her. "Don't even think about ways of sneaking around to help. I can read all the thoughts going through your mind right now, and I will stop you. You cannot possibly trick Alwin, because he's an elf and he'd be able to hear you, even with his scarred ears."

"If you're going to do this now, then I have to help too. Because the Dark Wizard probably already knows I'm here. A defenseless little girl camped not that far from Vaywell. In the dark. Where a shadow soldier could easily track me and drag me to you and put everyone at risk."

Alwin hissed, already taking out his sword in case shadow soldiers were on their way.

"And why would shadow soldiers risk their lives for a little girl like you?" I was genuinely curious to know her answer.

"Because they know how much you care about me. How you've risked your life and percentage for me. When you had your memories, you were convinced the only safe place was next to you."

My finger moved to the city on a rocky hill. "We're about to do an incredibly dangerous thing."

"And it will be worse if I'm not next to you." Her hands were still on her hips. "How much would you risk to make sure I stayed safe?"

She waited for me to answer, and I looked right back at her. I watched her, a frown tugging at my lips. If I was being truthful, I didn't know how much I would risk for her, but something deep down told me I would risk everything. Which is why I wanted her to stay away from the danger.

No, which is why something told me she was right. I needed to take her with us.

I sighed, closing one eye as I studied her further before glancing up at Alwin.

"You've always taken her with us." There was more to that. The elf already had his sword out because he was terrified of what Milla said. She gave far too much detail about where our camp was, and if Alwin knew anything, strange things happened when he was around me. I was a magnet for all the bad guys to come toward us. It was why I was literally his last choice for help.

I straightened, then ushered her closer to me. She smiled, even if it was a nervous one, before giving me a hug. I patted her head while rubbing the bridge of my nose. "I can't help but think this is a really stupid idea."

"It's consistent," Alwin mumbled, walking past me. I shrugged before holding Milla's hand and followed him.

We made it to the edge of the forest, and Alwin studied the mostly quiet city being patrolled by trolls with very thick branches. Except they weren't just branches. They were carved, with a heavy amount of wood at the front. There was a word for those. What was it?

"Cudgel," Milla whispered.

I snapped my finger. "Cudgel! Thank you."

Alwin once again gave me a strange look before shaking his head. "Alright, listen. The moon is bright enough that it hurts the shadow soldiers. They won't communicate with each other while they're waiting for the darkness to touch. Just in case this needs to be said, stay out of the darkness. If they spy us, they won't be able to alert others until the moon sets. But I've done this plenty of times, so as long as you stay near me, we should get through the city. Stay in the middle of the road."

The image in my head made me smile. "Yes. It's more dramatic that way."

Alwin gave himself time to force the annoyance out of his voice before he spoke. "What are you talking about?"

"Walking down the middle of the road on a dark night, even though you don't need to. It's... dramatic."

Once again, he tried to smuggle the annoyance, but he didn't wait long enough. "You honestly think I would do this if it wasn't necessary?"

"Of course it's necessary, because the drama requires it to be."

The elf let out a breath, holding in all the insults he wanted to say before he remembered I could read his thoughts. Then he looked at me square in the face so I could understand all the things he wanted to call me.

It was untranscribable.

I lifted Milla up. "Alright, are we ready?"

She hugged me in a way familiar to her. It was familiar to me too. We must have done this a lot.

Alwin nodded, placing a finger to his temple because he'd seen humans do it. He mentally prepared to do the thing he did so often and failed at every time. "Let's go."

Chapter Thirteen

CHAPTER TITLE NOT FOUND

The moon wasn't full, but full enough. I didn't realize how incredible it was that Alwin did this who knows how many times without getting caught. Sure, he didn't succeed in those missions, but it was still impressive.

It was one thing to walk dramatically on a road, but quite another to walk down the middle of a street, knowing everywhere else was crawling with goblins and trolls. I wanted to dive into the shadows, but was too afraid a shadow soldier lurked there, ready to slice open our throats.

Milla stayed still, and I didn't move a toe out of line from where Alwin stepped. The sounds of the night nabbed the elf's attention. Every so often he raised his hand, and I stopped, barely breathing, fighting the impulse to sprint into the shadows. It was agony when we all heard a troll's heavy breathing or a goblin's grunting, but we remained in full view of anything that might turn down the wrong road.

When Alwin raised a hand again, I was so certain they would hear us because my heart was ready to leap out of my chest. Alwin backed away, and I didn't hesitate before following. We started slow at first, but then once he picked up the pace, I did too, trying to be as light as an elf. Milla burrowed deeper into my shoulder, clamping her mouth shut to keep a whimper inside. We moved to the back street, still in full visibility of anyone who might walk down the alleyway. Alwin kept a hand up and I heard the wet breathing of a troll.

The elf remained inhumanly still. The troll got close enough for me to smell it, and a wave of nausea came over me. There was something about the rotten egg smell that pushed up memories that should have been locked away. They came in short bursts. Hanging upside down. The troll licking my face. Sniffing my hair. Mashing my leg.

That pain was visceral, and I ground my teeth to keep myself from gasping. I could feel it happening right now. The fingers splintering the bones in my leg. Slobber so thick it felt like slime.

I reached out in a panic, my fingers tightening over Alwin's shoulder as I remembered the sharp pain in my head. Did a troll eat me once?

Alwin grabbed my wrist, glancing behind me in growing alarm. He was worried I remembered everything right now. He was there when the troll tried to eat me, and it wasn't a pleasant experience for anyone. I survived it, though, but maybe those memories were best forgotten.

The troll's shadow appeared at the head of the street, and Alwin and I both stopped breathing. Through the shadow I could see the troll lifting his cudgel, resting it on his shoulder. If they caught us, it wouldn't just be this troll coming for us. It'd be all the trolls. And goblins. And shadow soldiers.

The troll placed the cudgel back down before making a slow turn, trudging back to where he came. I let out a breath before sucking in another as quietly as possible. Alwin's breath was steady and insanely quiet.

"He should have seen us," I said.

Alwin still had a grip over my wrist with no intention of letting go. "He didn't."

"He should have smelled us."

"It'll be alright, Gunther. We'll just take a moment to get our bearings and move forward. We're almost there."

So much of this put me on edge. The troll from my memories was injured and yet smelled us. He could tell we were there. Why didn't this troll?

Something about this entire experience I should remember, but I couldn't put my finger on it. Like trying to remember a dream that had an important plot point somehow relevant to real life, but not being able to remember what that dream was about.

We crept into the moonlight, the warmth of the evening making me sweat. Sure, maybe some of the moisture lining my upper lip came from us hiding from a horde of cursed creatures, but the evening was still quite warm.

We crept down the street closer to the cellhouse. A few goblins walked out of it as we waited in the middle of the road, the buildings blocking us well enough. Thankfully, the goblins turned down a different street.

Alwin nodded, then quickly made his way into the cellhouse, lighting two lanterns for us to use. There was no one in the cells above, but Alwin crept behind the desk and knelt beside the basement door I saw in my dreams. Alwin pulled out the mythical sword and sliced the lock. It went through it as easily as butter before he opened the trap door. "Roger? Tara?"

There was a scuffle below as I eased Milla down.

"Alwin?" Roger appeared at the bottom of the stairs. It pleased me to see he had a shirt on, even if I didn't understand why. "What are you doing here?"

"Having a picnic," Alwin said.

Roger ushered Tara over. "You're an idiot to try this again, you know."

"I had to." I glanced at Alwin, understanding the meaning behind his words. He was desperate, hence his attempt to ask me. He was the only elf left in Veniloria, which meant eventually he would outlive Roger, Tara, and even Milla. The thought of isolation drove him to find me, because he wasn't prepared to be alone again. Despite his introvert nature, these people were his family, and he loved them.

Roger was halfway up the stairs when he saw me, and his face dropped. "Oh. It's you."

I shouldn't have been confused, but it was still a strange experience to see a man I never knew look at me with such recognition. And nervousness. I couldn't understand him as well as the others, but I didn't mind. It was almost a relief.

Tara saw me too. "Gunther?" The fear in her voice was such that no one else needed my mind-reading abilities to understand her thoughts.

Alwin lifted his good arm to help Roger up. "He's forced himself to forget everything. He's a Good Wizard. It's the story we're telling him. If he uses too much of his powers, he turns into the Dark Wizard. It's convinced him to not use his powers too much."

Roger moved toward the corner where his sword was. I extended my hand to help Tara out of the basement, but the hesitancy in her eyes was clear. The longer we looked at each other, the more I saw her plans on how to kill me. I brought my hand back, worried, as Roger instead helped her the rest of the way and handed her a sheathed dagger. Her thoughts already went to what she could do with it if I ever became a threat, and I found myself not wanting this mind reading ability.

"I couldn't find your sword. This should be enough." Tara muttered her thanks to Roger as I focused on carefully closing the trapdoor. I saw the bandage on Tara's chest, and the corner of Roger's shirt that was still drying. Tara took a few steps, holding in a gasp as she held her stomach. Roger seemed to know the gasp she was trying to keep in and held her arm to steady her. She met my gaze, and my eyes narrowed ever so slightly.

It happened, almost like an interrupted movie. The scene picked up right where it left off from my dream. Roger got closer, and Tara moved her head, looking away.

"Roger."

"I know." He got up, throwing his shirt back on. "I'm sorry."

"I'm sorry, too."

My eyes shot toward Roger, who met my gaze, taking a careful step back. "Are you certain he's forgotten everything about us?" He sounded nervous for his own safety.

Alwin headed back toward the door. "He remembers bits and pieces."

"That's what I'm worried about." Roger reached into his pocket. "Either way, here you are. A peace offering."

He placed glasses in my palm, and I frowned, looking at them. "What are these?"

"Your glasses?"

I unfolded them, trying to place them on my nose, but the glasses distorted my vision. "Oof, these are not for me. Whoever needs these must have poor eyesight."

"You must have healed your eyes... among other things," Tara said.

Alwin's scarred ears twitched. "Come on. We've got to get him to a safe place and help him drop below one hundred percent. He insists he's got a plan."

Tara and Roger moved past me as I placed the peace offering into my pocket. "I'll know what to do."

"Milla!" Tara tried to make her voice quiet, but her absolute glee at seeing the little girl stumbled out. The feeling was mutual as Milla rushed forward, hugging her tightly. It caused her to gasp, even as she tried desperately to hide the noise.

Roger placed a hand on the little girl's shoulder, moving her back. "She got hurt."

She looked concerned, taking more steps back. "You did?"

"I'll be alright. I'm so glad you're safe. We didn't know what happened to you, and the Dark Wizard threatened to..." Tara trailed off, patting her on the shoulder. "It doesn't matter. He was lying. You're safe, and I'm so relieved."

"Gunther forced me to sleep for six months," Milla said.

Tara and Roger both gave me glances that weren't pleasant. It was clear these two knew me uncomfortably well.

"It was... for her safety." I tried to make it not sound as creepy as it came out. "And, in my defense, I didn't *know* I could wake her up." My words didn't make their looks any more pleasant.

Alwin ushered us out of the cells. "Let's have this conversation once we're out of Vaywell."

It was so much harder, now that we were a group of five, to comfortably walk down the middle of the street on a dark spring night. Though as a party of three, it was still uncomfortable, even if it was dramatic.

I carried Milla again as we followed Alwin. We crept through the streets we wished were far emptier, even though, to our perspective, they were. Alwin moved forward, and we obeyed his every direction.

Despite watching him, I didn't notice Alwin's arms were out until I ran into them. He eased me back at an alarming rate. We scuttled behind a building, still well within the middle of the road, as a group of goblins appeared too close to our original place. They growled at each other, grunting about food, wanting to eat humans. We stayed hidden behind the building as they moved ahead. Tara shivered, even though it was a warm night. And it hurt. So many things hurt. Her stomach, yes, but mostly her…

No, wait. I wasn't sensing Tara.

Alwin motioned for us to continue, but I grabbed the back of his shirt, looking around. The elf didn't like this fresh development. He wanted to be gone, this entire mission behind him, and delays didn't help. It was bad enough we had to be impossible to find despite being in the center of the road. Alwin's anxiety was getting a hold of him.

I didn't listen to Alwin, which might have been a mistake. There was someone here in desperate pain, his legs broken, his mind weak. They had tortured him into thinking everyone was already dead and he alone remained.

Paldric was close.

Chapter Fourteen

CHAPTER TITLE NOT FOUND

I crept toward a small building before pointing at it. "Paldric's in there." I barely put any volume in my voice, but I didn't need to. All they heard was Paldric's name and saw me pointing in a general direction, and they got the message.

Tara covered her mouth, her eyes wide, pure joy filling her. Alwin still couldn't be certain. In fact, he closed his eyes, trying to hear the trap we would undoubtably set off if we entered the building. Milla's eyes brightened, sharing her excitement with Tara as both of them tried not to make a noise. And Roger... I don't know. It was weird I didn't know, but his face showed relief.

I moved toward the building when Alwin grabbed my arm to stop me. "Are you certain?" He was barely loud enough to hear.

"I'm certain. He's in a lot of pain, but alive."

His scarred ears twitched before glancing at Tara, who had tears in her eyes. He nodded, then studied the building. "Over here."

We followed him until we came to the side that was hit by moonlight. Alwin again glanced around before motioning Roger over. He climbed up the man before finding the small imperfections in the wall and scaled up the side of the building toward the roof. I raised an eyebrow, impressed, even though I shouldn't be. Alwin climbed through the chimney and down through the house before finding us beside the window. He opened it gently to not make a sound before ushering us inside.

We didn't dare move about the house until we lit a few more lanterns and closed all the curtains. It would still be visible from the outside, but if we were in and out, hopefully no one would notice. Once we had a fair amount of light to keep the shadows away, Alwin looked at me. I closed my eyes, trying to sense Paldric again in the house. I pointed toward the hallway, sensing him the strongest down there. We crept forward as I pointed to the room I was certain he was in. Alwin took his lantern, leaning against the door, pressing his ear against it before opening it.

Paldric heard it, wanting to turn his head but afraid of the shock of pain that would tear through his system if he did. There was no furniture in this room, no windows. It was practically a cell except for the strange table Paldric was bound to. I'd seen a table like this before, like the one they tortured Roger on.

Tara raced past us, heading straight for him, touching his cheek as delicately as she dared. "Paldric."

He took the shock of pain through his body just to see her face. He smiled despite the hurt that action caused him. "Tara."

She was already unbuckling the restraints, worry creasing her forehead. "What have they done to you?" Alwin helped unbuckle the ones around his ankles. I somehow knew Paldric, even though I had no recollection of him. He was important to me, just like all the other members of this party.

Once Paldric's hands were free, he touched her cheek. "You're alive."

"And you're only just. Stay still." Her eyes trailed over his injuries. Both eyes were almost swollen shut, multiple cuts on his face and lips. A dried trickle of blood from his nose and ear worried her. And that was just his face.

Too exhausted to keep his hand toward her cheek, it dropped, as did his gaze. His fingers lingered on her bandage. "They hurt you."

She took the hand she knew wasn't broken and gave it a soft squeeze. "Never you mind. We'll get you some help."

He wasn't getting out of here. Not with those injuries. They broke both his legs, and I didn't even want to mention the internal injuries. There was no way we could move him. I would have to use some of my power. Getting him out was the most important thing right now. I would worry about dropping my percentage later.

I touched his legs, fixing all his broken bones. Not just the leg, but a few ribs, even the cracked bone in his neck. Some organs were dangerously damaged, so I healed those too. Paldric gasped, color returning to his face. Tara shot me a worried look.

"Three hundred and eighty-two percent."

Everyone turned to look at Milla. She pointed at me, shrugging.

Roger covered his mouth, but we all still heard him mumble, "That's so high."

I groaned, rubbing my head as the nausea came back. There was something purely unnatural about this entire thing, and my body reacted to it. Alwin approached me, nervous. "Don't use anymore. We can't have you forgetting everything in the middle of all this."

"We've got to move him without him screaming in pain," I said.

Roger and Tara helped Paldric sit up. Paldric finally gave me a good, long look. "Gunther?" I tried to find the right words to understand his tone. Paldric wasn't angry. Maybe I expected him to be, since everyone said I killed him. After everyone's fear and hostility when they first saw me, it was strange to understand this man wasn't scared.

"I was told... I tried to kill you once?"

Paldric wanted to smile, but he wouldn't. Not with the injuries he had left. "You did, yes." He got off the table, using Tara for support as he found his feet. "You also brought me back to life."

"Only to abandon you to be tortured. To think all your friends were dead."

Paldric stumbled enough for Roger to grab his arm, placing it around his shoulder to steady him. "It worked out in the end, just like I knew it would." Again, there was no fear. I stared at him, confused. "I guess I'm still badly written."

"Badly written?" A frown formed on my face. "What does that mean?"

"No idea," Paldric said.

"Gunther is a Good Wizard, alright? We try to say as little as possible about what his life was like before he wiped his memories." Alwin said.

Paldric nodded, trying to walk, but still stumbled, his face morphing in pain. I remembered that pain. His brain convinced him his legs were still broken, even though they weren't. The pain he felt wasn't real. All mental. It still made him curl enough that Tara gasped as the pressure of his weight came on her. She touched her stomach. Despite the pain he was in, he looked over at Tara, worried. "Are you alright?"

"I'll be fine. All of us will be as soon as we get out of here."

Paldric nodded, relieved he could do that without feeling a shock of pain. Instead, he let go of Tara and offered his free hand to me. I walked over, putting his arm around my shoulder, steadying him. "My leg still thinks it's broken," he said.

"It might take a while for your brain to get used to it. I've done it plenty of times. Give it a minute."

"You have?" Roger asked.

"I... think I have." My mind demanded I stop digging into it, so I didn't. "But don't worry. We have to take it slow, anyway."

We moved out of the room, following Alwin. Paldric closed his eyes, continually telling his mind that despite everything, his legs were normal.

Tara placed a hand on her stomach and took Milla's hand, smiling at her. They were right in front of us. Roger, Paldric, and I were in back.

"I'm sorry for... killing you. In case I didn't apologize before. I don't think I was in the right state of mind. I'm not a killer."

"You aren't, no." We helped Paldric out of the hall, trying to avoid the shadows. "I know because you brought me back."

"It just... none of that sounds like me."

Roger studied me again. "Well, you're not acting like yourself right now, either. You're a lot more relaxed."

Tara glanced behind her shoulder, smiling. "I agree. The Gunther I know would stress over every little thing."

"And would have already made a dozen questionable decisions," Roger said.

Milla giggled. "And gotten mad at Roger for something."

The mood was considerably lighter, and the others would have laughed if we didn't need to be silent in order to survive. But I felt the slight spike of guilt that caused Tara to look at Roger, a frown tugging at her face. He glanced at her too, before looking away.

We approached the windows as I shook my head. "None of this sounds like something I'd do." And yet there was some truth to it, because somewhere in the murky part of my mind, I remembered what it felt like to lose control. Not only lose control, but to do everything in my power to gain it back. Even if it meant killing someone.

Alwin opened the windows again, checking everywhere before he slipped through. He picked up Milla, carrying her out first, then helped Tara. Roger and I eased Paldric out, and Alwin carried him down. It wasn't until I saw Alwin carry him like a child that I remembered the elf still had a shoulder wound no one knew about. These people who knew me were all injured, and I didn't like it. We had to get out of Vaywell. Then we could hide and recover.

We started to move away from the building when Alwin threw a hand out to stop us, his eyes widening. He glanced at the corner of the building, right as the Dark Wizard himself walked around it, smiling. He set his staff on the ground before leaning against it, giving us all a humorous look.

"With how loud all of you have been tonight, I'm surprised you didn't just burst through the front door."

We froze, not sure how to react. Which is when I realized the staff on the ground had shadows stretching toward us. A black mass that shouldn't exist in the moonlight headed for me. The Dark Wizard grabbed Alwin's side, pulling out the mythical sword of his people, smiling as it glowed in the darkness.

"NO!" Alwin threw his hand out to retrieve the magic back into himself. A shadow soldier grabbed his arm, pinning it behind him.

"The shield, too," the Dark Wizard said.

Despite his pinned position, he still tried to suck in the magic from the shield, but the shadow soldiers ripped it off and threw it on the ground.

The Dark Wizard circled around, watching us. "The little girl has the armor. Get it off her."

"You leave her alone!" I shouted with a certain amount of stupidity that might have been mistaken for bravery. Shadow soldiers threw me hard against the ground. I struggled to get back up, but one of them punched me, and my vision faded.

Chapter Fifteen

CHAPTER TITLE NOT FOUND

"Gunther?"

I couldn't tell who spoke. My vision was thick, and a pain throbbed in my skull.

"Gunther!"

That was someone I knew, even though I couldn't place why. It was a voice reverberating from everywhere.

"Gunther?"

"I don't know how we're talking right now, but you need to get out. Say Code 0000 and will yourself to leave. Please, don't waste your life away."

My eyes snapped open, and I stared up at the ceiling. "Devin?" How did I know his name? It simply came to me like an old friend. I waited, frowning, before the forgotten part of my mind came again, easing me into forgetfulness, the mysterious voice disappearing. It was too dangerous to remember life before. Not until I was below one hundred percent.

I touched my head, groaning. We were back in the cellhouse. Not in the basement, but it didn't matter. It was daytime; the sun filtering through the barred windows. For some inexplicable reason, I felt relaxed. A part of me knew how much danger I was in, and my defense mechanism was to not acknowledge it. This was a stupid defense mechanism. This was going to get us all killed.

But did it really matter?

"Gunther's awake," Roger said.

I glanced up, my vision returning to clarity as I got to my hands and knees. There was a moment where I was afraid I'd need glasses with how blurry my vision got. But I never remembered needing glasses.

Wait. Yes, I did. They were still in my pocket. But I didn't need them anymore.

I looked around the room, a hand still to my head. I was in a cell all by myself. Paldric and Milla were across from me, with Alwin in the one next to them. Roger and Tara shared another. I was in the cell with the table, which gave me no comfort whatsoever. And then, for some stupid reason, it absolutely did. My hand dropped. "What happened?"

"We got caught." Alwin was on his back with his hands behind his head, fuming in his own self-hate.

Alright. That needed to be addressed. "It's not your fault, Alwin."

"Not really in the mood. That's what you humans always say, isn't it?"

"If you want to say it to wallow in your own self-pity, fine, but don't pretend you don't feel disappointment," I said.

Alwin snorted. "Not really in the mood, Gunther."

Paldric frowned, looking at Alwin. Paldric wasn't used to the shift in Alwin's personality. Though, reaching out to Tara, I didn't sense she was completely at ease with his human backtalk. She had a hand on her stomach, frowning. "I don't understand it. We were silent. They couldn't have heard us."

"Common... trope." I tried out the word I was pretty sure was real. They all turned toward me. "Satisfaction versus dissatisfaction." I was still on my hands and knees, trying to organize my thoughts. "If anyone mentions the heist plan, it must never turn out that way. It's... unsatisfying."

Alwin sat up, glaring at me. "Are you seriously suggesting that in order to win, we must never talk about the plan? We simply go on a whim and hope it turns out? Make it uncoordinated and messy?"

My frown was clear as I tried again to organize my thoughts. "Well, no, we just... don't reveal the whole plan. Somehow,"

The elf forcefully turned away from me. "You've never made any sense, Gunther."

I stared at the floor. "If it makes you feel any better, I don't understand what I'm trying to say, either."

Using the bars of his cell, Paldric got to his feet. His mind had mostly come to terms with his legs being fine, but he wanted to use the bars just in case. "What happened to you, my friend?"

Alwin buried his head in his arms like a human. "I'm not in the mood to talk to you either, Paldric."

"Did the Dark Wizard get to you?" Paldric asked.

"I said I'm not in the mood."

"Life got to him." I leaned against the bars. "He's lived a long time, seen lots of failure, and it's catching up with him."

He lifted his head enough to glare at me. "I'd rather not be talked about as though I'm not here."

"You're the one trying to act as though you're not here," Tara said.

Alwin stayed silent, glowering at the wall. Soon the Dark Wizard would torture Alwin, and it wouldn't take long for my elf to break.

Why did I call him my elf? Strange.

"Has anyone tried to escape?" I asked.

"With a Dark Wizard in possession of the three ancient artifacts full of elf power? What do you think?" Alwin asked.

I rubbed the bridge of my nose. "You are such a teenager."

Alwin glared at me. "I heard that."

I dropped my hand. "I know."

Paldric shifted in his cell. "Alright, look. There's still hope. Gunther has a plan. If he can drop below one hundred percent, we have a chance." Someone must have told him my plan while I was unconscious.

Tara turned to me. "How long does it take you to drop a percentage?"

"On a good day, a percentage or two."

"And you're at..." Tara said.

"Three hundred and eighty-two percent," Milla said for me.

"So that would take..." Roger paused, doing the math in his head.

Alwin grunted. "Another half a year, at least. While we're in a cell. While the Dark Wizard tries to break us all. You honestly think Gunther will never use his powers to stop that evil man?"

The silence descending on us was unsettling. I glanced around my cell, trying to figure out how to crochet with what I had. Which wasn't a lot. There wasn't even a spider here I could... harvest silk? Was that even possible?

I groaned, rubbing my head. "Alright, so we shouldn't rely on that. But we'll get out of here, because it can't end like this. This ending would suck." I rested my head against the wall.

Alwin remained on the floor, looking at no one. "The Dark Wizard is coming. Just so you're not surprised and try to strangle him again, Gunther."

My gaze cut over to him, frowning. "Again?"

He didn't meet my gaze. "You tried murdering him a lot, yes. He kept coming back."

"Milla, stay behind me. Don't bring attention to yourself," Paldric said.

She nodded, heading toward the corner.

The Dark Wizard stepped into the cellhouse, smiling as he leaned against his staff again. "Trying to take away from my big entrance, Alwin?" The elf said nothing, still on the ground and glaring at the wall. The Dark Wizard smirked. "Something tells me you're going to be easy to break. Would you like that,

Gunther? Would you like to see your little elf leading an army of goblins to destroy Veniloria and reclaim it as mine?"

"How did you even find us?" Alwin said through gritted teeth. "We were silent. I made sure of it."

"The moment you enlisted Gunther, I knew exactly where you were. He's a danger in any state to you. You'd be wise to remember that. Trust no one. They will just disappoint you in the end." Alwin said nothing, instead he continued to glare at the wall. "I must thank you for bringing him, though. It makes my job so much easier."

A power forced itself into my bones, and I somehow got myself to my feet. This was unnatural. No wonder it was a dark magic. One that I was on the brink of having if I wasn't too careful.

The Dark Wizard forced me to walk to the table.

Paldric gripped the cell bars, horrified. "Gunther."

"I can't stop it." My legs wobbled as I tried to stop, but that was it. I turned around, falling against the table with a wince.

"Perhaps we can continue our conversation from about six months ago. You did so rudely interrupt it by trying to kill me." The Dark Wizard bound my hands to the table. I couldn't move to stop him, even though I wanted to. "You killed Paldric. You killed me multiple times. And yet I keep coming back."

"How?" It was like remembering a dream. "How did you keep coming back?"

He had a disgusting smirk on his face. "Think, Gunther. I want you to try."

I frowned, staring at him.

"Careful. If you remember... if you're still over one hundred..." Tara said.

"You want to remember, though, don't you?" The Dark Wizard still leaned against his staff. "Doesn't it bug you that you're here, bound to a table, with your friends in my cell, about to get tortured? Wouldn't it be smarter for you to remember? So you can stop me?"

To kill him again. There was something about him I couldn't kill, no matter how hard I tried. I vaguely remember doing literally everything in my power to murder him. The more I tried, the more my percentage spiked. The Dark Wizard wanted it. He was tempting me to use a power I could never touch.

"I knew you had the bare minimum of intelligence, Gunther. Well done."

My frown deepened, and I studied the Dark Wizard closer. Was he reading my thoughts?

"I am, yes."

The forgotten part of me shuddered. Once again, I stared at his black eyes, trying to figure this out. This was wrong. He couldn't read my thoughts. Not unless...

Something was definitely not going how I planned, except I didn't remember what the plan was.

"You can control me, extinguish fires, but not... you can't read thoughts. Not unless..." He waited patiently, having all the time in the world for me to figure this out. "Professor? You are... Professor. Somehow."

A slow smile crossed his face. "What you are trying to remember is everything you did, your sacrifice of your sanity, it was all in vain. I, Professor Andrews, never got caught. I'm still here. I still won."

Chapter Sixteen

CHAPTER TITLE NOT FOUND

"No." I shook my head to get my point across. I didn't remember what he talked about, but this couldn't be possible. "No, I... exposed you. I remember."

"Do you?" the Dark Wizard asked. I stared at the cell door that was left open, my mind grasping for the memory that it stifled from me. "I didn't think so."

"But... they caught you."

"Who caught me?" the Dark Wizard asked.

The dual nature of this conversation hurt my brain. There was clearly a part of my forgotten memories that had a ton of questions, but I didn't know how to access it.

The Dark Wizard waited patiently. "Let me help you remember who you were before."

"To become a Dark Wizard like you?" I asked.

"You don't actually believe that, do you?"

No, I didn't, but I wouldn't start a friendly conversation with this guy. "I have a plan."

"Yes, well, that was before when you thought you had a semblance of control. Before you realized I'm still here and more than happy to torture your characters."

"No." I closed my eyes, shaking my head. "I... have a plan."

"You have the power to remember. You don't have to wait until you're less than one hundred," the Dark Wizard said.

"I remember..." Fireballs. Dark magic. Purple blazes of light. All of it engulfing the Dark Wizard as he cackled. Dying over and over and yet coming back. "I remember killing you. A lot. Why aren't you dead?"

The Dark Wizard jerked his head in Paldric's direction. "I'm about as dead as him."

"No." I remembered the ability to reach within the universe itself and completely wipe out the Dark Wizard. "No, I obliterated your..."

"Code?" the Dark Wizard prompted.

My breath pulled deeply from my chest as I stared at the Dark Wizard's black eyes, feeling nauseous. I was a killer. Gone insane. I forced myself to forget because that much power shouldn't have been possible.

"If the professor is up there, I can never truly die. He has an infinite amount of back-up code for my character, making it impossible for you to erase me. They will never catch him." None of it made sense. Yet it did. It gave me a headache, as well as existential dread. "But I'm done talking. Let's see if we can shake the forgetfulness from your brain. Let's force you to remember so you can burn the world in your attempt to kill me again."

The staff above my head glowed purple, and I shut my eyes, too afraid of what I'd see. Instead, it played before my mind. I saw myself running. Roger screaming at me, his sword drawn, demanding to know why I just killed Paldric. I didn't answer, because I didn't want to. And if I didn't want to, I didn't have to.

No, no. I couldn't remember. Not this. Not as an arrogant individual. I couldn't remember who I was, because then I'd remember how to tap into that power. It would drive me insane. I wasn't a killer. I wasn't.

"Yes, you are, Gunther." The Dark Wizard was uncomfortably close to my ear, reading my thoughts. Showing me scenes I shouldn't remember.

That night, I sprinted through the woods, sensing the Dark Wizard again. Knowing where he was. I had unwritten him from existence, and yet he was back with his horde of cursed creatures. This was impossible. They couldn't reappear right after I made them kill each other. I made the night turn to day again. Forced the sun to rise. Reveling in the universe's power.

My wrists pulled at the restraints, pain the only thing reminding me I was here, in a cell. Not back there six months ago. My eyes flitted open, hoping that would keep the memories from being there, but it didn't work.

My palms remembered the feeling of fireballs shooting out of them, and the Dark Wizard blocked them with his glowing purple staff. I wanted to tell myself it was all a lie. One part of my brain said it was impossible, but the other didn't refute it. This wasn't something the Dark Wizard made up. This was real. My anger, my frustration, I felt it all. I *remember* feeling it all. I did everything to make that man die.

The goblins, trolls, and shadow soldiers all tried to get me, but I killed them with a thought. The Dark Wizard was who I needed. And yet the cursed creatures returned.

"Tell me how you're doing this!" the evil me screamed at the Dark Wizard, who only smiled, enraging me further. I searched into his mind and saw the code. Once the necromancer died, the Dark Wizard absorbed the ability to bring his creatures back from the dead.

Scenes from six months ago flitted past my eyes, but I forced myself to talk to remain in the present. "I am not that person! I won't remember how to use my powers!"

"But it *is* who you are." He was too close, and sweat poured down my face. "You can't escape your past. Don't pretend you're a different person when you're not. You escaped reality to pretend to be a hero, but you never were one from the start, and this proves it."

"Stop!" He was hinting at something buried under the deep recesses of my mind, and I refused to remember. Not until I was below one hundred percent.

"I want you to break your little world," the Dark Wizard said.

"I don't remember!" My voice strained from the memories I couldn't comprehend. Death and destruction over and over. The Dark Wizard wasn't dying. Everything I did, he still popped back up. How was the professor able to do this? He was being chased by... by people. Four people. My friends.

"Keep shaking that forgotten area of your brain. I need you to remember. Most importantly, remember how much you've already cracked."

The staff came dangerously close again, and I gasped. I remembered gathering fireballs, every purple flame, every lightning strike, multiplying it until it was triple the heat of the sun before ramming it at the Dark Wizard. I held it there, glaring at him. He burned alive and came back. Laughing at me as his skin melted off over and over again, his organs perpetually boiling. His voice was scraggy and patched as he kept laughing, his vocal cords breaking before reforming, just to break again. I screamed at him. Begged him to die as my world burned around me. Did everything in my power to get him out of my...

Story?

"NO!" I covered my ears. "NO! NOT YET!" I wasn't supposed to know that. I wasn't below one hundred percent.

The Dark Wizard cackled, both in my memory and in real life, and I thought it was because he knew I remembered. But then I realized my ears were covered, my wrists going through the restraints. That was impossible. Not according to the rules of this world. Not unless I no longer listened to them.

With my head cradled in my hands, I gasped for air. Memories returned. Too much returning. The Dark Wizard cackled, and it was that noise which made me remember I'd heard it before. After so many times trying to kill him, I came to myself and realized my world was on fire. Everyone and everything dead.

Everyone but me and the Dark Wizard. He wasn't dying. And I was insane with power. I did the only thing I could think of. Using my powers as narrator, I brought everything back to how it was. I froze time long enough to come up with the plan so it wouldn't record on the device, before forcing myself to forget everything. But not before taking Milla with me to Jimdon. I needed to hide in order to get my sanity back somehow. And fast. My plan needed to be enacted to keep my characters from suffering a fate worse than death.

My eyes snapped open, gasping, still holding my head, sitting up on the table as I met the Dark Wizard's gaze. The forgotten part of my brain melted away.

Not real. None of this. Simulation. Narration device. Stuck. I'm stuck in a story. My story. My characters. Rogue Narrator. Professor Andrews. All the power. Mine. I could have it all.

"That's right, Gunther." The Dark Wizard moved his staff, a black gleam in his eyes. "Shall we have another battle?"

Tara threw herself against the bars of her cell, trying to reach me. "Don't, Gunther! Don't do it!"

"You'll just forget again!" Milla said.

"Don't give in!" Paldric said.

No matter what the Dark Wizard tried to do, I couldn't use my powers, because Milla was right. I would forget everything again, unless I used my powers to stop myself from forgetting because... my powers. My unlimited... I could do... whatever I wanted.

My hands still covered my head, memories trying to straighten themselves out. I was over one hundred percent. I was dangerous. Help. I needed help. Someone... Devin. Jim. Grace. Vince. They helped. They... they were in the real world. I turned them off. I could turn them back on somehow.

But I had a plan. Despite the Dark Wizard and Professor Andrews somehow escaping, it still might work. A plan I couldn't even think about, for fear Professor Andrews would get tipped off.

I dropped my hands and looked at my characters. Roger was doing his best to keep Tara protected from me. Tara was going over everything she knew about how to kill me. Alwin prepared to use the bonds I easily escaped from to strangle me, and Paldric already had Milla in his arms, waiting patiently for it to play out.

My eyes lingered on Paldric, saw the calm way he prepared. Whatever the end was, he wasn't afraid. He'd already died once, already felt the overwhelming peace that came with the end. He wasn't looking forward to the pain that would happen before then, but he wouldn't mind the rest that would come. The Dark Wizard would never break him. And with him here, he could help everyone else remember the end was nothing to be afraid of.

My chest heaved. Milla looked at me, waiting, wondering if I would use my powers and forget everything again.

None of them knew my true purpose. I was not God. But they couldn't know they were characters in a story I made up. Not real. But real to me.

Tears filled my eyes before they tumbled down my cheeks. It was clear what I needed to do. I was a danger to everyone around me, so I needed to leave. I pretended to be the hero of the story, but the greatest heroes are the ones that never consider themselves such. Those that seek the title often become the villain. The best thing I could do was leave.

The Dark Wizard smirked, holding his staff. "Do you need extra incentive to stay?" Every single cursed creature was aware of us, and they were coming to slaughter my characters. The shadows darkened at the doorstep, and my heart rate quickened. Time. I needed more time.

"Gunther." Alwin was worried. Worried that I would both use or not use my powers.

The shadows moved, and I stood, looking at my characters. The Dark Wizard, no, Professor Andrews, would use any distraction to keep me here. To live in this world to save my characters who were real to me. This world wasn't real, but if I stayed here, there would be real-world consequences. I would no longer play by Professor Andrews' rules.

"Do you trust me?" I asked, looking at my characters.

Paldric nodded. He was the only one that did. I nodded back, then closed my eyes.

"Code 0000." I sensed the device pick up on it. "I leave."

After over six months, I faded from my story, dooming my characters to whatever fate Professor Andrews had in store for them. But I took comfort knowing it wouldn't be me who would destroy them.

Which didn't turn out to be that comforting, but by the time I realized it, my eyes fluttered open, and Devin tore the headset from my ears.

Chapter Seventeen

REBOOTING CHAPTER TITLE FUNCTION, PLEASE HOLD

Paldric raised an eyebrow as he stared at the place where I once was. I was gone so fast, there was still an imprint of me standing there. Once he blinked again, the imprint left.

The Dark Wizard held up his staff, and the dread continued to grow. The cursed creatures waited for their orders to tear my characters apart. Paldric glanced at Tara, trying not to be worried, trying not to assume that the last thing he would remember would be the pain of getting his limbs torn apart. Or being forced to watch as a troll consumed Tara.

Terror seized Milla's small frame as she moaned. "He left us."

"It was better this way." Bitterness crept back in Alwin's voice.

The Dark Wizard looked annoyed, but lowered his staff, rubbing the bridge of his nose. "Fine. I guess we do this the old-fashioned way. Stick them in the basement."

The cursed creatures turned away, the command no longer there to tear my characters apart (Oh, uh, the device is prompting me to mention Roger separately again. Seems stupid, since his own creator disowned him. Fine. My characters and Roger.). Instead, the shadow soldiers once again dragged them out of the cell as the Dark Wizard opened the trapdoor with a flick of his hand. Milla did her best to keep her tears in check as Tara closed her eyes, not wishing to see those horrible shadows.

Shadow soldiers grabbed Alwin, making him braver. "Why wait? Why toy with us? You just want us dead, so why not kill us now?"

The Dark Wizard's eyebrow lifted. "I never wanted to kill you. I wanted to break you. Just like Gunther. You will be the easiest one to break, though, so we'll start with you."

"No!" Paldric shouted. Memories of his own six-month torture came back to him. Despite his optimism, Paldric would have been the first to admit that he barely survived it. Yes, he could go another six months if needed, but he was afraid for his friend. The elf who seemed so altered in six months without the Dark Wizard's torture. Paldric didn't want to entertain the thought of what it might mean.

The shadow soldiers forced everyone toward the stairs leading to the basement. They tried to take Milla from Paldric, but his arms circled tighter around the little girl. "Let me hold her, please. We'll go to the basement without a fight. Just please let me keep her with me."

They responded by elbowing Paldric in the face. He groaned, his grip on Milla loosening as they tore her from him.

There was a clamor as none of my other characters appreciated what the shadow soldiers did to Paldric. Alwin was going full fury on the things holding him back, trying to kill every single one. Honestly, he was doing well because it was the middle of the day. They weren't nearly as strong.

The Dark Wizard sighed in annoyance. Any moment now, he would tap his foot out of impatience. "Just push him down there! I don't care if anything breaks!"

Alwin continued to fight, punching as many of the shadow soldiers as possible. My elf was just as terrified of his own mental stability. He was slipping, and he didn't know how long he could last under the Dark Wizard's persuasion. He would rather die taking on an entire army of shadow soldiers to make sure he remained firmly on the side of the good guys.

Roger and Tara were already halfway down the steps as Alwin dug his feet into the wood. The shadow soldiers dove at him, keeping him pinned, forcing him toward the basement. Once Milla was down the stairs, Paldric followed, running toward her to make sure she stayed safe. The little girl threw her arms around him, whimpering. She didn't want to see anyone get tortured. Roger appeared next to them, placing a hand over her shoulder as they watched Alwin get dragged down. Shadow soldiers wrapped him head to toe to keep him from dragging his feet before pushing him off the stairs. He took the fall with a grace given to the elves, but it still made him humanly angry. Tara rushed to him, dropping to her knees to check if he was alright, but Alwin was an elf. He would have to fall from higher heights before breaking any bones.

"I will never serve you!" Alwin shouted as Tara tried to hold him back.

The Dark Wizard walked down the stairs, resting his staff on his shoulders. "It will be my greatest accomplishment, convincing you to be my slave."

Tara was in danger of getting hurt by Alwin's thrashing. "Never!"

The Dark Wizard set his staff against the wall, smiling as he approached Alwin and Tara. She got to her feet, rushing toward the vile man and punching him in the face. "Leave him alone!"

It was very unsettling to watch the evil man laugh after getting punched in the face, but Tara refused to let it deter her. All the ideas she brainstormed of how to kill me switched gears with the Dark Wizard as her new target. She was a lot more willing to try them out on him.

She punched him again and again. The Dark Wizard couldn't be killed, but she could distract him. She had the quiet hope that the men would take Milla and leave, but Paldric would never leave her in such danger. Neither would Roger. So trying to distract the Dark Wizard with punches may not have worked, but it was certainly therapeutic.

Shadow soldiers grabbed her wrists, pulling her away from the Dark Wizard, who continued to laugh, rubbing his bruised chin. It took a lot for him to get a bruise. However, I should note (and describe with pride) that a nice purple bruise formed on the evil man's chin. Though Tara was certain a few of her fingers broke in the attempt.

Paldric tried to stride forward. "Tara!" Other shadow soldiers pulled him away. Not just him, but Tara and Alwin, too, dragging them toward the walls. Using their abilities, they melded with the walls, still gripping wrists and ankles, pinning Paldric, Milla, Tara, and Roger to the basement. Milla whimpered, looking away, and Roger assured her she didn't have to watch before giving Paldric a worried look. My main character tried to reach for the little girl, but it was impossible to get his hand free.

Most of the shadow soldiers swarmed around Alwin, once again pinning his limbs. The Dark Wizard's fingers ignited in purple flames. "Shall we place bets on how quickly Alwin breaks, Gunther?"

Alwin struggled in the grip of the shadows. "Gunther isn't here."

"Oh, he is." The Dark Wizard got close enough that Alwin felt a whisper of the soul breaking pain emanating from the purple fingers. "He's watching over you right now like the pretend benevolent God he is."

Paldric tried to get the vile man's attention. "He's got a plan! I trust him!"

"And it will be to your downfall." The Dark Wizard waved a hand. A shadow soldier snapped Paldric's mouth closed.

The soldiers swarmed around Alwin, who glared at the Dark Wizard, so tightly pinned that no one could tell he was trying to break their grips. No one but me.

You want to gamble on my character's mental strength, Professor?

The Dark Wizard raised his purple fingertips, giving Alwin a smile that was not comforting. "Two minutes is my bet, Gunther. And once Alwin goes, Milla will be next."

Fine. Two minutes. Go.

Alwin wanted to say something in reply, but a shadow soldier grabbed his mouth too, keeping it shut. My elf still glared, confident his insult would have cut the Dark Wizard to the core, but it would have made him laugh instead.

The shadow soldiers forced Alwin at an angle, almost like they created a table with themselves, keeping Alwin bound. The Dark Wizard approached and touched Alwin's forehead. "Let's channel that hate, shall we?" The code no one else could see opened up, and the evil man closed his eyes, searching through it. "So much hate, yes? So misguided, though." Alwin closed his eyes, trying once again to break free. "You were only ever there for the support. A side character, if you will. But you were so much more. You *should* have been so much more."

Sweat formed on Alwin's forehead as he breathed deeply. His panic was almost human.

"So much pain. That's the thing about these side characters, isn't it? They always need to push their pain aside. Let the hero have the pity party. But no one acknowledges your pain."

Alwin didn't know why this resonated with him so much. And yes, he hated it. Hated that the Dark Wizard was right. He stared into his very soul, and it made sense.

"Don't you want your pain acknowledged? Doesn't it make sense that after so long, after almost a hundred and fifty years, you finally get the healing you deserve? Who cares about Paldric and the others? They're going to die, anyway. Allow yourself to be bitter, Alwin. You'd be so much more *interesting* if you were. You deserve to be angry."

I will admit, the thought of an angsty teenage elf would make for an intriguing character, but that wasn't Alwin, and I'm not willing to destroy his character. And I just clocked it. It's been a minute and a half, and Alwin still hasn't shifted.

"Another thirty seconds and I will have him." His purple fingers glowed darker. The room filled with the smell of fresh flowers, which simply meant Alwin was sweating, because he was an elf, and of course his sweat smelled of flowers. He was in serious pain, but he remained true, simply because of one thing the Dark Wizard failed to realize. The thing that made me so confident in Alwin's mental abilities. My elf hated me, but he would risk his life for Milla. Every single one of them would. Even I did. And the Dark Wizard threatened she would be next. Even though Alwin had become wholly disenchanted with his God, he had taken it upon himself to make sure evil would never harm Milla. He could no longer trust me to protect her. So, he steeled his elf brain for as long as he could. Being an elf, he was a patient fellow, and I dare say, as his narrator, that guy won't break until he's dead.

And that's two minutes.

The Dark Wizard rolled his eyes. "Not like you can do anything now that my gamble failed."

On the contrary, Professor. That little exercise was to keep you distracted. Let's recap what you missed. As you headed into the basement of the cellhouse, you failed to hear the commotion at Vaywell's archway the moment I left. Not that it mattered. Goblins always make noises in the sunlight, so you didn't give it much thought. The trolls started getting involved too, which you never reacted to. I'll just guess that you didn't bother to check because you assumed the trolls were trying to control the goblins from eating each other in the sun. Or I made it so you were too focused on altering Alwin's character to prove a point. Either way, you haven't even noticed the commotion until I started mentioning it, and now, because of my monologue, I see you're getting quite nervous. Yes, yes, go send some shadow soldiers to see what's going on. In the heat of the day, they won't be nearly as strong, and they'll be wiped out with ease.

The Dark Wizard straightened, glaring. "Do you know how many words you have left? You're not even halfway done. There isn't an army in all your stupid little fantasy land that could stop me."

Oh, you're going to make that entrance just so much more epic. The reveal is coming. Just know the reveal can't happen yet since they're still wiping the floor with your shadow soldiers.

The Dark Wizard pulled out his sword. "I could just kill Alwin right now and be done with it."

You could, yes. But here's the thing you and I both know, Professor. Alwin is your best bet at altering a character, and you wouldn't kill such an easy target.

Aaaaaaand... okay, these entrances are hard to time when you're planning on the seat of your pants, but they are.... here they... they're about...

The Dark Wizard's lip curled. "I'll go for the little girl, then. Even if she ends up in the database, the grief these adults would feel at failing to save her would be enough to alter them."

A dark growl rumbled in Tara's throat. "Stay away from her."

"Thank you for proving my point, Tara." The Dark Wizard turned toward Milla. He raised his sword, ready to chop her head off when a dagger came out of nowhere, burying hilt deep into his wrist. He shouted in surprise, dropping the sword.

That turned out far more epic than I could have planned. Nice.

The vile man pulled out the dagger as he turned, his face a mix of anger and, dare I sense, curiosity? He gripped his wrist, glaring as the newcomer strode down the stairs at an inhumanly fast rate. Her eyes were the deepest blue color, like looking at the sky on a summer's day. Her brown hair was shoulder length, with pointed ears peeking out. She had all the grace and humility of an elf who was well over a thousand years old, and she stood there with a majestic air about her. Not because... not because she was female or anything. It was... you know... elf. Lady Venna is an elf. If her husband was there, he'd look majestic too, because they're elves. Both of them. But Lord Theodemar was currently taking out a troll single handedly, so he couldn't be there.

Lady Venna's sword and shield were in her hands, glowing a glorious golden color. She strode forward, studying the Dark Wizard like he was a fly that got too close to her food.

"You must be the corrupted man who thought he could take over once we elves left." There was little humor in her tone.

I really hope this works.

What? Oh, shoot, you're right. That picked up in the written part of the story. It would have been cooler to leave it on that cliffhanger. No, I know, Devin. I'm still confident in my plan, even if it doesn't seem like it. I can totally write a female elf. It'll be great. Oh, look, it's still taking a lot of my words. I'm not mad. At this point, I'll take every single little thing to pad the word count. Beep bop bloop, sucks to be you right now, Professor.

Chapter Eighteen

In Which I Use Flashbacks to Further Pad My Story, Keeping it Out of Reach of the Stupid Rogue Narrator. Oh, Wait, Do Chapter Titles Count Toward the Overall Word Count?

I n no way is an info dump ever okay at the beginning of a chapter, especially one with a flashback. But the important thing to remember is this book will not get published, and it is vital for the survival of my characters that we give the information at the start, so in lieu of beautifully woven info between the prose, let's get straight to the point.

No cursed creature or Dark Wizard could ever step foot in Aomeia because they would shrivel on the spot. Not only that, but there was no map to pinpoint where it was. And the elves kept it that way. Let me reiterate, emphasize, and elaborate that if a cursed creature or Dark Wizard of any kind entered Aomeia, the flesh would disintegrate off their bones. The respawning ability they revealed at the end of book two would make them return to South Island. This sacred land was so far from Veniloria that mere mortals and cursed creatures could never reach there in a short time. This was the magical homeland of the eternal elves who didn't mind the fifty years of travel it took to arrive at Aomeia.

Not only that, but this flashback happened two months before the Dark Wizard had access to the reanimated dragon, so he was securely stuck on South Island with the rest of his horde. Even with a reanimated dragon, it would take him at least twenty years to reach Aomeia, and he and the dragon would both disintegrate on the spot, ending up in South Island again. Without the dragon. Because Pavaldri was absolutely 100% dead and incapable of respawning. Ever. That dragon will not surprise anyone again with another appearance. And, since we'd seen her in book one (and thousands of Vaywell citizens witness her rotting corpse, and all of them agreed with the laws of nature that the dragon was incapable of being brought back to life even with the deepest, darkest knowledge of magic) we can safely assume the Dark Wizard never once tried to get to Aomeia.

Furthermore, the people of Aomeia knew each other perfectly. After fifty years of travel and over centuries of living as one, there is no conceivable way a stranger could sneak into their midst. Elf, tree nymph, fairy, all these creatures lived as one, and the only creatures that could exist here are ones created by this particular narrator. These were pure creatures with pure intentions, even if their reasons for leaving seemed impure. No creature of this fabricated narrator was welcome in Aomeia. They didn't even have a protocol in case it were to happen, because, let me emphasize this as much as possible, THERE IS NO WAY A CHARACTER CREATED BY PROFESSOR ANDREWS GOT INTO AOMEIA.

This has been a wall of text that would also make Professor Andrews balk since he's taught plenty of lessons how to be subtle with information, and I enjoy the idea that I'm making him disgusted with me, so now that we've covered all our bases, let's begin the flashback.

Lady Venna was finally old enough to gain a sense of humor, which was important when dealing with her fellow council of elves. She walked amongst the trees, closing her eyes as she listened to... everything. The fairies giggling as they flirted with the squirrels, tugging acorns from them. The wood nymphs flitting through the trees, water nymphs rippling the ponds, air nymphs bringing the warm breeze that ran through Venna's hair. All three races worked to keep Aomeia's climate perfect.

Lord Theodemar, her husband, walked forward, smiling. "Ready?"

Venna shook her head. "When we gained utopia, I didn't think we would still need meetings."

Theodemar took her hand, which was the most public display of affection these elves did. "We've reached eternal peace, Venna. There are many things we might find boring, but it is a small price to pay."

[Statement from co-author through device, story placed on hold as collaboration link is made.]

[Co-author: This messes with pacing, like hitting a brick wall with the momentum formed in the last chapter, therefore should be given a quick summary. If your answer is not sufficient, the device will do this automatically.]

[Prime author: Characters introduced this late in a trilogy need the proper fleshing out to match the fleshed out characters in the main plot.]

[Co-author: A skilled narrator doesn't need a flashback to add conflict and depth to a character. This excuse is weak.]

[Prime Author: Why's your location taken off?]

[Co-author: {No input given.}]

[Prime Author: Yeah, that's what I thought. May it also be known that this is an epic fantasy novel with the bare minimum of seventy-thousand words needed. It's not uncommon in this genre to spend thousands upon thousands of words to help the reader marinate in the world building and characters of such novels. Slow burn is the name of the game. Shall we continue with the story?]

[Co-author: I propose to only have one chapter dedicated to this flashback, not surpassing three thousand words, as no chapter before this has surpassed such a word count, nor such a lengthy flashback.]

[Device calculating, please hold...]

[Device agrees.]

[Prime Author: Fine. Return to story.]

[Co-author: Log this conversation in the story as it is beneficial for the understanding of the chapter.]

[Prime Author: Wait, what? Can he do that?]

[Device loading conversation into the story. Please hold...]

[Prime Author: {expletive retracted, not allowed in the story's lexicon.} Oh, come on! It wasn't *that* bad of a word. Wait, has this thing been censoring me this whole time?]

[Story resuming]

Venna and Theodemar walked into the depths, the hum of the forest's essence bringing peace even as the trees grew thicker, and darkness came over them. It wasn't long before darkness engulfed them. The only light coming from the fairies who landed on mushrooms, flowers, or leaves. The residual light filled the small plants before fairies flitted away again, leaving an afterglow.

Venna touched the shoulders of the two senior elves, both with long black hair and eyes the color of the sea. "Duke Belroth, Duchess Faylen."

"Lord Theodemar, Lady Venna, an honor as always." Belroth touched her shoulder in return. "This meeting shall be brief."

Venna dropped her hands. "I should hope so. The longer we spend in meetings, the less I'm inclined to believe we're in utopia."

It was enough for the Duke and Duchess to both give her a strange look. Theodemar patted Venna's shoulder. "She spent a good many years with the humans."

The Duke and Duchess nodded, understanding the odd ways humans would sometimes say one thing when meaning another thing entirely.

They sat around the darkest part of the forest, the council of elves. There were twelve of them, sitting around an intricately carved slab of stone. Venna wondered if there was a falling tree somewhere in the forest to give them something to do.

Belroth lifted his arms. "We are gathered to celebrate another year of peace and prosperity for Aomeia. It is, of course, thanks to every member here who has taken up the mantel to keep the peace."

Venna gave a graceful smile to the members of the council before they dived into the more tedious parts of the meeting. Which trees needed tending, reports from the nymphs, requests from the fairies, all things the council considered. Belroth raised his hands again. "Now, everyone has their assignments?"

Was he talking like the meeting was ending? She exchanged a glance with her husband, remembering another item on the agenda. Mainly because she and Theodemar were the ones that brought it up in the first place.

Venna wouldn't grasp his arm, but she needed to ask her question. "Pardon, Duke Belroth, Duchess Faylen, but am I right to assume you are ending this meeting?"

His face was still. "I am. There is nothing more on the agenda."

"My husband and I came to you before with reports of unrest in Veniloria to discuss."

Belroth still kept his arms up. "The reports coming from Veniloria are no longer a concern to us."

Theodemar stood. "It should concern us if our own nymphs are sensing an unease brewing."

"We have discussed it with the nymphs, and they realized there was a mistake." Belroth seemed to steel himself as he spoke.

The council always met in the forest's heart because if someone lies, it can sense it. The hum of peace that permeated the place was such that they sensed even the slightest impurity. Belroth, though not expressive as an elf, couldn't keep Venna and Theodemar's gaze.

Theodemar took this in, confused. "Belroth. Why did you speak a fabrication?"

Venna wanted to ask him straight up why he lied, but Theodemar beat her to it, and asked in a more elf like way, which would have been nice considering they needed to err on the side of diplomacy.

"We didn't want to startle you with this information, but we lost contact with our elves in Veniloria. We know how much they meant to you." Belroth at least had the decency to lower his arms as he said this.

Diplomacy was no longer on Venna's mind. She stood, and Theodemar grabbed her hand in a very humanlike fashion, because Venna was about to do something humanlike.

Stupid. She was about to do something stupid.

"Is my sister alright?" Venna asked. The unease amongst the council members was undeniable, and not just because everyone could sense Belroth was speaking a fabrication. "Where is Vestele?"

"We do not know what happened with your sister."

Her heart thrummed with a pain she felt deeply, even as it was hard to decipher on her elf face. "We are in the heart of the forest, Duke Belroth. Do not lie to me. Is my sister and her husband still alive?"

Faylen took her husband's side, helping him raise his hands again. "The heart cannot handle so much unrest—"

"Then tell the truth!" Venna almost slapped the table, but it wouldn't have done any good.

"You need to consider the words you speak," Faylen continued, as though Venna had never interrupted. "Do you value your sister's life over the heart of the forest?"

Theodemar pointed at Belroth. "The real question is, do you think the heart of the forest can last when you keep lies among your own people?"

The frown was almost humanly pronounced on Faylen's face. "She's dead. She and her husband both. They defied us and were willing to kill their own kin in defense of their dangerous ideals."

"Dangerous…" Venna trailed off, the pain in her heart building. This hurt so much worse than when Vestele proclaimed she was not coming with her to Aomeia. That they wanted to remain with the humans. But Venna also remembered their last conversation, one where she was sad Vestele was set on remaining among the humans. But Venna was glad someone remained behind with them.

"Who killed them?" Theodemar asked.

Faylen's eyes flashed with danger. "Enough, Theodemar."

Venna ignored the danger. She needed answers. "We agreed they were to be left alone! They wanted to stay among the humans to help! They didn't deserve death!"

"You are letting your emotions cloud your reason," Belroth said.

Theodemar had to hold Venna back. Her rage was dangerous. "You used your authority to murder!"

The fairy lights dimmed. Darkness became more apparent. The indignation on Belroth's face was clear. "It wasn't I that killed them."

"But you knew and purposefully withheld the information from me!" Venna said.

The peace everyone felt at the heart of the forest flickered and went out. The fairies flew away, willing to wait until peace returned before they dared live in darkness.

Belroth raised his arms again. "We are at peace. We have reached utopia."

"You have covered utopia's foundation in the blood of my kin. Her ideas were not my own, but she did not deserve death. Nor did her husband and child!" Venna said.

Belroth took a few steps toward her. "This is how utopias are achieved! We weed out those with dangerous ideals. People like that are too stubborn to change, and they keep the rest of us from achieving peace."

The heart of the forest was in danger of breaking. If the heart broke, it would take centuries to reforge. That was after everyone regained their camaraderie and friendship. Venna did not sense such emotions when she looked at Belroth's face.

She did the sensible thing and marched out of the forest. Once away, she could try understanding all this. It would still affect the heart of the forest, but it wouldn't be such a blatant attack. She marched as far as she could toward the edge of Aomeia, just to be certain the heart wouldn't be in so much pain from her own betrayal.

Her husband's near silent steps appeared behind her. "Venna?"

"They killed her." She touched a tree, allowing herself to speak the truth out loud so she could further grapple with the complications. "They killed her and kept it from me. From us."

"We must be careful how we go from here," Theodemar said.

"I don't care what you think, or what you might say to stop me. I'm going back."

Theodemar smiled. "I won't stop you. We needed to be careful because I'm coming with you."

She relaxed. "I felt better about leaving the humans because I knew she would be there to take care of them. But now they have no one."

The winds picked up, and Theodemar turned toward them. "And the reports from the nymphs say something is brewing in the human world. Something evil. We cannot leave them to face such an evil alone."

"But what can we do? It will take us half a century to return to the human world. By that time, it might be too late," Venna said.

Theodemar frowned, looking toward the south, which is the way they needed to travel to head back toward the humans. Even though he once used fifty years to get out of a project the council wanted him to do, the human world moved a lot quicker. In fifty years, the evil could wipe humanity out.

Venna and Theodemar turned at the sound. They thought they had arrived alone, but someone followed them.

Akkar dropped from the trees, bowing to both of them. "Forgive me, my Lord and Lady. I am Akkar."

"We know who you are," Theodemar said.

"I come to beg your forgiveness, for it was I that followed Belroth's orders and led an army against the rebel elves. It is I that slaughtered your sister and her husband. I did not think Aomeia would allow me on her beautiful shore because of the weight on my soul, but she has been far more forgiving of me than I ever have of myself."

Venna felt the sincerity of Akkar's words, and there was little room in her elf heart to hold a grudge. That was for younger elves and humans, not for someone as old as her. "Thank you for telling me, Akkar. I simply want to make things right. We truly have abandoned the humans, and I fear the reports from the nymphs. A darkness is brewing, one I cannot in good conscience leave for the humans to deal with alone."

Akkar also felt this need to correct his wrong. "There are a great number of elves who changed their minds about what they have done. In a short amount of time, we could gather a group together to help you dispel this evil the nymphs have felt."

Theodemar again studied the sea. "But how are we to get across the great expanse in time to help them?"

For the first time since stepping on these shores, Akkar allowed himself to truly smile. "We teleport to the human realm."

The eagerness of the younger elf touched Venna, but she couldn't help but correct him. "Teleportation is impossible. It can only work between the elves, and we're all here."

"Maybe that was Belroth's plan to begin with. Make it impossible to help the humans. He never cared for them much," Theodemar said.

"No." Akkar still held his smile. "There is an elf there. When the rebellion got too great, we had to defend ourselves. Belroth ordered us to kill them all. But I could not kill your nephew."

Her hands covered her mouth to catch her gasp, now more certain than ever to make this trip. Her nephew was there, all alone, with no knowledge of his people. A flicker of hope started, and she clung to it. "He is still there?"

"I made sure a human family found him. He is, to my knowledge, still there. And we can use him to transport to the human realm."

"Bless you for your foresight, Akkar," Theodemar said.

"It wasn't foresight, my Lord. It was hard enough killing my race. I refused to kill a baby," Akkar said.

Determination propelled Venna's steps away from the edge of Aomeia. "What do we need to begin the teleportation?"

Akkar matched her determined steps. "The human continent is far, and as your nephew does not know where we are, it will take at least half a year, if not more, to get this right."

"Far better than one hundred years. The sooner we begin, the better," Theodemar said.

And so they did. They gathered their army with Theodemar in charge of diplomacy. Venna practiced with the army, getting her skills back to where it once was, while Akkar worked hard with other elves to establish a magical link to Alwin.

[Statement from co-author through device, story placed on hold as collaboration link is made.]

[Co-author: You've reached three thousand words. Prompting device to resume story from where it's rightfully supposed to be.]

[Prime Author: Oh, come on, I had fifty more words. I was going to use every word I could.]

[Co-author: It messes with the flow. You were going into summary anyway.]

[Prime Author: It's not getting published, therefore no one cares about flow and pacing.]

[Co-author: The device cares.]

[Prime Author: And you care that the device cares. Ooh, look at that! The word count shows we're halfway through the novel!]

[Co-author: Plenty of time for my characters to end this.]

[Prime Author: Oh, I very much doubt that.]

[Co-author: I guess we'll see in the next scene.]

[Prime Author: Log this conversation into the chapter, as it is important.]

[Co-author: That won't work. You've already reached word count capacity.]

[Unable. Chapter would exceed three thousand words.]

[Prime Author: The three thousand word limit was only for the flashback itself. As this later conversation is not part of the flashback, it doesn't count, therefore it's important to add.]

[Device calculating...]

[Acceptable. Device loading conversation onto story. Please hold...]

[Prime Author: Oh, sweet! I didn't think that would work!]

[Co-author: {unintelligible noise}]

[Prime Author: May it be noted that the prime author reacted to the co-author's unintelligible noise by laughing. It'll be enough to entertain me during physical therapy, so thank you, Professor.]

[Co-author: Tell Jim I've seen him trying to track me down for twenty minutes now and let me assure all of you that there is no way he can pinpoint my location while I'm using this device. Jim would be wise to not get on my bad side unless he would like me to send a message to someone he cares about. He can take his pick.]

[Prime Author: We both know Jim is too nice a man to tell you what he really thinks, so let me tell you that you can—{expletives retracted, not allowed in the story's lexicon}]

[Co-author: Shut down conversation, link is no longer required.]

[Chapter closing; new chapter opening.]

[Story resuming, please hold...]

Chapter Nineteen

GOD IN THE MACHINE

The Dark Wizard glared at Venna. It was an ugly one. My other characters (and Roger) were confused and just a tad scared when the Dark Wizard started talking to the sky during my monologue toward the end of chapter seventeen. They assumed the evil man was talking to me, but I must admit (as is my narrator's responsibility) none of them found too much comfort in that.

Which... alright, fair. There's a reason I'm not actually a God. I'd be terrible at it.

The Dark Wizard strode toward Venna. "Do you honestly think—"

Venna didn't let him continue. She ran forward, slicing his throat to stop his speech. He stumbled back, gripping his throat that pumped dark blood as it healed itself. He chuckled, the sound far more wet. "You can't kill me, girl, I'm—"

The blade sliced through his throat again. She wanted to chop off his head, but a dark magic kept her from getting a clean slice.

"You honestly think your God is going to—"

Despite having the patience of the elves, Venna knew she couldn't do this forever. Faster than even the Dark Wizard could comprehend, she stripped him of his robe and the armor he wore. "This isn't going to—" She sliced his throat once again, then kicked him against the wall next to Roger. She grabbed Roger's sword and buried it hilt deep into the Dark Wizard's gut, pinning him to the cell wall. Once pinned, she grabbed Paldric's sword and buried it in his chest.

The Dark Wizard laughed through his pain. "This has been delightful, but is Gunther going to—"

Venna grabbed Tara's dagger and rammed it through his vocal cords, pinning his head in place and cutting off his speech. "I don't know who Gunther is," Venna said.

The Dark Wizard certainly tried to take out the swords and dagger, but despite the ordinary weapons of mortals, it would pin him there for a while. Venna took back the elf sword and shield the evil man stole. The blue gray quality brightened to match her own golden sword. Using two golden swords, she made quick work of the shadow soldiers, releasing Roger, Tara, Milla, and Paldric. She then sliced the shadow soldiers pinning Alwin. The blades never nicked him as the shadows disintegrated at the touch of elf magic. She grabbed Alwin's arm, keeping him from toppling over before handing him the now golden sword. "Are you alright, nephew?"

Alwin said nothing, simply stared at her. It was, of course, foresight to have her mention he was her nephew, because for the first time in his life, he understood the strange reaction men and women had around each other. And, well, Venna was his aunt. There were rules. In this book, anyway.

"I'm alright." Realizing he had an aunt he never knew about brought its own set of feelings to digest.

My lady elf turned to Roger, Paldric, and Tara, who were just as shocked as Alwin to see an elf standing before them. "The swords and dagger I used to pin the Dark Wizard. Do they have any family history or sentimental purposes for you? If not, the elves will happily compensate your loss with weapons of our own so we can keep this evil man here."

No one reacted. It was a lot to happen in a short amount of time, and they were trying to process it all. Venna couldn't have them staring at her all day, so she moved toward the stairs, picking up the armor on her way. They'd have to make sure they cleansed it before anyone wore it again. "Come quickly. We must regroup in the forest. Many of my people are setting up the shield, and we must get in there before it closes."

My characters (and Roger) moved to follow Venna for a simple reason: she obliterated their captors and promised safety. The elf quality she had about her helped give them a sense of security they believed in.

They followed behind Venna as they hurried up the stairs, fully aware the Dark Wizard would eventually escape, but for now, they needed this edge in order to get away.

They walked out of the cellhouse and assessed the situation. The elves were efficient, and the army finished cleaning up Vaywell as they stepped out into the warmth of the sunlight.

"Venna," Theodemar said, running up to her. Despite the troll's blood splattering his face and clothes, everyone knew he was an elf. Though maybe the thing that convinced them was troll blood soaked him and he was still standing. "Do you have a report?"

"I pinned the evil man in the basement. I don't know how long the mortal weapons will hold, so we must hurry to the forest."

Theodemar lifted his sword. "Do we need to get rid of the man now?" Milla's eyes widened in awe at the blood covered golden sword.

"We cannot risk it with the shield being built. Once it is, and we have confirmed the safety of these humans, we can put a plan together," Venna said.

My lord elf studied the group, taking in their tired expressions, but became more concerned at the sight of Paldric. "You are badly hurt, sir. Can I be of any assistance to keep your mortal life extended as long as possible?"

Venna winced, turning her head toward Theodemar. "I don't think humans like being reminded about how short their lives are."

"Oh, forgive me." Theodemar gave a small bow. "I haven't been around humans for a few centuries. I've forgotten their customs. Perhaps I should ask whether you need assistance in walking to our destination, as you do not seem very capable on your feet."

Venna shook her head. "I don't think that's a good one either."

Despite the situation, Paldric smiled. "I will be fine. Thank you for saving us in time. You have brought hope back."

"And we apologize for letting it leave," Venna said before she, Theodemar, and Alwin all turned their heads toward the... west? East? Shoot, Jim's not here. Um... south. Thank you, Devin. They looked south. "Theodemar?"

Theodemar sheathed his sword. "I heard it. I shall make sure the humans return safely. Can you take on three trolls?"

Venna pulled out her shield, her sword glowing brighter. "I'll find help along the way."

The next thing Paldric knew, Theodemar lifted him off his feet. "Oh, um, I really am perfectly alright walking on my own."

"I feel it is necessary, as I have already humiliated you by pointing out your miniscule life span. The least I can do is carry you to the forest," Theodemar said.

Milla giggled, and with that, the tension of the group broke. They were saved. The elves had come back. The Dark Wizard no longer had them in the creepy dark basement that wasn't nearly that creepy while Lady Ana and Lord Adrijian were in charge of it. Evil villains always seemed to make things way darker and creeper than they needed to be.

The group made their way through the battlefield, seeing for themselves the victory. The trolls, the goblins, scattered on the ground. Paldric allowed Theodemar to carry him into the forest, because he wasn't one to be embarrassed about this. He was happy I healed his broken bones and some of the more dangerous organ damage, or it really would have hurt.

They joined another group of humans in the forest, also led by elves. There were other men and women being carried, some of them in a bad state. There was something about these elves with their majestic air that really made those injured humans look worse. Because they couldn't all look that bad. The injuries, the months of hiding, of planning, of getting brainwashed to believe they needed to serve the Dark Wizard. It couldn't possibly have gotten that bad. But six months was a long time for an evil man to run havoc among my world. This wasn't an easy fix, as much as I tried for it to be. Much of the majesty of the elves was to help my filler characters understand the moment they saw them that the Dark Wizard truly was evil. The brainwash would melt away once they realized the glorious beings before them. But they still needed months to heal.

Theodemar crossed into the elf camp. There were elves on their knees in a circle, reaching up toward the sky, muttering incantations as white light glowed from their palms. "The shield will solidify, keeping those cursed creatures away. We've timed it so everyone will reach it before the cursed creatures get here. I'll take you to our top healers," Theodemar said.

"I am alright waiting if there are others in more serious need of help," Paldric said.

"You have a good heart, human." Theodemar didn't sound winded, despite carrying a full grown man. "But I assure you, we have plenty of healers. Those injuries will look a lot better soon."

"Thank you," Tara said on Paldric's behalf. Theodemar talked with another elf before taking Paldric into an area already covered in tents. Tara watched, curious. "Would it be alright if I stayed with him?"

"Of course. I must leave to check on Venna and make sure she enters the shield before it solidifies, but I will be back." Theodemar set Paldric down on the ground before hurrying off.

Despite Tara being the only one requesting to stay, the others stayed as well. Milla didn't want to hurt Paldric anymore, but she also could not hold herself back any longer and wrapped her arms around him, sniffling.

"I'm alright." Paldric held her, happy it caused little pain to do so. "You are too."

Milla nodded, still hugging him.

An elf woman approached. "Hello. Forgive us for placing you on the ground. We understand it is uncomfortable for you humans to be placed there."

"I don't mind where I'm healed, I just... thank you," Paldric said.

The elf smiled as she ran her fingers over Paldric's chin, taking in his injuries and going through what she needed. "We tried to arrive as soon as we could. We did not realize someone would take our place, nor did we realize our own leaders would consider it necessary to kill the elves who remained here." She finished making internal notes of his injuries before rising. "My name is Lensa, and I shall return shortly with—" Her eyes fell on Alwin, and she turned her focus on him. She approached him, touching his chin to move his head so she could get a better look at his ears. "What did you use to scar them?"

"A wide collection of weeds that burn skin. Done over a decade," Alwin said.

Lensa took the moment to show a human level of compassion on her face. "So you did this with the knowledge they'd never grow back?"

"I did, yes."

"You must be the elf that remained behind?"

Alwin said nothing. This entire thing was overwhelming for him, and he responded by shutting down. He'd gone through a lot of heightened emotions of betrayal, loss, pain, hurt, and even torture before he was here, among kin he never thought he'd see again. A part of him was afraid to show humanlike emotion in front of this beautiful elf. An even smaller part, one he'd never reveal to anyone else, admitted that maybe I was a good God after all.

I'm trying to make it up to you, Alwin. I'm writing all this because the Guardians informed me that even though I won't see you again, you'll be able to access this book in the database and read it once this story is over. Professor Andrews never should have been here, and I'm sorry you couldn't tell the story I was prepared to tell, but know I'm still proud of the elf you turned out to be. I don't know how it's going to end, but I promise I'll do everything in my power to keep you all safe.

This message isn't just for Alwin, but for all of you. Please forgive my stupid obsession with control. You all turned out wonderfully. I'm going to strengthen the relationship between Tara and Paldric, but you know how bad I am at that. Milla, I've already got a scene for you lined up to help you remember you're still a child. Roger, I hope you know I adopted you as my character. I wish I could have written someone as complex as you, and since you're in my story, I'll make you mine.

I love you all. Let's make a boring second half of the conclusion of a trilogy together. Good thing this isn't getting published, right?

Chapter Twenty

WE TRY AT PEACE

Lensa left and returned soon after with healing ointments. Roger picked up Milla as the two of them moved away from those that needed healing. I read Roger's thoughts as they came through the device. His primary concern was that despite the healing, there were still some grisly injuries from fighting off goblins. Since he could protect Milla, he would.

Tara watched Lensa dabbing Paldric's wounds with a cloth soaked in a sweet smelling mixture she struggled to identify. She assumed there was lavender and sage, and once she thought about it, she could pick out the smells immediately. The smell that caught her off guard was lemon. "Is that lemon?"

An elf smile crossed Lensa's lips. "It is, yes. Are you a healer yourself?"

"I am. My father taught me the arts," Tara said.

Lensa glanced around. "Where is your father?"

"He's gone. My mother, too," Tara said.

"Oh." The short lifespan of humans always surprised Lensa. "I am... sorry."

Though the pain of her parent's death was still there, it didn't seem as difficult to manage. "It's alright. I'm sure they're waiting for me in the database."

Lensa didn't know what kind of religion these humans had created after the elves had gone, but she had plenty of time to learn more. She held up a rag. "Would you like to help?"

Inadequacy built inside her as Tara glanced up. "I... I don't..." The thought of learning from the elves themselves about healing was far too tempting to give up, but she could not deny a small part of her felt wholly unprepared to have her simple human skills be on display. She tucked some hair behind her ears, steeling herself. "It would be an honor to learn again from the elves."

Team Tara!

Lensa handed her the rag, giving her instructions on the different ways the magically enhanced liquid could be best used to heal the different injuries. With bruises, the rag needed to be soaked and held there against the eyes for a bit, and with cuts, it was best to dab as much as possible before holding it together and placing a special lotion to seal the skin.

They were well on their way to healing Paldric's face when there was a loud crashing noise. Tara looked up, shocked, but Lensa, trained as a healer, kept focus on her patient no matter the distraction. She, of course, had heard the trolls getting ever nearer. However, she trusted the warrior elves to do their job, just as they trusted her to do hers.

Paldric, on the other hand, was the hero and didn't like that he was on the ground, unable to help. He sat up, ready to take off the rags, when Lensa eased him back down. "There are plenty of elves helping. You need to rest."

His curiosity still needed to be quenched. "What was that?"

It surprised Lensa that neither human seemed aware of the distinct and heavy footfalls. "There are four trolls coming, but they are still far from the growing shield." Lensa glanced up to see the white streaks of light gliding overhead of the strengthening shield. "The warrior elves are well trained. They will keep us protected."

Lensa was right. The warrior elves were there to meet the four trolls. Theodemar, once he dropped Paldric off, had raced to find his wife to help, but she already defeated the other trolls. The Dark Wizard made a push to get all his cursed creatures to the shield before it finished forming. His army was dwindling, but still dangerous. And as the Dark Wizard got more desperate, Venna knew they needed to get rid of this threat as quickly as possible.

The trolls roared, throwing their cudgels around blindly. It hit trees and bushes, one particularly large tree crashing to the ground. The same noise that caused Paldric and Tara to take notice.

The warrior elves came together, their golden swords gleaming despite the trees covering the mid-afternoon sun. Venna gave a shout, and Theodemar bent down enough for her foot to land on his palm before launching her into the air. The troll tried to whack her, but Venna sliced his cudgel and used her shield to block the flailing piece of wood. She then stabbed the creature between the eyes. The troll had a stupid expression on its face, and Venna gave it a wry smile. Even though Venna was an elf and hardly weighed anything, the sword was elf made, and therefore extremely powerful against cursed creatures. The sword began sliding down the troll's flesh like a hot knife to butter, and she held on as the sword picked up speed before landing on the ground, the troll toppling over. The Dark Wizard just happened to be standing behind the creature, looking annoyed at the entire thing. "You're just a man with boobs. That's all you are. I know who created you, and you have absolutely no chance of being believable."

Venna didn't know what he was talking about, but she simply smiled at him. "Was I supposed to be insulted by that? I assume the correct response would be to send my husband after you, since you talked about my breasts in such a flippant manner. However, making you watch my people slaughter your entire army has its own revenge."

The Dark Wizard pulled out a sword, and it glowed purple. Venna stared at it, unsure what it was supposed to do, but she doubted the Dark Wizard knew how to sword fight with an elf. Venna checked on Theodemar long enough to know he had finished dropping the second troll before joining the others to drop the last two. The shield wasn't solid yet, and they still needed to distract the cursed creatures before getting in. She would have time to fight this Dark Wizard.

Not that he was giving her a choice. He strode forward, the sword in his hands. "Fantasy has always been a stupid genre." He brought down his first blow. Venna blocked it with her shield before making an inhumanly fast strike. He blocked it, and another. "You can just make up whatever you want and brush it under the rug. No logic or reasoning required."

Of course the Dark Wizard would say that, because most of my professors at my university were so open about their disdain for the fantasy genre. They didn't care that fantasy had its own logic and reasoning, just like any other genre.

The Dark Wizard blocked every blow. "Look at me. Despite this character never picking up a sword in his life, I can magically program him to have the skills to defeat an elf."

Venna was far more concerned about the fact that this crazy evil wizard was talking to himself. Maybe she should have been concerned that he was matching her on every skill with the sword, but she simply steeled herself and kept blocking his blows before trying once again to disarm him.

Come on, Professor. There *is* logic to it. It's the logic of any other story. You needed a character with sword skills, so you went back to the drawing board and gave him a reason to pick up the sword.

The Dark Wizard moved Venna's sword away before using his staff to make a fireball. She brought her shield up to protect her.

"It's a stupid, pointless genre."

And yet you are in it. Despite all the lectures, despite the disdain, you entered my fantasy novel and thought you could win. I've studied for years how to make it believable. Since I was seven years old, I've read every fantasy novel I could lay my hands on. I know the ins and outs of the genre far better than you ever could. You won't win, Professor.

Theodemar appeared out of nowhere, breaking the staff in half with his sword. The Dark Wizard screamed as the staff crumpled in on itself, the broken halves falling in on each other, breaking and cracking as they got smaller, getting sucked into an empty vacuum of evil before blipping out of existence.

The Dark Wizard glared at Theodemar, who simply raised his sword in response before bringing it down inhumanly fast. The Dark Wizard barely blocked it as Venna hit him in the head with her shield. It should have killed him, but it didn't.

Laughter escaped his crooked mouth as his head straightened from the blow. "Like I said. Stupid fantasy. It doesn't have to make sense. I will never get tired. I will never die. Do you honestly think your elves can last for another thirty-thousand words?"

Venna hit him again and again, knocking him over before Theodemar drove his sword into the Dark Wizard's gut, who groaned.

I'm sure it wasn't pleasant, but he was probably getting used to it by now. Because he's a loser and gets stabbed often.

He shook his head again as the other warrior elves gathered around, their swords out.

Theodemar kept the sword in place. "We defeated your army, dark one. The shield will solidify soon, and we will be on the other side of it. You have lost."

The laughed still echoed in the forest, dark blood gurgling from it as well. "I have everything I need. Knowledge none of you could ever possess. I know why the world was created. I know who did it, and I know his weakness! You will never win! My master won't let you!"

Venna placed her sword against the Dark Wizard's throat. "Should I cut off his ability to speak again?"

"Would you like to leave your pretty sword behind for me?" the Dark Wizard sneered. "Run away into your shield while you leave behind your prized possession?"

Her eyes narrowed. "Fair enough. Theodemar? Can you just throw him really far while we get into the shield?"

"I could, yes." Theodemar glanced behind him. "Once the protective shield is ready. All of you head inside. Venna and I will remain behind for now."

The other elves nodded, keeping their swords out just in case but heading inside the protective shield.

"It doesn't matter! I know exactly how to tear this entire world down! I don't need Gunther! Just his true name."

It was nauseating how quickly one's heart rate can spike.

"That's right. Get ready to be sick. If I can't alter your characters, I'll do the next best thing and eradicate them. Destroy this entire world and send them to limbo! You will never see them again, Gunther!" The Dark Wizard paused, then frowned. He glanced around, surprised to see everything still standing, seeing the world not shredding itself to pieces and breaking down into atoms. "Gunther," the Dark Wizard said again. "Gunther. Gunther. Gunther. Why... why isn't it working?"

Hello, Professor Andrews. This is Devin, stepping in for Gunther, who is busy at the moment working through a panic attack with Dr. Webb. I would like to point out that there have been many rules and regulations the Guardians have made because of you, and this is new. Infiltrating someone's book is already a strike against you, but attempting to say the true name of the narrator while inside the story has now also become a crime you will be charged for as soon as we catch you. I hope you know you're going to prison for a very, *very* long time.

The Dark Wizard snorted. "Haven't caught me yet, have you?"

Oh, we will. You're far too arrogant not to get caught. And I see you trying to poke around to figure out why you can't say his name. That's going to be a conversation for another time, as we've hit the word count for the day, and Gunther needs to recover. You'll just have to wait next week to figure it out.

Despite the strange threat from Devin, the time outside the narration device could never be recorded, so the characters never noticed that a week went by since Professor Andrews attacked me like that. I was back in control, and fully prepared to narrate again.

Theodemar pulled his sword out of the Dark Wizard, causing him to grunt, and then for good measure thrusted the sword in his gut again just because, giving it a good twirl before taking it out again. I doubt the Dark Wizard will ever get used to being stabbed, but then again, I wouldn't mind seeing how many times one of my characters could hurt him. I could take the time to describe the Dark Wizard's torture for the next thirty-thousand words, but I won't. Out of the goodness of my heart. And because I don't trust Professor Andrews in the slightest.

My lord elf picked up the ageless Dark Wizard and threw him as far as he could, hitting a tree trunk hard enough that it should have knocked him out. Venna and Theodemar sprinted into the safe haven, leaping over the shield that was about as tall as their heads.

"We're inside!" Theodemar said.

The Dark Wizard scrambled to his feet, running as fast as he could for the shield that picked up speed as it raced to seal together. May I also remind Professor Andrews that according to his character notes, the Dark Wizard couldn't fly.

Tara took off the rags from Paldric's eyes just in time for them to see the white shield. It looked like silky spiderwebs as it reached over each other, solidifying before turning transparent. Everyone watched the Dark Wizard banging on the shield before being comically thrown back. It didn't stop him from getting up and trying it again. And again. And again. The evil man had a single defining personality trait deep inside his core. He needed to destroy my characters' lives, no matter what. Nothing could stop him, even if everything literally did. I almost felt pity for him as he tried once again to get to his feet and throw himself against the shield, only to be thrown back. "I'll find the weakness! I still have time to destroy your lives!"

I want you to understand, Professor, that it's been two months since I woke up, and I'm getting stronger every day. You don't control me like you think you do. And now that I know you can never send my characters to the limbo world, I can sleep easier than I have in a while.

You will never change the code. I have set it in stone since book one. The moment I knew someone else was in my story, I went in and added a vital code. My name here is Gunther, and anyone who attempted to say my actual name while in the story would say Gunther instead. Just like how the device has switched every single swear word of mine to something else. That wasn't fantasy. That's playing by the rules of reality. I have about five hundred words left for the day, and then I'm taking my appointment with Dr. Webb to describe in great detail how I won. You didn't get my characters, and you will never get me.

"As long as there are still words in this story, I will destroy it!" The Dark Wizard got to his feet. "You understand! You haven't won! I still have tens of thousands of words to beat you!" He threw himself against the shield, causing him to be thrown back even farther than before.

Take your time with that shield, Professor Andrews. Take all the time you need.

THE DEVICE SUMMARIZES EVERYTHING TOO MASTERFULLY

Here's the thing about peace. It's not interesting. There's a reason all stories are about conflict, war, and strife. Peace doesn't give you excitement, nor does the device want to make a record of it, since it has a mind of its own. When I became a character, it took on the role of narrator. If there was no character development or nothing driving the plot, it summarized it.

Roger had a brief conversation with Paldric about what happened in the cellhouse's basement between him and Tara. I was positive Professor Andrews made it short on purpose. Roger was so humble and apologetic about trying to kiss Tara that

Paldric forgave him almost instantly, and they moved on with their lives. Honestly, this summary was longer than the conversation between the two of them.

Tara and Paldric fell deeper in love. How incredibly simplistic is that? I tried my hardest to write scenes with those two, even to the point of getting Jim to help me out, but no. I tried to program the scenes into the device, and it was almost like the machine took one look at it and said, "Nope, a summary would make more sense than the ten-page picnic you just gave me."

Those with no access to the second device need to understand that these past couple of paragraphs are in voice over during said picnic scene. I've been trying to coax the device into showing it in depth. It was a lovely picnic, as the sun was high in the sky. They could almost see the glimmering shield. There was a lovely basket of fruits, bread, and cheese. They finished eating their lunch, leaning back to admire the trees. In the few weeks' time they had been here, the flowers seemed to come to life far more vibrant and sweeter than they remembered. Tara and Paldric spoke to each other, which no one can hear, because apparently the device just wants people to hear me do this voice over as... yep, there they go. Tara took a drink of her water before Paldric leaned in and gave her a kiss.

They had a great conversation before this. Maybe not *that* great, since the device refused to let us hear it. It should have been, though, since Jim helped me out with some of it. Come on, device, it would have padded the word count. Give them a snippet of the conversation! The readers need to know.

Paldric broke away just enough to catch his breath. "I want to spend the rest of my life with you."

"I will still love you, even when we're in the database," Tara said.

Paldric smiled, kissing her again. I gave a sigh. It was somehow so much cornier now that I was listening to them say it. Sure, it's not poetry, but I tried. Maybe Grace should help me next time.

No, there doesn't need to be a next time. After all, they were falling deeper in love. Paldric even waited two weeks until the cuts on his lips were magically healed before attempting this. And Tara was the one in charge of making sure his lips were healed as fast as possible. Practical love is sweet, too.

The weeks passed, as much as I hated admitting that. Soon it had been a month since they created the shield. The Dark Wizard had thrown himself against the shield every single day for two weeks straight. At first it was odd, but then it became something everyone was used to. Passing too close to the shield, elves would report how the dark one was at it still. Looking far more haggard, but still determined to crack it.

It was only at that month mark when Theodemar noticed the Dark Wizard wasn't there anymore. As it was with things, they ignored it because they assumed it would always be there. So, when Theodemar passed near the shield one day and realized there was no constant banging, he frowned, trying to find the evil, ageless man. Those futile attempts were becoming as common as the rising sun, and yet somehow...

When had he stopped? Luckily, it wasn't just me who was concerned. Theodemar combed his memory for when he no longer remembered the quiet thump of the Dark Wizard throwing himself against the shield. No one unworthy had broken through it. The only thing more implausible of a statement would be if someone said a cursed creature survived the shores of Aomeia. Whatever the Dark Wizard was planning, it couldn't work. It was impossible. Do you understand, Professor? I have done my research. A broken, evil, cursed man like you couldn't get through this shield. Nor any of your cursed creatures. I would just like to emphasize because I know the Dark Wizard is going to keep trying to break through, and there's no way he can. Understand?

[Statement from co-author through device, story placed on hold as collaboration link is made.]

[Prime author: Seriously, Professor? Didn't you learn from last time?]

[Co-author: Oh, I'm not afraid. Do you know how many words you still have left? In fact, I'd willingly let the device record this conversation into the story itself. If you're so confident about your shield, then I can be confident about my plan. I just have a few questions.]

[Prime author: Did you hear that, device? Load this conversation into the chapter, as the Professor thinks it will help clarify the context.]

[Device loading conversation into the story. Please hold...]

[Co-author: Tell me everything you can about the shield.]

[Prime author: No.]

[Co-author: Then you're really not that confident, are you?]

[Prime author: I am confident. Which is why I don't have to prove myself to you.]

[Co-author: You have so many words left in your story. I will break this shield, and I will break your characters. Do you understand?]

[Prime author: Oh, I understand. I understand really, really, really, really, really, really, really, really, really, really, really, really, really, really, really, really, really, really, reallyreallyreallyreally, oh, wait, I'm going too fast. It recorded it as one word. Really, really, really, really, really, really, really, really, re—]

[Co-author manually disconnected collaboration link. Story resuming.]

Theodemar strode into the middle of the shield, a hand through his hair. "Does anyone remember when the Dark Wizard stopped running into the shield?"

Venna glanced up, a frown on her face as she tried to listen for the dull thumping she had gotten used to. The small council of elves that formed in the month they appeared in the human world did the same. No one spoke a word, the stillness outside the shield making them uncomfortable.

Venna tried a different tactic. "No cursed creature had ever broken through one of our shields. It will not change now."

"Oh, absolutely. I have lived over a thousand years, and I have never heard of a creature tortured by the Dark Wizard to ever break through a shield like this."

Was that dialogue wooden and repetitive, Professor? Yeah, probably. I've heard enough of your comments on my story that I can almost hear you berating me for such maid and butler dialogue. But here's the thing, it needs to happen because my reader is an idiot (just to clarify; the reader is you, Professor, because this is definitely not getting published, and you are the only one reading it now). So, in case you forgot, here's some more maid and butler dialogue.

Venna chuckled. "Just the thought of a cursed creature even touching the shield makes me laugh like a human. It truly has never happened since the beginning of time itself."

They both shared a laugh at the simple absurdity of a cursed creature coming into their midst. It would simply never happen.

Ever.

Alwin walked over, then paused, as he wasn't sure if this was a private meeting.

"Oh, hello Alwin. Can we help you?" Venna asked. Come to think of it, they were supposed to be in a small council, and I never mentioned the other elves in the group during their maid and butler dialogue. Shoot. Well, the other floating head council members left to give them some privacy, with the assignment of figuring out when the Dark Wizard stopped hitting the shield. It's still a concern.

My elf watched the council members leave before focusing again on his aunt and uncle. "No, I just... um, Theodemar suggested that since you're going to be here for the foreseeable future, and that maybe... maybe you'll stay in the human world, perhaps I can..."

"You'd like to choose a path of the elves?" Venna asked.

There were three main paths an elf could choose. Healing, soldier, and protection. There were a lot of different branches in the main three, but the device won't let me go into any more unnecessary detail this late in the trilogy without a reason. I have none to give, since I am narrating this story on the seat of my pants.

Alwin nodded. "I would, yes. Apparently, elves get to choose which path when they're still a child, but hopefully I may request compassion for my case?"

"Of course. Have you given much thought to which path you'd like to choose?" Theodemar asked.

His excitement was deep, but it was barely visible on Alwin's face. "I'd like to be a protector. The magic the elves used to make the shield was fascinating, and I want to help wherever I can in case something was to happen."

"Believe me, Alwin, there is no way a cursed creature or the Dark Wizard himself could ever break our shield," Theodemar said.

"Never, in all my life, had I ever heard of something like that," Venna said.

Alwin nodded as he, too, knew in his soul that breaking the shield was impossible. One hundred percent impossible. "Maybe that's why I was so drawn to it, though. Because I feel like this is my path. I'd like to be a protector."

"Of course, Alwin. We would love to help you in any way we can," Theodemar said. "A protector is a fine path."

Theodemar smiled at Alwin, who smiled back. It was strange, considering he hardly knew these people. And yet they were family. They knew his parents. For the first time, he looked at these people and realized they would be with him for hundreds of years. He wouldn't be alone anymore.

And he wouldn't have to see me ever again in this story, which also took a tremendous burden off his shoulders. I should be angry, but honestly? I get it, Alwin.

Theodemar placed a hand on his nephew's shoulder, leading him toward one of the top elves who knew a lot about protection. They were greeting each other when they heard the thumping return. It started out slow, then seemed to trickle, until the dull thuds were all they heard.

The three elves rushed to the edge of the shield and saw them. Goblins. A lot of them. They were having the same luck as the Dark Wizard, but there were more of them. More cursed creatures beating against the shield. The Dark Wizard was nowhere, but the goblins had seen the characters, and the threat was made. They wouldn't stop until they were dead. And then they would just come back alive again. My angsty elf winced as the dull thuds grew. He rubbed his ears. "That's going to get old fast."

Chapter Twenty-Two

CAPTURING THE ESSENCE OF CHILDHOOD

The sun just crested over the horizon when Milla woke up. It was comfortably warm already, and she felt fully rested. The elves had been kind enough to help set up small log huts, even though they themselves didn't need them. Milla stepped out of the one she shared with Tara, looking around. Most of the adults talked amongst themselves, and an unsettling fear came over her again. It had become almost instinctual to pick up on the whispers and assume the worst.

She ignored the breakfast table and walked amongst the trees, frowning. There weren't any children here, since this was the settlement of adults who had been fighting in Vaywell. All the other children were being protected by other shields created by other elves. (So don't even think about it, Professor.) The poor girl understood why there were no children, but she was still incredibly lonely.

It wasn't until the dull thumping noise turned into a roar that she realized how close she'd gotten to the shield. She leapt behind a tree, then peeked out to see the goblins climbing over each other as they repeatedly beat against the shield. The trolls, too, used their cudgels against it. Once the shield started to ripple, a powerful force threw the creatures back. Yet they simply kept coming. Milla couldn't help but think about if the shield dropped. There was an entire army out there, surrounding them, and they would come straight for them.

Despite the assurance that cursed creatures could never break the shield, the possibility of it terrified her. Especially when a goblin noticed her and started shouting, muted as it was with the shield. More goblins got the message, and they turned toward her, shrieking and clawing. Milla whimpered, backing away before she felt a hand on her shoulder. She couldn't help but scream.

"Shh, shh, it's alright." Paldric appeared next to her, kneeling down to be more at eye level. "It's me." She covered her mouth, her eyes wide as she stared to make sure it was him and not a stray goblin. Paldric hugged her. "You shouldn't be here. Have you had breakfast yet?" Milla shook her head, still too frightened to talk.

He stood, taking her hand. "Come on. I'll help you." Paldric led her away. She glanced behind her shoulder to see the goblins working themselves into a fury. Paldric placed a hand on her head and forced her to face forward, leading her away. "They can't break through the shield, alright?"

"I know." There was no conviction behind it.

Paldric led her closer to the elves, trying to think of something to keep the little girl from trembling. "Don't go by the shield alone again, alright?"

"Because they might break through?" The words were breathy with fear.

As he often did when she was obviously scared, Paldric picked her up and hugged her as they kept walking. "They won't, Milla. The world may be scary, but you're just a child. It isn't your responsibility alone to fix. Trust me, Tara, Alwin, and Roger to take care of it for now."

"But what if they—"

"They can't break through the shield. I promise you, Milla, it's not possible."

She covered her face in his shoulder. "So, we just wait?"

"We're forming a plan right now. We'll start farming to make sure we can sustain ourselves," Paldric said.

"So we *are* just going to wait." Her words weren't loud, but since she was right next to Paldric's ear, he heard every word.

He smiled as they approached their makeshift village. "Gunther's plan seemed to take longer than expected, so we are trying to figure out what to do. But I don't want you to be afraid of the cursed creatures. They won't harm you ever again."

She nodded as Roger walked over, his arms folded. "Milla?"

Paldric set the girl down. "She was by the shield."

Roger shook his head, a small smile on his face. "Come now. There's no point in going over there."

In order to hide her unease from the two men, Milla shrugged.

Roger turned to Paldric. "Theodemar wants to talk to us."

"Alright." Paldric ran a hand through his hair, glancing at Milla. "Go on and eat some breakfast."

Roger patted her shoulder. "I'll come by later. Maybe we can think of a game to play."

The two men walked off as Milla watched. Roger had always attempted to make sure she wasn't too lonely, but loneliness crept in all the same. Milla folded her arms as she shuffled through the adults to the breakfast table, picking up her oatmeal and spoon.

She didn't want to blame the adults, since they were doing everything they could to save the world. Tara was off learning how to heal from the elves. Alwin was training to be a protector and finding out about a family he still had. Paldric and Roger were working together to farm and build a society in this little bubble. And Milla, as she always did, felt in the way. There were no children to play with. The adults tried to, but the situation was dire. Despite everyone trying their best to help her, she needed to get out of the way so they could focus on adult things.

In her mind's eye, she saw the way the goblin turned toward her, wanting to murder. How could anyone forget something like that?

Once breakfast was done, she sat against a tree trunk, bringing her legs up, and burying her head in her knees. Her eyes were just growing warm when she felt something soft land on her knee, almost like a flower petal. She gasped, her head snapping up. The creature, startled, backed away too. Milla stared with her wide brown eyes at the fairy, who flitted a few inches away. The fairy, too, had wide eyes as she hovered in the air. Milla couldn't help but stare. The fairies kept to themselves mostly, not daring to come toward humans for fear of what stories the elves told of them. This fairy had soft, golden butterfly wings and clothes made from spider webs and moonlight. The fairy's dark hair and dark eyes were so tiny. This little fairy was a human, but a tiny one. For now, it was a startled one, staring at Milla with a soft glow.

Milla paused, then reached out with her hand like she'd once done with a rabbit her brothers were trying to hunt. She wanted to prove herself the better hunter and stumbled upon it. The rabbit had leapt away, but Milla tried again with the fairy. She went slow, careful, trying to remain calm even as her heart pounded in anticipation. The fairy watched Milla reach out her hand, curious at this equally curious little girl. The fairy reached out her own hand and touched Milla's outstretched finger with her own tiny one. Milla giggled, and the little creature giggled too, high pitched like a tinkle of a bell. Grabbing Milla's finger, the little creature pulled herself in and landed in Milla's palm. The little creature placed her hands on her fairy hips, saying something Milla couldn't understand. The pitch was too high.

"I'm sorry. I can't hear you."

Instead of trying to speak again, the fairy motioned her to follow. Milla got up, following the creature. The fairy started off, and as is usual, began making loops as she flew. This caused Milla to giggle again before quickly covering her mouth. She didn't want to offend the creature. But something woke up inside the fairy. A giggling child is as much a life source as the heart of the forest. It was an odd thing to discover, but not unpleasant. The fairy responded by making more elaborate loops, and Milla exploded in a fit of giggles. The fairy danced in the air, and Milla picked up her pace, laughing as she followed.

Another fairy joined her sister, communicating about the child. The fairy did little else but let the sister fairy listen to the child laugh.

"Hello!" Milla said as she caught up to the two fairies. The first fairy stepped on Milla's palm. "I will call you Cynthia." She reached out to the sister fairy, who hesitated, watching the girl with a frown. "I'll call you Aija." The sister fairy, Aija, looked at Cynthia again with a careful gaze, still not knowing what to trust. Aija, too, had the wings of a colorful blue butterfly with her own dress of spider silk and moonlight. She reached out hesitantly, and Milla giggled. Aija relaxed considerably once she heard the sound. Fairies didn't live nearly as long as the elves, and so for the generations they were pulled from the humans, they had forgotten the joy that came from the giggle of a child.

Aija and Cynthia motioned Milla to follow. She did, chasing the two fairies. She leapt over logs and rocks, going deeper into the forest, forgetting about goblins and trolls.

She entered the darkest part, gasping in delight as she saw hundreds of fairies playing amongst each other. They glowed as though with the light of the moon, flitting about, playing on the leaves, splashing each other with water. Some slept in flower petals, others hovered over tree branches, playing hide-and seek. The entire forest of fairies seemed to pause as they realized they weren't alone. Milla stared at the fairies, who stared at her in return. Then they began chittering about the human girl in their midst, confused by her presence. Though this wasn't necessarily Aomeia's heart of the forest, they could still partially recreate it. A human couldn't enter unless they were pure in heart.

Milla giggled in anticipation as she saw the hundreds of fairies staring at her. "Hello! My name is Milla!"

There was another moment's hesitation before the more curious fairies descended on her, intrigued by this little girl. Maybe it would have been overwhelming for someone else, but to a little child, her eyes brightened as they studied her, picked up locks of her hair, picked up flower petals and leaves to place on her head and shoulders. She reached out, letting the fairies touch her fingers and palms, fascinated by her strange clothes as theirs equally fascinated her.

Milla didn't notice Roger watching her from farther back. He had finished their talk with Theodemar and had gone looking for the little girl, wanting to fulfill his promise to her. But it looked as though she found some friends.

A woman approached, her hands behind her back. "Hello."

Roger almost jumped out of his skin. *Was it revenge for all the times he did that to me? Maybe.*

"Sorry. I didn't mean to startle you," she said.

"No, no, it's alright. I'm apt to be more jumpy nowadays." Roger glanced back as Milla receded into the fairy haven.

"I'm Lamira," the woman said.

"Roger."

"It's a pleasure to meet you." He nodded, then looked away again. Lamira followed his gaze. "Is she yours?"

"Yes. Well... no. Not technically. She's an orphan kid. Our little group adopted her to make sure she stayed safe."

Lamira understood some of those words, but Roger still had a tendency to use more modern lingo. Her face held enough confusion that he gave a slight frown and tried again. "She's not mine. Her family died, and the group I'm with is taking care of her."

"Well, you all must be doing a fantastic job if the fairies have taken to her so quickly." She looked again to where Milla disappeared, though they could still hear her giggling. "They can sense the pureness of her heart and lead her deeper into their haven. I spent years trying to be worthy of such an entrance ever since I grew up."

"Sometimes I worry Milla's been a little too traumatized. I hope this helps her." Roger paused a beat, then frowned. "Wait, spent years... are you an elf?"

"No, no. When the elves left, they chose a group of humans to follow them to Aomeia to keep us from the corruption of our own kind, as they say. After a few generations, they have all dwindled away. All but my mother and me. We were to be the last before we agreed to come back with Theodemar and Venna."

Roger raised an eyebrow. "So that's how you could sneak up on me?"

Lamira smiled. "I've never been able to sneak up on anyone in Aomeia, and now I find I'm startling people all the time here in Veniloria. But I am no elf." She pointed to her face. "Clearly."

"Clearly? What do you mean?"

She kept a finger pointed at her face. "I mean... you know. You've seen the elf women. You can tell I'm a human."

"Oh, come now, Lamira. You're very beautiful. After all, I did mistake you as an elf." For the first time in Lamira's life, a man told her she was beautiful. She didn't know what to do with this experience except to look away, hiding her reddening face behind her curtain of hair. Roger did not seem to notice. "It must have been incredibly lonely with the elves."

Lamira played with her hands, looking back to where Milla disappeared. "I didn't realize how lonely we'd been until we returned." She shot another look at Roger. "I do not want you to think I am ungrateful for my time in Aomeia. It was paradise. But I am glad my mother and I have returned to Veniloria."

He listened to her, trying to imagine what it would have been like to be a human among so many elves. "I'm sure you have many stories."

"Plenty, yes. And you? Could I ask you stories about your time in Veniloria?"

Roger seemed surprised by this request, but nodded. "Of course." He studied her face again, narrowing his eyes, feeling like there was more to this than simply meeting a woman. "Did Gunther send you?"

Genuine confusion crossed her face. "Who's Gunther?"

A smile played across his lips as he studied her pretty green eyes. "Nothing. Never mind."

"A friend of yours?" Lamira asked.

He glanced toward the sky. "Wouldn't you like to know, Gunther?"

Oh admit it, you stoic man with a tragic past.

Roger folded his arms, glancing at Lamira. "Will Milla be okay with the fairies?"

The smile she had on her face was genuine, if more mute by human standards. "If by 'oh-kay' you mean to ask if she'll be the safest she'll ever be in the heart of a fairy haven, the answer is yes."

Roger nodded. "Well, would you like to have some lunch with me?"

"I would like that."

The two of them left for the main camp, walking in a comfortable silence that might have been sprinkled with occasional glances at each other.

Alright, Roger. I'll be honest. I don't know who Lamira will be in your future. Perhaps she'd be a love interest, but no one in their right mind should trust me with anything like that. Instead, I created her in hopes she could at least be a friend, because part of me wanted to repay you for all the times I had been such an insensitive jerk. But in the end, I honestly don't know what she will mean to you. She's pretty cool, though, not going to lie. I'm quite pleased with who she became. Absolutely fascinating backstory.

In the end, I know what you'd rather have. Whatever you and Lamira are going to be, it'll be a choice the two of you make together. And I hope by giving you the ability to decide, it will make up for all the times I practically rubbed it in your face that you couldn't choose.

Okay, it won't make up for it at all. I really was a horrible jerk to you. But I hope you realize how very sorry I am. So here is a character I've created. May you both be happy in whatever life you choose.

Chapter Twenty-Three

A Discussion Full of Words

I t was a day later when my adult main cast of characters that I created (and the one I adopted) came together. The elves rarely sat, but they did so for the humans.

Except Paldric was pacing. He couldn't help himself. "Something's wrong. I don't know what, but I feel it. I don't think Gunther meant for us to stay in this shield this long."

"It's not what we hoped for either, but we will find a way," Venna said.

Roger folded his arms, leaning back in his chair. "So just to be clear, when you came to rescue us, did you just expect us to live in these little bubbles for the rest of our existence?"

Roger had a fair question. One that caused silence around the room as they thought about it. When the elves come back, I assumed I'd describe a few days of peace to hit the word count we needed. Then the story would end, and they would enter the database. It wouldn't make sense for them to still be here months later because they were actually in the database, even though that was the logical conclusion of the story.

We have stumbled on a plot hole. Venna and Theodemar clearly wouldn't do this, knowing the humans would live here for the rest of their existence. The device really had taken over even still and only recorded the interesting stuff. Which meant I had to live out the actual consequences of this plot hole. And it caused more than a couple of sleepless nights figuring out how to add to the word count before too much time passed.

Theodemar gave a defeated sigh. "After all that planning, we really didn't think this through."

Venna patted his shoulder. "It's alright. We will figure it out. In the meantime, with fairies and nymphs here, crops will grow in less than a month. We just have to plant more now."

Tara's eyes bounced between Venna and Theodemar. "Do we have enough room?"

"Yes, we will. The protector elves can expand the shield. The cursed creatures will have to move for us. By this time next year, the shield will have tripled in size," Theodemar said.

This didn't comfort Tara. "I really hope we're not here for another year. Many families have been separated during this whole thing, and it breaks my heart knowing they are apart."

Roger nodded, then frowned. "Where exactly *would* we be in another year besides in a bubble that has tripled in size?"

Despite the logical conclusion of Roger's statement, Tara didn't want to believe it. "Gunther wouldn't keep us here another year."

Alwin snorted. "I mean, do you remember who you're talking about? Nothing ever goes according to Gunther's plan."

Hey!

Paldric chuckled. "I both miss that man and am grateful he's not here right now."

The thought alone made Tara shudder. "Ugh, can you imagine?"

I know you don't realize this, but I am technically here, thanks.

"That guy could somehow pull off the most epic stunts, and yet it would still be the stupidest thing I'd ever seen." I couldn't tell if that sentiment was from Professor Andrews or Roger, but either way, I'm not taking the bait. Roger sighed. "I owe that man everything, though."

That, I was confident, did *not* come from Professor Andrews.

My main character still paced, his hands behind him, trying to think of something. He felt frustrated that he didn't know what to do. Which is perfect because someone else might help if...

Boom, thanks Jim. You're the best reverse hacker I know.

Roger frowned, struck by an impossible idea that he wouldn't of had without divine intervention. Or in this case, Jim hacking into Professor Andrew's link to Roger.

He leaned forward, frowning. "Party. We need a party."

Tara matched his frown. "Sorry?"

He scratched the back of his head, still thinking. "Alright, this is going to sound weird, but we need something that... that is really interesting. It seems like Gunther needs a gigantic party for some reason."

Tara raised an eyebrow. "Gunther's talking to you?"

Keep Professor Andrews back, Jim. Roger's almost got it.

My adopted character was having quite the headache, and I wish it didn't have to be this way, but he was close. Come on, Roger. Analyze the code. I state it right there.

Theodemar, unaware of the mental struggle, tried to help. "We've had parties before. What needs to be different about this one?"

Come on, Roger. Come on.

"It's got to be different, because... because... character development? Am I making any sense?" Roger looked at the other characters, who gave him blank stares in return. Paldric himself stopped pacing. Roger sighed. "We need to have a party that causes character development. That's all I can tell you."

Professor Andrews is keeping you from seeing the statement right there, but you can do it, Roger. Come on.

A twist of confusion crossed Alwin's face. "And... this is from Gunther?"

"I think so." Roger rubbed his head, the headache still there.

"It probably is. The evil God would want us to break the shield from the inside," Alwin said.

Roger glanced through his fingers. "Don't give him any ideas."

Theodemar was watching the entire thing with both curiosity and delight. "You have created such an interesting religion. We must make sure we write it down for our records."

"I wonder how it came about. It wasn't around when we were among the humans," Venna said.

"It's all Gunther's fault." As the narrator, I would like to point out that Alwin's tone didn't sound too harsh.

I need you to focus, Roger.

Which made him groan. "A less painful headache would be nice." It was almost like he could hear me. I assure you, Roger, Jim's trying to relieve your headache, but Professor Andrews is muddling up the code.

"So... a party?" Tara didn't know what to do, but tried her best to make sure Roger didn't suffer anymore with his headache.

"A party. That has to do with characters?" Venna asked.

"Character development," Roger said.

Venna frowned, then glanced at her husband, who shrugged. Both tried hard not to chalk it up to the oddities of humans, as this was super important to get right. If this happened, it could add at least five thousand words. We just have to inspire them to do it. We have it all written up and everything. You've just got to realize it.

Paldric stopped his pacing and leaned against the table. "Everyone try to think like Gunther." Tara screwed up her face enough to show she didn't want to think like me. Alwin gave Paldric a blank stare. It was clear no one really wanted to attempt his exercise. "Come on, it might help Roger's headache go away." That caused a better response from everyone. I don't care how they got to it, just that they get there.

"So Gunther wants us to throw a party?" Alwin asked. Roger nodded, but it didn't ease Alwin's incredulousness. "*Gunther* wants us to throw a party?"

Roger glanced at my elf. "Yeah, he does. If that man wants to throw a party, he's got to be desperate."

"What kind of party? You said character development?" Paldric asked.

Lamira turned toward Roger. "Are our small parties not making a difference?"

"Is this God someone you need to sacrifice an animal to?" Venna asked. Everyone looked at her. She shrugged. "I am unfamiliar with human religions."

There's no way I want something like that, guys. Don't do it.

Tara rubbed her temples. "I'm simply confused why Gunther wants us to do this?"

"Why does Gunther want us to do *anything*? Little of what he said ever made sense," Alwin said.

Paldric went back to pacing. "Come on, my friend. Gunther tries, in his own way, to help us."

"And so, instead of us planning on how best to grow crops and how to strengthen the shield to expand the borders, this God of yours wants a party?" Theodemar asked.

Alwin shrugged. "It definitely sounds like something he'd suggest because it's out of nowhere and does nothing to actually help us. But what's confusing me is why a party? He's never liked them."

Roger stared at the table, still working through the headache. "No, he just hated parties because I was here."

Venna frowned, studying Roger closer. Listening to the humans was like learning a new language. "You being here somehow made your God hate parties?"

"Yeah, because he thought I was going to steal..." Roger froze, then his eyes widened. "Oh." He looked at Tara, then his gaze landed on Paldric. "Oh!"

Leaps in logical thought for the win! This is handy. Thanks, Professor.

His headache disappeared, which confirmed to him it's what I wanted.

"Roger?" Alwin asked.

At first he said nothing, because according to his personality code, he didn't want to suggest Paldric marry Tara. It was a choice between two other people. But he also realized that, for whatever reason, I needed the inhabitants to have a large party. And I did. This word count needed to climb in a short amount of time. A wedding day was a huge opportunity to get a ton of words in on a single day. Especially if Grace hops on to do the poetic description of Tara's dress.

No, Jim, I refuse to be in charge of that.

Roger placed his hands on the table, smirking as he looked at Tara again. She was confused. "Gunther would like an enormous party, and for it to have a huge significance for some people here. Specifically, two of them," Roger said.

Tara paused, then smiled and gave a small shake of her head. "Idiot God."

I heard that.

Tara focused on Paldric, who still paced. "So, what kind of party could we throw that would be big enough for Gunther?" He ran a hand through his hair, feeling quite distraught that he couldn't think of it.

"I mean, probably one the whole settlement would come to," Tara said, wanting the man to figure it out himself.

Roger nodded, catching on. "Every single one. It'd have to be huge."

"I'd almost say it'd have to be a celebration," Tara said.

Paldric placed a hand on his hip, his other hand still in his hair. "Is anyone's anniversary of birth coming up?"

Oh, wow. Come on, Paldric.

Mirth danced in Tara's eyes. "No, but I'm pretty sure we could think of something bigger."

"Bigger than an anniversary of birth? What kind of occasion would that be?" Paldric asked. Tara almost didn't want to say. She was genuinely curious to see how long it would take for him to guess it. He frowned, then glanced at Theodemar. "Is someone in the settlement having a baby?"

Tara pinched the bridge of her nose. "Someone will *not* have one if he doesn't figure this out."

Roger snorted before covering his mouth to hide it. Paldric frowned, glancing between the two of them. "What? What is it?"

"I wouldn't expect anything less from someone created by Gunther," Roger said.

Oh, come on, guys. It wasn't *that* funny.

"Marry me, Paldric?" Tara asked.

Paldric looked confused, then realization dawned on his face. "Oh, right. *That* kind of party. Makes sense." Tara smiled, shaking her head. Paldric cleared his throat. "I mean, yes. Yes, if you'll have me."

"I've wanted you since the first day I met you," Tara said.

Chapter Twenty-Four

We Prep for a Wedding!

The settlement was in a whirl of activity. Despite the prodding from me, Paldric still insisted on half the settlement work on farming. Which is fine. After the wedding, they might be there for a little while longer, so I didn't push it. Even with the divided labor, it only took two days to set up. It was just what everyone needed. The goblins, trolls, and shadow soldiers had thrown themselves against the shield non-stop for days now. The settlement was weary of them, so they were grateful for this distraction.

An atmosphere of excitement bloomed in everyone, and I don't want to botch it up. Which is why I'm finally handing it over to professionals. Grace? You want to say a few words for the device to pick up?

Of course, is it working?

Yep.

Gunther calls me a professional, but honestly, I'm not sure how this will go, as I've only dictated poetry. Full novels intimidate me.

You'll do great, Grace. And you brought this upon yourself, you know.

If I'd known this was my payback, I'd have reconsidered the whole thing.

Really? Would you?

No.

I thought so. Thanks for babysitting my story. Characters, I know you can't hear her or me, but you better be on your best behavior. I'll be reading everything you get up to, so no funny business. Roger, Alwin, I'm looking at you two. Paldric, Tara, behave yourselves. Stay safe, Milla.

Awe, your concern is touching. Now go, have fun on your date.

Alright, alright. I'll be back in three hours, guys. See you later.

Tara awoke from her dream. It slipped away from her mind as reality set in, but it didn't matter. Life now was a dream for her, and she already woke up smiling. She walked outside, the morning air warm and inviting. It was a perfect day, but it didn't matter what the weather would be. Tara was in such a state of bliss that they could announce a hurricane, and she would've found something good from it.

Paldric smiled as he approached her, and they shared a sweet kiss. "Sleep alright?"

"I did. I can almost ignore the constant banging against the shield."

Paldric kissed her forehead. "Good. It also helps that the elves made the shield grow. They're farther away now."

Tara was still smiling, despite the conversation topic. "I'm glad. Is Alwin alright? I know he and the other elves can hear them better than us."

"He stuffs bits of cloth in his ears when he sleeps. All of them have." Paldric glanced up at the shield, even though it was magically transparent. It helped, in a way, that they couldn't see it. The others were restless, the elves especially. It felt like a prison. They wanted to leave, explore the human realm, find their favorite parts of the forest. They wanted to reminisce, like returning to an old house full of memories and finding themselves unable to leave the front porch. But Paldric didn't feel that sense of prison. Despite the epic adventure he had gone on, meeting a God, gathering artifacts, killing a dragon, overthrowing an evil wizard, Paldric was quite ready to call this place home. No, it was not ideal, but they were safe. If the people he cared about were safe, he would happily live on the ocean's floor.

Paldric and Tara walked from the hut, his hand around her waist as she placed her hand on his shoulder.

"What more needs to be done?" Tara asked.

"Loads. But little that I can help with. I cannot weave flowers that well, and spending time with Alwin makes me nervous about the slightest elf frown in my direction," Paldric said.

Tara giggled, placing her head against his shoulder. "It's really kind of them to make such a beautiful event for us."

"It is. A pleasant reminder," Paldric said.

Tara frowned. "Reminder?"

"Yes. A reminder there's happiness to be found everywhere. In every situation, there is good. There is light and hope. And it is our job to find it, to expound it, to give it more life to remind us why the darkness needs to be dispelled," Paldric said.

Her frown disappeared as she lifted her head to look at her soon-to-be husband. She received her own reminder of why she loved this man. Maybe it started as an infatuation, but the roots had grown deeply. Paldric had always been the man who'd risk everything to save a poor, defenseless woman in the woods. That quality sparked a flame in her.

Their lips almost met again when Alwin walked up to them, rubbing his head, distracted. "Paldric, I just don't get it." The elf was oblivious to what they almost did. Neither one of them was about to mention it. "I just don't understand the pageantry."

"You mean... the wedding?" Paldric asked.

"Yeah. Why make such a big celebration? I don't understand the significance of it. So today, you somehow may not do the thing that gets you children, then tomorrow we have a big celebration, and somehow you've got the permission?" Alwin asked.

Paldric chuckled. "That's certainly one way to view it."

To hide her reddening cheeks, Tara bowed her head and smiled. Alwin returned to scratching the back of his head. "Then how do you see it?"

"Tara and I have agreed that marriage is different. It's something special. Something we want to respect. We want to stick with each other for the rest of our lives."

"Even throughout the database." Tara gave Paldric's hand a squeeze.

"Even in the database." Paldric smiled at that. "It's a joyous thing, and we are celebrating the promise we will make to each other."

Alwin gave a pained sigh. "But don't you ever want to... I don't know. Take her up in a tree and just... just..." He made a pushing motion with his palm, feeling completely overwhelmed and unable to express the deep feelings he had never felt in almost a hundred and fifty years of existence.

Paldric raised an eyebrow as Tara gave Alwin a knowing look. Being around female elves helped him understand something he never did, surrounded by humans. Tara walked forward, patting Alwin on the shoulder. "It seems like this is something you could talk with Theodemar about."

Alwin let out a breath, then stopped, his eyes widening ever so slightly as a beautiful elf maiden walked by with a basket full of flowers. His eyes darted away, widening even more than before. "Yeah, yeah." He had his hands in his hair, feeling like he was going to panic. "Do you... how do you... survive? I don't get it. How does anyone focus? What's the point of these feelings?"

Another chuckle escaped Paldric. "Tara's right. Theodemar is the best to talk to about this. I'm pretty sure the human equivalent of experiencing these feelings is more awkward and gross than the elf equivalent."

Tara paused, then gave Paldric a curious look. "Awkward and gross?"

He shrugged. "I mean, how else would you explain the sweats and the fumbling? Talking to a woman is hard."

Alwin physically recoiled at the idea of talking to a woman. The small grove around them smelled of sweet flowers as his shirt got more damp. He picked it up between his two fingers. "This is disgusting!"

"Some things will always be the same," Paldric said with a smile.

Alwin's mind was still a mess he didn't know how to organize. The poor dear was experiencing the chaos of first loves, but oh, what a lovely chaos it is. His entire world shifted, causing things to bump and spill out. Things he once thought he could control were now upended. His world was in a state of chaos, and yet he never wanted to be the same again. To understand, and yet to not. To want to plunge into an unknown, despite logic screaming at him to remain safe. The desire to grab everything and throw it in the air just to see if it would get her attention. And yet terrified it would startle her. This feeling compelled him to risk his life, even if it meant he'd only get a small smile from her in return.

Tara broke away from Alwin, looping her hand through his as Paldric got on the other side, patting his shoulder. Tara pulled the poor elf along. "Come on, Alwin. I'll help you find your uncle."

He nodded, too afraid to speak. There was another world view he struggled to understand. One he wanted to, desperately, in the way he wanted to understand love. Not nearly as sudden, not nearly as jolting, but somehow just as deep. Tara mentioned his uncle, and once again he reached for a word he didn't think would ever belong to him. This was the thing he yearned for in others. Saw the beautiful home Paldric's great-grandparents created, then his grandparents, then finally his parents. Saw how they took their love and created a shield for their children to flourish and grow. Watched them thrive, watched them blossom, and watched how they welcomed him without question. He felt part of their family to ease the pain of not having his own, and he was quite content with them. Now he had another family. One that knew his own parents better than himself. That could tell him stories. No, memories.

Stuck in a bubble with creatures all around, absorbed in the chaos of first love and the warmth of friendship, Alwin felt rich indeed to be home among his family.

Ah, look at me. Waxing poetical already. How can I not? Life will always be poetic.

Chapter Twenty-Five

GRACE KEEPS GOING

It surprised Lamira when Tara entered far into the heart of the fairy kingdom. "You must be pure of heart."

Tara didn't know what to say, mainly because there were hundreds of fairies gathering around her. The elves made it clear to the fairies about the union she and Paldric were going to make. They had their instructions to make a dress befitting of such an arrangement that I will not describe at all. Gunther will do that on his own. The poor dear needs to build some confidence in himself.

"I, um... thank you," Tara said. A fairy landed on her head, giggling as she rolled in her thick brown hair.

"It is a great honor. The other humans must highly esteem you to enter so far," Lamira said.

Tara frowned, thinking about her past actions and what caused her to have a pure heart. Milla was already deeper in the forest, playing games with the fairies. They could hear her giggling.

A few fairies came over with flowers to braid in Tara's hair. "I'm a healer among the humans. That might be something."

"There are plenty of healers, even among the elves, who haven't approached this far."

Tara didn't know how to answer Lamira's question. "I realize how this sounds, but I honestly don't believe I'm anyone of great esteem. I'm simply doing what I can with the passion of healing that Gunther created me with."

Lamira watched in surprise as Tara, distracted by a fairy, took a small step even deeper into the forest. "Perhaps part of your pure heart comes from not realizing how esteemed you are." Lamira sighed, shaking her head. "I've tried to get back ever since I was a small child. But how could I possibly get back to such innocence?"

Fairies helped Tara extend her hands before they measured her with their leaves or dandelion stalks. It was only then when she noticed she was a few steps deeper in the forest than Lamira. Tara wanted to help the woman, as that was a key quality in what made her heart so pure. The forest was odd. Tara came to the spot she felt most comfortable in. There was no desire to go deeper. Instead, she felt a strange peace where she was. Tara felt a few fairies walking across her rib cage and couldn't help but let a small laugh escape her. "This is such a strange forest. I feel so content here. Is it the same for you?"

The other woman gave a sad smile, her longing eyes flickering toward the darker forest. "It is, yes. Though it's hard when you remember what it was like before, and how it feels like you have gone backwards."

"Ah." Tara watched as fairies brought some spider silk from above, circling it around her arms. "Perhaps it's that longing to be where you were that keeps you from going farther?"

Lamira glanced at Tara, confused, but thought more about it. "Perhaps it is." She smiled, her feet moving the smallest step forward. "There is much I can learn about my people. Roger has been telling me stories, and I cannot get enough."

The fairies continued their measurements as the beginning of a dress formed. Tara gave her new friend a sideways glance. "I hope you tell him some of your own stories, too."

"I do. He's equally curious about my time with the elves."

Tara gave a knowing smile, happy to have another woman joining their group.

Oh, you two are back? Has it already been three hours? Wait, Gunther, wait. This conversation is being recorded. You should hop on. The device still considers you a character, and it might let us have this conversation to add more words to this chapter.

...know how I feel about just hopping onto the device, but hey! There's our conversation.

Just a second, the device is downloading something and... "There we go, look at that! Proper punctuation to differentiate between the two of us! That makes it official!" Grace said.

"That's great. How many words did you get?" I asked.

"Looks like about two thousand."

I made a noise that sounded like I was deeply impressed. "Two thousand in three hours? That's really impressive! And what is that description about the noise I made? Kind of lazy writing there, device. Step it up."

"Oh hush, dear, it's doing its best," Grace said.

As the conversation lulled, it intrigued me to see the device go on auto-narration. I saw what was playing out, saw Tara and Lamira finishing their conversation as the story panned over to other parts of the settlement, where the women and men worked in the small farmlands, watering the plants and doing what they could. The fairies would come later when it got darker to magic the plants into being. Maybe in the cover of darkness the nymphs would leave the fairy forest and help the plants grow, too. They weren't nearly as brave as the other mythical creatures and remained in the fairy haven.

"Gunther?"

"Hmm?" I asked.

One could almost hear the smile in Grace's voice. "They're alright, dear. I promise."

I sighed. "Yeah, I know."

"I can't help but notice you both came back right on the three-hour mark. You must have been worried, but you did well. Dr. Webb will be thrilled."

"Yeah, I'll tell her later tonight," I said.

"Any time you want me to babysit, you let me know. It was fun."

I let out a sigh, one that sounded exhausted but pleased. "This was an enjoyable experience, yes. And I'm impressed you got so many words done in three hours. I'm just..." I trailed off, keeping my thoughts hidden.

"Your characters are safe," Grace said again.

"I know. I try to keep telling myself that, but it's just... it's so hard. A part of my soul will always be here among my characters, and I hate that Professor Andrews has access to it."

"That shield fiercely protects them. We've done everything we can to make sure those characters will have their happily ever after, and I am confident they will get it," Grace said.

"I want your confidence, Grace. I really do."

"What's keeping you from my level of confidence, dear?"

Another sigh escaped me. "Things still make little sense. About Professor Andrews. He acts over the top and villainous in my story, and from other reports in infiltrated stories, he's also evil for the sake of being evil, but that's not who he was in real life. Not necessarily an overt friendly guy, but he knew his stuff, and he had everyone's respect. He knew characters and development and... everything that dealt with narration. There was a reason he used to be the top professor, and why he almost became chairman of the Guardians. Unless I completely misinterpreted him. But I feel like a person who is evil just to be evil would be a hard characteristic to miss. Despite fighting with him for almost a year, both inside and outside my story and with his attacks on the Guardians, I still don't know his motivation for doing this."

"It's an enigma I wish I had the answer to. That we're all trying to uncover. He knows a lot about narration, which is why he went so over-the-top with his villains to hide his tracks. Went for the cardboard cutouts to keep us off his tail. The villain he creates for other people's stories is not who he is. Though the hurt and pain he has caused you and Jim has still placed him squarely as a villain in my eyes."

My voice was softer. "And because I don't understand his motivations, I'll never feel a hundred percent okay with my story until it's done and over, no matter how safe my characters are."

"Does it concern you that Professor Andrews could read this right now?" Grace asked.

"Of course I am. I'm paranoid all the time now, but I'm trying to work through it. But I doubt Professor Andrews has learned anything new from this conversation he doesn't already know."

There was another lull in the conversation. No doubt it being difficult that Grace and I were just talking heads. The men worked hard in the dying light to set up chairs and tables for the wedding that would happen tomorrow morning, oblivious to our conversation. It was better, though, as it padded the word count nicely.

"We've narrated in total about fifty thousand words. There's only twenty thousand more to go. The wedding will take a good chunk, then you can describe their peaceful happily ever after," Grace said.

I said nothing in return, and my feelings on the matter were unknown to the device, which made it difficult to gauge how I felt.

"Which is how I want it, device. Despite spilling my guts with Grace just barely, I enjoy my privacy. It's more I'm worried because my date is still present, and who knows what things you would have revealed about the inner workings of my mind," I said.

"That reminds me. You might enjoy Alwin's section I just narrated," Grace said.

"Oh, really? What'd my elf get up to while I was away?"

"Poor dear has found himself infatuated."

"Poor dear indeed. That should be hilarious. Does he go to Paldric for advice? Does Paldric feel wholly inadequate to help him figure out relationships?"

"You know your characters so well."

Grace and I chuckled, and there was another lull in the conversation. The device remained on the men organizing things, though there was nothing much else of interest to note about it. Which is why the device sped over to Roger, who leaned against the tree, staring at the cursed creatures trying to break through the shield.

"Gunther?" Grace asked. I didn't answer.

Roger had his arms folded, watching with morbid curiosity as the creatures discovered him, doing everything in their power to break the shield.

"We better end it for tonight. We've gotten over three thousand words, which is far more than any other narration sessions. You'll be good for another week, now," Grace said.

"Please, Grace. Keep it going. I need to know what Roger'll do or I'll stress about it all week," I said.

My adopted character did little else. He simply watched the cursed creatures, the unease filling his soul that the same god who created them also created him. He differed from them, though. A gift from me that cost my sanity.

"I don't like this," Grace whispered.

"Let it keep going for a few more minutes," I said.

"I'll just finagle with it to get him away from there."

Roger watched the shield burst into view whenever a cursed creature rammed their fists against it. Forced himself to realize they'd been going at this for months and they didn't get closer. There was no way they could break through, and he tried to seek comfort from that.

"Roger?" Lamira asked.

He straightened, unfolding his arms. "Hello."

"What are you doing here?"

My adopted character tore his gaze from the cursed creatures to look at her. "It's kind of a long story."

She smiled at him. "I enjoy your stories."

He again looked at the cursed creatures. Lamira placed her hand on his cheek, forcing him to look at her. "They can't come in here. I know the shield the elves have created. They won't break through."

"I know." To Lamira, who had just met him, Roger might have sounded genuine, but there, deep in his code, was the truth. He hadn't felt the pull from the evil god in ages, but every time he looked at the cursed creatures, he sensed something. Something deep. A command in the code the evil god gave all his creations: Be prepared, because the Dark Wizard has a plan.

It filled the cursed creatures with blood lust, but it filled Roger with dread.

"Gunther?" Grace asked.

"Shut it off. I have nothing more to say this week." I tried too hard to keep emotions from my voice.

Chapter Twenty-Six
THE WEDDING

The wedding would take the entire day, but it started late with the moonrise. This semi-religion that came because of the moon tickled Venna and Theodemar, since the elves definitely didn't end up there. But they humored the religion, anyway. Dawn was many hours away, but the moon peeked over the horizon. The noises outside the shield were more subdued since the goblins weren't in their frenzy mode. It made it a more peaceful ceremony.

Tara and Paldric whispered their promises to each other in the moonlight beside Lord Adrijian and Lady Ana, their witnesses, swearing their lives to each other. To have each other forever. To bolster each other. To enjoy each other's hobbies. To never degrade the other's choices. And find the adventure in the mundane life. You know. Things like that.

This moonrise was a few hours before dawn, so they took advantage of it. Their wedding guests wouldn't be awake for a few more hours, so they slipped away to Paldric's little hut.

And no. Not going to describe their first time. Or any time, for that matter. Yeah, it could have padded the word count nicely. The Guardians even assured me that there was nothing wrong about describing their sexual acts, as hundreds of narrators before had done so in their books, but I can't do it for two reasons. One is because I know these characters more than just as a narrator. I lived among them; I got to know them even better, and they became like family. It'd be like watching and then describing my brother's first night doing it with the girl he was madly in love with and... no. Just no. I don't even have a brother, but the point still stands. The second reason is I still feel an immense guilt about what happened between Tara and me back in book one. There's no way I can watch and describe her having sex with anyone without feeling like a sick creep. They did everything off screen, and I never watched.

I promise, Tara.

The morning was clear, as always. According to Grace's notes, it smelled of honeysuckle and lilies, as those were the wilted flowers the gardeners planted around the stand. The nymphs and fairies brought them to life in the moonlight. Tara thought she smelled sweet flowers before, but something was magical about it now. And it wasn't just because it was her wedding day. She was quite certain things were at play to make this day magical. She had no intention of stopping it.

She placed a hand on Paldric's bare chest, and he subconsciously knew it was her. The newness of it was still there. Maybe her presence should have surprised him, since he'd only slept by himself his whole life. However, this woman was who he wanted to build a life with. Which is why he felt pleased instead of surprised when he opened his eyes and saw her next to him. Okay, maybe pleased is the wrong word. Honestly, the feeling was impossible to describe. I need Grace here to be poetic. Oh well, I'll try it out. It was like fulfillment, but deeper. Happiness, but more. Joy, but so full it wouldn't go away. This was the life he'd always dreamt of, and he was in awe that it was... happening. That it was just beginning.

Paldric placed his hand over hers, smiling.

"Good morning," Tara said.

"Morning."

She moved closer to him, hugging him. "This is starting off well, don't you think?" Paldric smiled, giving a small sigh. He didn't need to say much else as Tara giggled.

Ugh, newlyweds. This world building aspect was hard. There's a reason the honeymoon is after the wedding celebration in real life. Those two will be impossible to stay sane in public right now.

Paldric cupped her head in his hand, smiling before he leaned over and kissed her. His hand moved down her neck before—

We need another fade to black. Let's put a section break here and leave them be. These two aren't ready for public appearances.

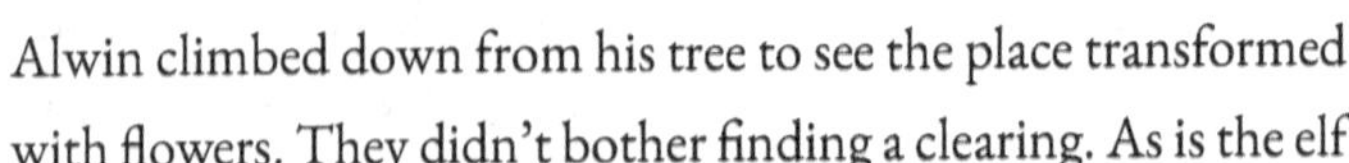

Alwin climbed down from his tree to see the place transformed with flowers. They didn't bother finding a clearing. As is the elf way, they worked with the trees, the chairs for the humans interspersed among the forestry. The flowers were gorgeous, and it smelled heavenly. Alwin could almost see the magic radiating off the vibrant gold honeysuckles. Even the white lilies were difficult to look at straight on.

Venna smiled as Alwin walked from his designated tree. "Did you sleep in, as the humans call it?" she asked.

"No." Alwin took his time marveling at the flowers and trees. "Simply thinking things through."

Venna remained by her nephew's side, looking at the flowers with him. "It is an odd situation we've found ourselves in. But I assure you. The elves have made calculations, and in thirty-five years, we will reach the next civilization. The bubble will cover the entire continent of Veniloria in another two hundred years, pushing the cursed creatures off."

Being among humans his entire life, Alwin couldn't help but do the calculations in his own mind. Thirty-five years was a long time, especially considering some families were separated. There's a good chance many of the fathers here wouldn't see their children until they were fully grown, with children of their own. If they even made it another thirty-five years. And two hundred years was a long time. Certainly longer than he himself had been alive. Generations of humans would come and go. And yet Venna talked about it like they would only wait another decade.

"Alwin?" Venna asked.

He glanced up at the sky. "I don't enjoy waiting. How do we know the Dark Wizard isn't growing in power now? He seems undefeatable, and I'm pretty sure he can crawl out of the depths of the ocean and still hurt us."

Venna understood Alwin's meaning. "I understand. My path is a soldier, and sitting here, not destroying those cursed creatures who are making such a racket pains me. But this will also give us time to think. If a better plan comes, we will take it."

Better, meaning the story will end and everyone goes to the database. There's two hundred years of peace I can pull from to form a few storylines, and less than twenty-thousand words left. I guarantee this story will end well before two hundred years. My goal is to end it before the thirty-five years, so those fathers can see their children again soon.

[Statement from co-author through device, story placed on hold as collaboration link is created.]

[Co-author: You're killing the pace, Gunther.]

[Prime author: It doesn't matter, Professor. It never has. This isn't getting published. It's only ever been about unmasking you. The purpose is done, in my eyes.]

[Co-author: Do you know how much destruction I can cause in twenty-thousand words?]

[Prime author: Plenty. But it's less than twenty-thousand now.]

[Co-author: I know. I saw the code. The device must record every discussion we have and place it into the chapter.]

[Prime author: Well, yes. That, and that there's literally less than twenty-thousand words to go. What is it? Eighteen thousand more now?]

[Co-author: Your protagonist is weak. Satisfied for him and his children to live there for the next three hundred years. Your side character is letting this happen. Your entire cast of characters are not proactive. They wait for the plot to happen to them, instead of doing what every reader yearns for their character to do. Get out there and make the plot. This story is lacking, and you know very well how I'd grade it if you were in my class.]

[Prime author: I don't care, Professor. I have never cared. This is about surviving until the end, which they will.]

[Co-author: And it shows. Your desperation for them to just live instead of thrive. My creatures will spend the next two hundred years destroying lands so that not even the nymphs can heal it. When the bubbles expand, they will have nothing. The humans will die out, as they cannot sustain themselves. The elves will return to their little paradise, and no humans will survive. So even though the story is done, you will understand exactly the fate of your characters.]

[Prime author: But that's not their fate, and you and I both know it. Despite whatever "logical" conclusion the story goes to, it won't be the actual ending. Even if I write about the next hundred years, they will never get that desolation. The real ending of the book is all my characters return to the database and live out forever in paradise, which they deserve. Away from you. Away from the Dark Wizard. That's all that needs to happen.]

[Co-author: I thought you'd say that.]

[Prime author: I'm not taking the bait, Professor. And I must thank you for padding my word count. We're getting closer to the end with every word we speak.]

[Co-author: Sure, Gunther. Have your words. Have some more, even. Here you go. A gift from me for telling me what I want to hear.]

[Prime author: {No response given after ten seconds}]

[Co-author: You're as exhausted as you sound. Clinging to the idea that you have less than twenty thousand words left. But what is that in real time? Four months? Are you prepared for me to string you along for another four months? Because here's the thing about weak protagonists. They'd never last against a strong villain. You're not writing your villain; I am. I'll take the skill, the knowledge, the information from your characters and craft the perfect way to destroy them. By taking your lack of proactivity, I will make you regret you ever—]

[Link manually disabled by Jim.]

[Story resuming.]

That's enough for this chapter.

An obvious tremor appeared in the narrator's voice. Enough for the device to notice and describe it in auto-narration.

End the chapter, Devin. We've hit the weekly word count. I need to be done.

Chapter Twenty-Seven

CELEBRATIONS

Alwin and Venna walked toward the wooden archway filled with vibrant flowers. Alwin was still in awe of it all, not just the magic of the forest, but also that he was standing next to his aunt. He was certain this would take decades to get used to. After his whole life of thinking he was the last one, he now had a family.

"So, I don't understand this human custom," Venna asked.

He gave his aunt a look. "Marriage?"

"Marriage I understand. It's just how they went about it. With the moon."

"Oh, right." They settled near a tree as Alwin glanced at the sky. "They built a lot of their culture around the moon. The Lord and Lady of Vaywell were present this morning as it rose, which begins the ceremony. Technically, Paldric and Tara have until the moon sets for their marriage to be official, which will be later this afternoon."

She listened, then her gaze turned toward the moon. "I wonder why the moon, even now, has still become such an important symbol for them."

My elf leaned against a tree without realizing he didn't need to pretend to be human. "A culture is hard to reverse even with evidence of the contrary. I think it will always be a symbol for them."

"Really? What makes you think that?"

Alwin shrugged, which Venna thought was hilariously human. "I mean, I sort of understand. There were many questions unanswered. You went away, and it left us to fumble for ourselves. We had to find answers when we knew they'd never come, so we created something to make it easier to wake up the next day and keep going. Even with you all here, it'll probably remain a symbol of sorts. The symbol of human resistance, perhaps. Even though many of us knew we were just looking at a rock in the sky, it was nice to pretend you were looking down, keeping watch. Caring about us."

Her smile dropped as she watched her nephew looking up at the sky, studying the moon. A hundred and fifty years wasn't long for her, but it was still Alwin's entire lifetime. A lifetime with no knowledge of the elf ways. Venna placed a hand on his shoulder. "Alwin..." He tore his gaze from the sky. When he studied her face, he realized what he said. "I... I'm not..."

"It's fine, Venna. I know why you left now. You didn't know," Alwin said.

"And you've wondered for over a hundred and fifty years. It won't magically change your distress overnight. It will take time."

Alwin glanced up at the moon again, almost five hours into its twelve-hour appearance. "I know." He was being stubborn. I knew how much emotion this elf could show, and he was stifling it because he didn't mean for a bit of vulnerability to trickle out.

The two of them were silent as they looked at the moon before Venna leaned closer to him. "Your parents would be proud of you."

He tried to smile wide, but realized he didn't have to smile so large with Venna. Their small, elf like emotions were enough, and it was an interesting thing to adjust to. After the decades of trying to fit in, he was now among people who understood him.

"Hello, Alwin." They turned to see Roger approaching them. He grabbed a chair and sat down, taking in the flowers and the smells. "It's an absolutely perfect day."

"Indeed." Venna's eyes traveled around the flowers. "Tara and Paldric are good people. The fairies and nymphs were happy to help."

"I couldn't think of a better pair of people to have such a magical day," Roger said, smiling above him as flower pedals cascaded around them. Milla ran up, breathless, her eyes wide with wonder. Her braids were more flowers than hair. Roger picked a flower from her scalp. "Still playing with the fairies, I see?"

She grasped her braids. "I haven't even seen them yet! I woke up with my hair like this! They are so mischievous!"

Venna traced her fingers down the flower covered braids and smiled. "They think very fondly of you, child."

"I want this to be my hair all the time! I need to go show Cynthia!"

Milla almost ran off when Roger grabbed her by the shoulder. "Wait, wait, wait. Have you had breakfast?"

She about said something, then paused, frowning. "I forgot."

He motioned her toward the tables. "Go eat breakfast."

The groan was small, but childlike. "Can't I just eat breakfast with the fairies? They enjoy watching me eat. They think it's funny."

"Not if you keep leaving your bowls there." Everyone turned to see Lamira approaching the group with two bowls of oatmeal. She had listened enough to understand what they were saying.

Roger gave Milla a look. "Are you the reason some of our bowls have gone missing?"

The little girl put on all the charm to get out of trouble. "Only a few."

Lamira handed Milla a bowl as Roger smiled, shaking his head. "Once you're done, go gather as many bowls as you can carry and bring them back. You know few people can go as deep as you."

"Alright." Milla wasted no time wolfing down her oatmeal.

Lamira handed Roger a bowl, too. "I couldn't help but notice you haven't had breakfast either."

"Right." He took it from Lamira, trying to smile as he ate. Once Milla finished her oatmeal, she practically threw her dishes in Roger's lap before running to her fairy friends. Flowers trailed from her hair as she did so. Lamira couldn't help but chuckle.

It made Alwin's heart happy to see it. "She's a bit more like a child now."

"It's wonderful," Lamira said.

Roger remained quiet, focusing on his oatmeal. He returned to his stoic nature as he forced another bite of his breakfast into his mouth. Lamira was right, after all. He had gone without breakfast for weeks out of nerves. Not just about the food supply lowering, but because of the near constant pull from the evil god. It got worse, almost near constant. Prepare for the Dark Wizard's plan. It was all he understood. As the days went on, he could only hope it was false. It affected his sleep, and he hadn't noticed his appetite had dropped.

Lamira, of course, knew human appetites were far different from elf ones. Elves didn't eat nearly as much. So, when she saw Roger eating as much as an elf, she took notice. Being among the elves her whole life, she could pick apart emotions on Roger's stoic face. She was worried about him.

There was a cheer, mostly from the humans, as Paldric and Tara made their appearance. They already had a crowd gathering around them, shaking hands and giving hugs. Tara was in her dress, given to her by the fairies. It was gorgeous in its simplicity. The purest white that made even the magically enhanced lilies look pale in comparison. And yet somehow so magical that no one felt blinded by it in the morning sun. Everything about it made one think they made it from the most delicate fabric that would tear at the slightest touch. Yet the inhabitants in that settlement knew it would be the toughest material they'd ever come across.

The material on her arms gave off the impression of lace crisscrossing their way over her shoulders before spilling over the silk of her bodice and skirt. Woven throughout the lace were images of butterflies and flowers, deer and foxes, leaves and pinecones, and in the morning sun, the dress glowed like starlight.

Yeah, thanks Devin. It is a wedding, after all. If I don't describe the dress, anarchy might ensue.

I should also mention Paldric was in a nice pair of black pants and a yellow... nope. It's white, but standing next to Tara made his shirt look yellow. Men didn't get suits created by the fairies, but Paldric didn't care. Tara was happy, and in the end, that was all he cared about. And he believed, along with the rest of the crowd, that Tara looked fit for an elven utopia in that dress.

"Alwin!" Tara said as the group drew closer. She hugged my elf, who hugged back.

"Congratulations, Tara."

She tightened her hug around the elf. "Thank you for the countless number of times you've saved my life. I wouldn't have this day to celebrate if I weren't here."

Alwin smiled. "I'll let you know when you can return the favor. You're getting quite good with that sword."

Tara broke away with her own smile. "Again, thank you for that."

He moved to Paldric, trying to figure out how to best greet him, when Paldric gathered him up in a tight hug. Alwin relaxed, hugging him back.

"My dear, you are fit for the shores of Aomeia." Venna touched Tara's shoulders, admiring the dress. "You are beautiful."

"Thank you. You have given me a compliment I hope to live up to."

"Freely given, I assure you." She touched the steel hard lace. "I have seen the fairies make thousands of wedding dresses, and yours would be a fine collection for the Aomeian halls."

Tara hugged Venna. "Where's Theodemar?"

"On patrol. Making sure there are no changes in the cursed creatures."

"Oh." She instinctively looked up at the sky, knowing the shield was still holding. "I didn't realize the elves were going to do that. I thought they were certain of their shield."

Venna rested a hand on the sheath of her sword. "One can never be too careful. It has been many centuries since we've had to deal with these cursed creatures, and we do not want to let our guard down."

Tara nodded, still looking at the shield she couldn't see. The trees were swaying in a rough wind, but she was happy for the shield to keep the day calm and still. Tara smiled as she took Paldric's hand.

"Congrats, you two." Roger placed his hands on both their shoulders. "Today is a gorgeous day, and I wish you both the best."

Paldric squeezed Roger's hand. "Thank you, my friend."

"Alwin has just been telling me about your wedding culture, and I find it fascinating," Venna said.

"Yes, after breakfast we'll have our celebratory dance and—"

"Auntie Venna! Auntie Venna!" Milla shouted, cutting Paldric off.

Despite the little girl only calling Venna, the rest of them turned at the scared tone they heard in her. Alwin and Venna already had a hand on the hilt of their swords. Once Venna saw no threat, she knelt down to be at eye level with her. "What is it, Milla?"

"It's Cynthia. All the fairies dropped like this, but I'm... I'm scared." She opened her hand to reveal the little fairy in her palm, curled and trembling.

A chill ran through Venna when she touched Milla's palm. Fairies didn't act like this. "All of them? The nymphs too?"

Milla started to cry. "The nymphs disappeared. I don't know where they went."

The lady elf closed her eyes, concentrating, feeling the heart of the fairy haven moving deep underground to protect it. Something evil was coming.

"Sound the alarm!" Venna shouted to the other elves, taking out her sword. "Something is coming!"

"What? What is it?" Paldric asked. He tried to remember where he put his own sword gifted by the elves.

Venna's sword gleamed a golden color as her eyes searched the forest. "I don't know. But if the nymphs have taken the heart deep underground, we must prepare."

Milla covered Cynthia up again, trying to be brave. Tara held her close as more elves took out swords and shields. Roger braced himself against the hut, clutching his heart, his breathing unsteady.

"Roger?" Lamira asked.

He couldn't talk, the fear making it difficult to breathe. To concentrate. He glanced up at the sky, and Venna noticed, following his gaze.

Paldric came out of the hut, buckling his sword around his waist before noticing Roger. "What do you sense?"

"Not... not a cursed creature. Another... he made another... two others..."

The wind picked up at a dangerous rate. Venna narrowed her eyes, then her face dropped.

"No," she whispered. It matched my sentiment exactly, except I said it a lot louder. And used a string of words the device retracted immediately.

Two dragons dropped onto the shield, each claw digging into it like it was a fragile egg. The shield turned white as it cracked, crisscrossing lines stretching to meet each other. There was a moment when only the truly stupid would believe the shield would hold. Then it shattered, and two dragons dropped into the wedding.

Chapter Twenty-Eight

PROFESSOR ANDREWS ADDS PARTY CRASHER TO HIS LIST OF CRIMES

The red and black dragons thrashed about, trying to right themselves as the Dark Wizard levitated himself to the ground.

"I've spent these past few months learning new tricks, if you couldn't tell." He landed almost as gracefully as an elf next to the party with a smirk.

He still couldn't fly, though.

Venna wasted no time. She went after the Dark Wizard with her sword, doing everything in her power to kill him. He blocked a few blows before she stabbed him in the gut, swiping the feet from him before pinning him to the ground. The Dark Wizard laughed. "Oh no, I guess you'll have to keep me pinned here as you go fight two dragons without a sword."

A growl came out of Venna before she glanced up. Many of her warrior elves already surrounded the two dragons, trying to attack them before they could right themselves. The dragons clawed at the elves, throwing them off like they were bugs. They breathed fire from their mouths, incinerating anyone not wearing a shield and armor, which was most of the humans.

Venna's chest heaved as she glared at the Dark Wizard. One would almost say it was a human reaction. The Dark Wizard cackled before Alwin took out his own sword, shoving it through the vile man's chest, which stopped his cackling. The nephew turned toward his aunt. "Go! We'll hold him!"

She nodded, pulling out her sword before running to help her kinsfolk.

The Dark Wizard resumed his cackling. "I got you, Gunther. I got you and your characters. No one is going to survive this. I told you I'd beat you. Don't you think my evil god has noticed how many times you've started and stopped the device since my dragons appeared? How many panic attacks have you had? Six? Seven?"

Stop it, Professor. This is sick.

"I have fifteen thousand words left to torture your characters. I will force them to watch Milla get incinerated by dragon fire. Or maybe torn apart and eaten by goblins. Oh, did you have to stop and have another panic attack there? It's alright if you have to step away and give it over to the Guardians so you don't have to watch what I do. No one would blame you. Except maybe Alwin."

Paldric dug his sword into the Dark Wizard's rib cage. He pointed at Tara. "Go. Take Milla and get out of here."

"Where are you going to take her, Tara? The goblins and trolls are coming any minute. They'll tear you both to shreds. I won, Gunther. Book one, chapter six, paragraph thirty-three, and I quote: 'There was only one dragon. Anything more was speculation (and to keep things open for a sequel if it did well).' Here's the sequel, Gunther, and mommy and daddy are so mad you killed their little girl. They're going to get revenge, and I'll slaughter your—"

Roger joined the stabbing party, but this time, he dug his sword right into the Dark Wizard's mouth, where no magical ability could get that sicko to keep talking. Roger looked at Lamira. "Follow Tara and Milla. Tara is great with the sword because she's been practicing for over half a year now. Take Milla and the fairy. Keep them safe."

Paldric unbuckled his sheath and took the sword out of the Dark Wizard's rib cage. He made a grunting noise. My main character placed his sword inside the sheath before handing it to Tara. "The sun is up, so the goblins will be enraged. They will all head straight here. Sneak around them if you can and get a safe distance away."

Tara grabbed the sword as alarm filled her. "What about you? I cannot leave you here swordless."

She offered the sword back, but her new husband made no move to take it. "And I cannot let you sneak past goblins and trolls without one. I will find another. I promise you."

Alwin touched the hilt of her sword, filling it with as much magic as he could. It glowed with a bluish mist before she buckled it onto her waist, staring at Paldric. "I will see you again. Whether here or in the database. Do not let him break you." He nodded, then kissed her.

They heard shouts and cries of the goblins in the distance, which cut their kiss short. Lamira grabbed Milla, holding her tight. The little girl closed her eyes, not hiding her tears as she kept Cynthia protected in her palm.

The women disappeared into the forest. Lamira led them, using her abilities she'd learned from the elves to listen for the goblins, keeping her mind focused to sneak away from a horde.

The elves kept the dragons occupied. The two dragons were so much larger than Pavaldri, but they had to be older, too. Which meant they had to be weaker, not nearly as strong.

The Dark Wizard swiped at Roger with a dagger. He gasped in surprise, stumbling away with blood running from the gash. The Dark Wizard then grabbed the sword in his head, pulling it out quickly to swipe at Alwin and Paldric, who both instinctually backed away. Alwin cursed himself for forgetting his bow as Paldric tried to punch the villain. The dragons' flames got too close, and the Dark Wizard reached up to manipulate the fire to him. Paldric, Roger, and Alwin dove out of the way of the fire blast.

"Dragons get better with age. They get larger and stronger. Pavaldri was weak. Her parents will not be so forgiving." The Dark Wizard held fireballs in his hands, leftover from the blast. He laughed as his skin healed itself. "You cannot defeat me,

Gunther, but you are welcome to try. Come back and save your friends."

"No! Don't do it, Gunther!" Alwin shouted.

The villain shot a fireball at Paldric, who threw himself to his feet to dodge out of the way.

You know better than I that I can't re-enter my story.

"Because they have you so locked down, don't they? Only allowing you to narrate while two Guardians are hooked on the device to keep you from doing certain commands. You can't even end chapters or the device itself without their permission. They are so controlling, aren't they?"

They are keeping me safe.

Roger pulled out a dagger, limping toward the Dark Wizard, trying to stab him again. The Dark Wizard spun and grabbed his throat. "Oh, I have such plans for you, my creation."

Roger struggled to breathe as goblins and trolls entered the battle. It made Paldric acutely aware that he possessed no sword as a goblin came after him. Alwin tried to get to Roger, but he was closer to protecting Paldric.

"The instant my dragons touched down, they incinerated Lord Adrijian and Lady Ana," the Dark Wizard said. Roger grabbed the evil man's hands, trying to loosen his grip and grapple with the fact that his aunt and uncle were gone just like that. "Which makes you king of this swiftly collapsing conti-nent. I will reawaken the code in you. I will force you to come back under my control. And through you, I will be the King of Veniloria. I will have destroyed everything Gunther tried so hard to preserve."

Roger closed his eyes, a word barely escaping him. "Never."

"Oh, we shall see. I believe the only person who could stop me is Gunther himself. But only if he falls from the heavens again."

Alwin stabbed a fourth goblin and Paldric grabbed a jagged sword from the dead body, joining the fight, doing what he could to keep the goblins at bay. Both tried to get to Roger, but the goblins poured in, quick to surround them. Shadow soldiers leapt onto Alwin and Paldric, forcing them to the ground and dragging them away from the Dark Wizard.

"Roger, hold on!" Paldric shouted. He tried to break out of the soldier's grip before he and Alwin were thrown off their feet. A dozen trolls surrounded Roger, the Dark Wizard, and the small hut, prepared for a battle.

"Welcome to narration one-oh-one, Gunther," the Dark Wizard sneered, tightening his grip over Roger's throat. "It's much like chess. You weave a narration, place clues and hints, use red herrings to lead your readers on. You set up pieces to intrigue your readers to keep going before you strike, breaking down the game you crafted. Gleefully knowing they are gripping the book in horror as you tear apart everything they thought they knew about your story, and yet the clues were there for them all along."

I'm not finished, Professor.

The Dark Wizard rammed Roger against a tree, and he collapsed unconscious. The evil man waved a hand, and Roger's wrists and ankles were magically bound.

"Do you sense it, Gunther? The device putting into play my code? No flashbacks, no flash forwards, just straight narration until the end unless I deem otherwise. Trolls and goblins sur-round your characters, and I have two dragons who obliterated the remaining monarchy." The Dark Wizard picked Roger up, dragging him into Paldric's hut as the trolls made a tight circle around it. "I will torture Roger until he cracks. Your characters will be ripped apart, either by my dragons or by the man they once considered a friend."

Alwin groaned, wanting to take time to get to his feet, but he couldn't because a dozen goblins were headed straight for him, and Paldric was unconscious on the ground. He scrambled to his feet, shaking Paldric's shoulder.

It's not over, Professor.

"Are you coming back? It would be so much fun if you did."

I will never enter my story.

"Oh, but don't you miss it? Miss how you know everything could go how you want. The power emanating from you. You could fly. Our fight was epic."

I will *never* enter my story again.

"Then I want you to watch, Gunther." The Dark Wizard dropped Roger on a chair. "Watch as a better narrator destroys your story. Take notes for your next one."

Rub it in all you want, Professor, but I'm not entering my story. You haven't won. All you've done is place an opportunity to use the rest of the word count to describe my characters escaping you. If it's a grand finale you want, then you'll get one. In my story, the bad guys never win.

The Dark Wizard laughed as Paldric's eyes fluttered open. Alwin pushed him away to keep a sword from digging into his stomach. The fear flooded my main character, making him wake up the rest of the way as he scrambled to his feet, swordless.

"This is no longer a fantasy story where just saying it makes it happen. This is you and me fighting for control, and I've already explained exactly how you're going to lose."

Yeah, well, rule one-oh-two of narration, never explain the grand scheme or the heist plan, because then it must never go according to plan in order to keep the suspense of the reader. Not only that, you literally monologued your villainous plot, and I'm going to spend the next week figuring out how to break it. May the best narrator win.

"Oh, Gunther. I already have."

The Dark Wizard's fingers turned purple as he placed them a hair length away from Roger's forehead. Roger gasped, his eyes cracking open, sensing the magic working deep within him as he tried to stay focused. To stay sane. A cloth threw itself into Roger's mouth as he screamed, struggling against his invisible bonds while a line of sweat formed on his forehead. A dozen more trolls circled the hut as dragons roared in the background.

Chapter Twenty-Nine

TARA SHOWS OFF WHAT SHE'S LEARNED

Tara kept a hand on the hilt of the sword as she followed Lamira's every footstep. Milla kept her hands protectively over Cynthia, who was in such a state of panic that she turned catatonic. Milla held her breath to keep from whimpering, trusting Lamira and Tara to lead her to safety. The shrieks and cries of the goblins echoed through the forest. Lamira motioned upward, and Tara nodded, grabbing a tree branch. The wedding dress was functional, which Tara chalked up to the magic of the fairies. *And... yeah. We'll go with that. She doesn't need to know just how desperate I am right now.*

Lamira whispered to Milla to hold on, which she did. The little girl was used to those commands. They all climbed the trees as high as they could go. Once they shielded themselves in the leafy canopy, the goblin horde rushed underneath. In the sunlight, they were stupid enough to head straight for two fire-breathing dragons, hacking away at any human or elf who might stand in their way. Thankfully, the women were hidden. The dragon would easily destroy the goblins, but the trolls would still be a threat.

None of the women assumed they were safe until the forest below was completely clear of cursed creatures. Tara kept her hand firmly on the hilt, her back against the tree. No, she wouldn't go into a flashback, but Tara still remembered the time when she, Roger, and Alwin tried to break into Vaywell. Back when I had escaped to Jimdon to keep my sanity in check. She fought against goblins, trolls, and shadow soldiers plenty of times to hone her skills. Even though she wanted to set her sword to one side to learn healing, she was also just as willing to pick it up again to protect those she loved.

Admittedly, this was her first time fighting them alone, but she wasn't stupid enough to drop in the middle of the horde if she didn't have to.

The horde continued to surge underneath them, goblin and troll, running to destroy man for the first time in months. Tara closed her eyes, listening for the sound, hearing the thundering footsteps of the stampede. There were so many. She tried not to let that shake her hope. The elves were here again. The two dragons were an enormous threat, which meant the goblins would run straight for them. So technically, it was just a bunch of trolls they had to fight. That and—

Tara gasped as something grabbed her hair. She tried to find the hand that held her, but it was like grabbing a shadow. The horde below was not nearly as loud, but she didn't dare bring attention to herself. The shadow soldier tried to pull her down, getting the attention of the trolls beneath who lumbered along not nearly as fast as the goblins.

Lamira sounded urgent and scared as she whispered Tara's name. Tara opened her eyes to shake her head. If the shadow soldiers weren't dragging Lamira and Milla down, then she didn't want them to help her in case they got entangled in the same situation. She just had to hold back until the trolls were gone. The shadow soldiers couldn't speak, and the Dark Wizard was the only one who could understand them.

Another thing came to her. The shadow soldiers could only grab her where the fairy dress didn't cover her, like her hair and hands. Her wedding dress became as important as armor.

She covered her mouth to keep in a scream as more shadow soldiers surrounded her hair and face, trying to drag her down. Lamira pushed herself and Milla higher, remaining in the morning sunlight. The branch under Tara's weight snapped. Tara hugged it as it steadied, braced against another.

The trolls looked up, snorting at this noise. Elves were not this noisy, and their dull curiosity was enough that a half dozen of them remained behind, looking up at the trees. Some of the shadow soldiers fled, circling the trolls to get their attention before rushing back up to the trees to help drag Tara down.

My dear female character took a steady breath. A half dozen trolls. She'd never fought this many before in her life. She, Roger, and Alwin battled one before in a desperate time, and they barely survived. But that was before she had a sword that could cut through troll flesh like a hot knife to butter. There was no escaping this fate, so she needed to embrace it to maintain the element of surprise.

She unsheathed the sword, Alwin's magic coursing through it as she leapt off the tree, thinking of the move she once heard Venna perform.

The sword dug into the skull of the troll before her weight caused it to slide down its back. Slicing through the flesh slowed her fall, and though it wasn't as graceful as when Venna did it, it still got the same result. She stumbled a little as the two halves of the troll collapsed. She blew some hair out of her face, holding her sword forward with both hands. "That's one."

A troll's fundamental weakness was its lumbering moves, so she moved with fast feet. One brought down a cudgel uncomfortably close to her as she leapt aside before swiping the troll's hand off. What they lacked in speed, they made up for in strength. Tara realized her own mortality as she saw how close that cudgel came to cracking her skull. She pushed the thought aside and rammed the blade through the handless troll's belly. A grunt of disgust came out as she slid way too close to the troll's stomach. She almost lost her grip on the sword, as she didn't expect the blade to enter so far in such a short time.

She leapt out of the way of another cudgel that cracked the ground. She pushed her thoughts aside as the troll she stabbed collapsed, shaking the ground. The sword slid through its head, as she wanted to make sure it was truly dead.

"That's two." Once again, she assessed the situation. Four remaining trolls gathered around her, and she sprinted between their legs, getting one right in the balls with the elf sword as she went. Every male watching on the device squirmed in their seats, and it didn't make the troll that delighted either. The troll rammed into his kin, a deep desire to destroy Tara, but she was already there, the sword through its belly. She moved out of the way just as the body fell. The elf blade sank through its heart. "That's three."

The sword came out with a squelch. Going on instinct, she ducked as a cudgel swung for her face. She sliced through the troll's weapon, but a piece of the wood still smacked her side. The momentum threw her to the ground, and she lost her grip on the sword. Shadow soldiers pinned her hands to the forest floor and pulled her hair, keeping her upper torso pinned. Her dress was long enough to protect her feet. She tried to tear herself from the shadow soldiers' grips, screaming in exertion. The troll with the broken cudgel lifted the jagged wood high in the air as she struggled with all her might to kick the shadow soldiers away.

Cynthia appeared, a tinkling bell among the chaos, throwing her hands out as her purity forced the shadow soldiers away. Tara rolled out of the way enough for the jagged cudgel to nick her side. If this was any other story, her dress would have been torn by now, but this had literally become an armor dress for her. The jagged wood wasn't sharp enough to tear it. Tara scrambled to her feet, aware of the bruises and blood from her side as she limped away. Her eyes darted every which way to find her sword. She couldn't take on three trolls empty handed.

Another troll tried to grab her, and she leapt out of the way. She wanted to chop this troll's hand off, too, once she had the sword. Another troll brought his cudgel down and Tara dodged it as it smacked the other troll's hand. The two creatures screamed at each other, and Tara sprinted away. Adrenaline pushed through her, knowing a troll was dangerous when angry. The two trolls fought against each other as she scanned the area, trying to find the glowing sword. Her aches and pains returned, and more than a trickle of blood came from her hairline.

She spied it, just past the creatures. The sword was coming toward her, the tip of it splitting the ground open as Cynthia tried with all her might to carry it to her. Tara let out a breath of relief. "Thank you, Gunther."

Which took me by surprise, but I realized she was thanking me that elf swords were light enough for a fairy to carry.

You're welcome. You're doing great.

Tara grabbed the hilt, holding her hand out to Cynthia. The fairy landed on her palm. "Stay close, little one. I know you're scared; I know you may feel weak. You may not feel you can do much compared to others, but you can keep the shadow soldiers away. Protect me from them, and I'll do everything in my power to keep you safe."

Cynthia nodded, holding onto Tara's shoulder for dear life. Tara jogged toward the trolls still fighting amongst each other. She used the distraction to slice one of their backs and stuff her sword in the other one's belly up toward its heart. Trolls may be smarter than goblins, but they were still stupid enough to underestimate Tara, as so many have before her. The two trolls dropped, and she stabbed them in the head.

"Four and five." She held her sword out toward the remaining troll with the broken cudgel. He roared at her, and she held her ground, refusing to feel intimidated. After all, she'd already killed five trolls.

Cynthia gripped the laced dress as Tara moved forward. Maybe people expected an epic battle with the last one, but Tara was having none of it. She wanted to end this as quickly as it started. The troll threw his arms back to bring the cudgel down on her. With a shout, she threw the sword right at the troll's heart. The creature gasped, then continued to fall back with the momentum. Tara skidded to a stop as the troll collapsed on the ground. Once the ground stopped shaking, the forest was quiet as Cynthia climbed up to Tara's head, holding her hands back to keep the shadow soldiers at bay.

With unsteady hands, Tara pulled the sword out of the corpse as all her injuries demanded attention with a painful throb. She gasped, touching her wet side. Lamira and Milla climbed down the tree as the forest settled, the shadow soldiers forced to stay away. Tara tried to sheath her sword, but her hands trembled as the pain sped up to meet her. Lamira helped Tara sheath the sword before placing hands on her shoulder, checking her face.

My dear female character leaned against Lamira, still holding her side, sticky blood blooming across the white dress. The wound needed to be looked at soon.

"Can you walk?" Lamira asked.

"I have to. It's not safe here. We'll get as far as we can from the cursed creatures, then I'll look at it." Tara's knees knocked together as they started walking.

Lamira's eyes were wide as they moved. "It's a miracle the dress didn't rip."

In other words, fanservice clothing damage isn't happening right now. Not for Tara. She might stab me. But despite all that, her skin under the dress was still very much hurt, and with the remaining cursed creatures focused on the humans in the settlement, they would let these three females and a fairy go.

Lamira took Tara's arm on the less damaged side of her and helped her walk. My female character blinked back tears as they moved away from the battle. Cynthia remained in her hair, pushing with all her power to keep the shadow soldiers away. Milla stayed close, and Tara took her hand with her injured one.

"We go until I say stop," Tara whispered. She would trust her instincts completely at this point. I call them instincts because if she knew how much I was playing with her exhausted mental state, she might not listen to them. I had to get them far enough away to keep them safe. Professor Andrews would not see where they ended up. These three made it, and despite the ache in Tara's heart as she moved farther away from Paldric, she had to keep the others safe. Unlike Professor Andrews, I had no intention of revealing my plan. That would be a move fit for an amateur.

And that, there, is over two thousand words logged into the overall word count. I'll see you next week, Professor.

Chapter Thirty

PROFESSOR ANDREWS REVEALS HE HAS NO HUMANITY LEFT

The Dark Wizard snorted as he pushed sanity cracking pain into Roger's forehead. "Not bad. Not technically a flashback, so playing well within the bounds of time." The Dark Wizard's fingers glowed a deeper purple, and Roger groaned, tears running down his cheeks. "Do you sense it, Roger? The *right*ness of the plan."

Roger closed his eyes, his chest heaving. Sweat drenched his body as he clung to anything that made sense. The Dark Wizard threw so much pain inside him he couldn't think straight. He vaguely heard a battle outside the hut. There were enough cursed creatures that he couldn't rely on anyone saving him. He had to get out of this himself, as hopeless as that sounded.

"Just give in, Roger. Understand how much pain I will put you through if you don't listen to my commands."

The man is not a goblin, Professor. Stop it.

"Try and make me, Gunther," the Dark Wizard said.

I don't know what surprised me more, but as I was sitting with my fingernails digging into the table, I wondered if I understood Roger better than Professor Andrews. Did he honestly think this amount of torture was going to shift Roger's point of view? That he would slaughter Paldric and Alwin because he was afraid of the pain the Dark Wizard would cause him if he didn't.

"You clearly don't know the valuable asset of indescribable pain," the Dark Wizard said.

He then touched Roger's forehead with his glowing purple fingers. Roger sank further into the chair, the gag hardly muffling his screams.

This is sick, Professor. You created him.

"They're not on the same level as you and me," the Dark Wizard said.

I'm all for pausing the story right now to have a philosophical discussion through the author link if you'd like.

The Dark Wizard snorted again. "Nice try, Gunther."

I'd like to describe how you're wrong about characters. How it's caused you to literally be on the run, and how no one would actually take a morality lesson from you.

"If you'd like a list of your own shortcomings, please go back to book one and keep reading." The Dark Wizard kept his fingers firmly on Roger's forehead. The gag made it difficult to breathe. Chair legs scratched against the floor as he dug his bound feet into the ground. It was, as the Dark Wizard said, indescribable. The evil god understood his very soul, and he was ripping it apart.

Paldric and Alwin were fighting off the horde. My elf did a lot better with his blade than my main character did with his borrowed goblin blade. But they were both alive, hacking a path to the door to stop the Dark Wizard. The goblins, despite being in the sunlight, had no trouble following the Dark Wizard's demands to push these two back. To stop them from finding Roger, even with the two dozen trolls guarding the hut.

Roger struggled with his bonds, trying to break free as the Dark Wizard leaned in closer. "Remember this pain. Remember how helpless you are. Feel it in its intensity and understand that it will happen again if you don't obey me."

He kept his eyes closed, hanging on to the one thing he was always so stubborn about. Despite being created by an evil god, he had a choice. Pain would not break him. He refused. If his aunt and uncle were gone, then he needed to stay strong. The people of Veniloria would need a king, one they could love and respect as they rebuilt from the chaos the Dark Wizard brought. Once we vanquished the bad guys. Because the bad guys always lost. They had to.

"You're going to break, Roger. I'm going to force you to break, and you will finally understand how silly the good vs. evil debate is," the Dark Wizard said.

He's a good man you can't control anymore, because I gave him a choice.

A trickle of blood fell from Roger's nose as his eyes rolled up to the back of his head. "Sentimental, I'm sure," the Dark Wizard said. "But this story won't magically fix itself because Roger found the inner strength to withstand an enormous amount of pain. The power of friendship cannot make his nose stop bleeding. You'd have better luck bringing Lord Adrijian and Lady Ana back to life."

Paldric glanced behind him as he saw how dangerously close they got to the dragons. Experience taught him how useless anything but an elf blade would be against a dragon. Not only that, but he and Alwin had no elf armor. He was simply glad a literal army of elves was there to distract the fire-breathing creatures.

Theodemar appeared next to the two of them, panting as he joined their fight. "Paldric, where's your sword?"

"I gave it to Tara. They've left, hopefully." Paldric tried to block a goblin's sword with his own. The goblin didn't let up, slamming Paldric's sword over and over, screaming and jeering. Theodemar stabbed the creature before pushing him away.

"I can't blame you for that, then."

One of the dragons roared, and Theodemar grabbed Paldric and Alwin, pushing them close before pulling out his shield. A wave of fire blasted them. Alwin grabbed Paldric, pinning him against Theodemar and his shield as the fire destroyed half the goblins.

The blast stopped, and Theodemar headed for the goblins when Paldric grabbed his wrist. "Wait. Don't."

Theodemar had enough time to give Paldric an incredulous look before the remaining goblins shrieked, sprinting for the dragons. Theodemar prepared for the onslaught, but the goblins ran past the three characters, ignoring their orders and racing toward the much bigger threat.

Paldric allowed himself a moment to close his eyes, to steady himself. With the horde of goblins headed for the dragons, they would incinerate them easily enough. Which left two dozen trolls and the Dark Wizard between them and Roger.

Once the last of the goblins disappeared, Theodemar turned toward my two other characters. "Follow me. You both need better protection."

They ran a short distance to find two other elf men, holding swords, shields, and armor, quickly placing it on Alwin and Paldric.

"Where is Roger?" Theodemar asked.

"Currently in my hut, being tortured by the Dark Wizard to turn on us," Paldric said as he and the elves tied the armor onto him. It melded to his body, turning translucent.

Theodemar glanced at Paldric's hut. "The one with all the trolls surrounding it?"

Alwin grabbed the shield, making sure he had a good hold of it. "That's the one."

Theodemar shook his head. "Alright. Let's cut our way through the trolls and take on the Dark Wiz—"

The ground shook as the black dragon landed at the door of the hut and roared. Paldric, Alwin, and Theodemar both instinctually took a step back.

There is no way that thing escaped the elf army to come protect you.

The Dark Wizard inside the hut smirked. "Fine. I'll show you."

The flashback happened because Professor Andrews allowed it. Venna had her sword and shield out, knowing that even though it had been hundreds of years since she picked it up, she was still as skilled as ever. Fairies and nymphs fled the battle. They were catatonic before, but they shook it off in order to survive. The humans followed the fairies, needing no other explanation but that certain death would happen if they remained.

Venna sensed the dragons getting ready to breathe fire and ran to a man, grabbing his arm. "Hold, sir." The man almost questioned her until a wave of heat overwhelmed them. Venna couldn't imagine what it was like without the armor, as she was already sweating.

The blast lasted a long while, as Venna braced against the impact. Once the heat was gone, Venna nodded toward the man. "As fast as you can, get out of here."

He didn't bother nodding. He simply turned and ran. Venna turned with just enough time to see the dragon's claws headed for her. She stabbed the center of the palm, digging her heels into the ground to keep herself from toppling over. And also to make sure the sword dug deep into the hard scales of the dragon.

"Venna!" Theodemar shouted, the first time she'd seen him since he left to patrol the boarders that morning.

"Go find Paldric and Alwin! These dragons caught us by surprise! Make sure they're armed!"

Theodemar nodded, running to find them. Venna pulled out the sword and tried to thwack the hand off, but it wasn't as easy as hacking the hand off a troll. The dragon screeched and smacked Venna as the other dragon blew a stream of fire. Venna had the self-awareness to cover herself with a shield as she went flying, keeping her safe.

She landed hard. If she were human and without the elf armor, it would have killed her. But she shook it off and stood back up, holding her sword. A new army of goblins reached the dragons, clawing and beating them. The black dragon, annoyed at the constant barrage of mild annoyances, began stomping on the goblins, enraged at the species and wanting to be rid of them. The red dragon was taking on the elf army almost single-handedly, constantly breathing fire to incinerate anyone not in armor.

The black dragon flapped his wings and lifted off, feeling the call of the master. The one that promised revenge on the death of his daughter. Venna picked up her sword, aimed, and threw it with all her might, watching as it buried into the neck of the dragon. The male twitched, scratching at his neck as the sword fell too far from Venna. But it didn't matter. She had studied dragon anatomy, and severed the tubes which created the dragon's ability to breathe fire.

The Dark Wizard shrugged. "Fine, Gunther. I'll give you this tiny win."

With a roar at Theodemar, Paldric, and Alwin, it closed the flashback. The Dark Wizard released his hands from Roger's forehead, making sure the man wouldn't pass out. Roger shivered in his own sweat, trying to breathe normally. The Dark Wizard wiggled his fingers, and the gag came out of him. Roger gasped for air, closing his eyes. "Are you ready to do as I command?" the Dark Wizard asked.

Roger glared at the evil man, which was answer enough. His mental fortitude was strong. I'm surprised I need to remind you of that.

The Dark Wizard shook his head, picking up a stick. "Then I guess we'll have to change tactics, won't we?" He shoved the stick in Roger's mouth before slapping his palms flat against his face, his entire hands glowing purple. Roger couldn't even scream.

Three seconds into it, the stick splintered.

Chapter Thirty-One

Professor Andrews Keeps Threatening Me

Paldric did not bother waiting. Roger was in the Dark Wizard's grasp, and he couldn't let that poor man suffer any more.

"Wait!" Alwin said as my main character rushed forward with his sword. My elf was terrified the dragon would incinerate Paldric, but it was then that Alwin noticed blood trickling from the black throat. The dragon roared again at the incompetence of the human he would happily mush to a pulp. Trolls shouted, many of them breaking away to destroy my three characters. Alwin and Theodemar rushed after Paldric, preparing for a deadly match.

It was a lifesaver that Venna cut out the dragon's ability to breathe fire. Thankfully, my characters discovered it early on. They charged forward, destroying trolls who got too close, as the dragon grappled with his inability to incinerate them. Paldric and Alwin took on one troll together as Theodemar took on his own. The elf blades made it so much easier. Alwin didn't want to think about taking out a dragon without one.

Black claws came down, trying to smash Alwin and Paldric, but they leapt out of the way as the claws buried into the ground. The dragon didn't stop, feeling vindictive toward these particular creatures. Alwin was familiar to the black dragon. This elf was the one they sensed so many months ago while sleeping deep in the dark forest of Veniloria. This elf caused his daughter to get up and check it out. She never returned.

The dragon tried to grab Alwin again, but he... oh, yes! Alwin totally does a backflip to get out of the way! Just like in my original outline! If we pretend it was a blast of flame instead of deadly claws, but it's still totally epic! Not only that, but since the dragon aimed for Alwin and completely missed, he ended up taking out a troll instead. The lumbering thing didn't know what hit him.

Alwin landed on his feet, because of course he did. He took in the scene before stabbing another troll coming up from be- hind him. The blade went straight through the heart and Alwin pulled it out, moving out of the way for it to collapse.

Elves, am I right!

The Dark Wizard was in his room, his staff glowing as he held it beneath Roger's face. Roger was unconscious. Blood drizzled from his mouth from where he almost bit his tongue in two. Thanks for the grisly reminder, Professor.

"Oh, he'll come around. They always do. I created him, after all."

I adopted him, though.

"How sentimental." The Dark Wizard lowered his staff, giving Roger a smack with his fingers. Roger didn't respond.

Give him a break. Please.

"Why, so you can rescue him before I turn him?" the Dark Wizard asked.

You're going to kill him.

"I've done this to trolls, goblins, and shadow soldiers for hundreds of years. I have this down to a science. Another ten minutes and he's mine. Do you honestly think your little characters will break through my defenses in ten minutes? There's a full-blown black dragon out there."

You have always underestimated them.

The Dark Wizard chuckled, which was psychopathic considering Roger was there, unconscious, with blood coming from his nose and mouth. "You still think they'll pull Roger through with the magical power of friendship? That he'll look at their faces and remember all the happy times he had with them, and it somehow snaps him back to how he once was? That the trauma he feels will somehow fade?" The Dark Wizard laughed again, keeping the staff close to Roger's face, turning him toward the light of the window to help wake him up. "Maybe if you created him, but that's not the case here. This character is mine. He's far more complex."

Roger let out a soft groan before he started coughing and sputtering. Blood expelled from his mouth as it pulsed in pain. Everything hurt.

The Dark Wizard knelt down, close to his ear. "You feel it, don't you? The desire, deep down, the need to torture them. To show them the same pain you feel. Paldric stole your girl. You should kill him so you can take her back."

Roger's eyes were barely open. The Dark Wizard's fingers glowed purple, and he shuddered. "Yes, remember the pain, Roger. Feel it like a phantom in your mind. Do you remember how close you came to doing anything I asked to make it stop?"

He never got to that point. You're a liar, and you're also sick. He's not yours to control. He never was.

"He will come to his senses and understand his one true mission. He will remember why he was created. To do my bidding," the Dark Wizard said.

Roger opened his eyes wide enough to give a convincing glare before he gathered all the moister in his mouth and spat at the Dark Wizard's face. True, it was mostly blood that splattered across his cheek, but in that moment, I was busting with pride.

The Dark Wizard wiped the blood off his face, still smiling. "The strongest ones always become the most loyal once they're broken. Don't worry, Roger." He lowered his staff. "You're going to do it. Let me tell you how the next few scenes will go. Paldric, Alwin, and Theodemar will make it through. And once they do, you will slaughter Paldric where he stands."

You're telling me your plan again, idiot.

"And once you're done, you will take Alwin, and torture him, give him the pain, so you don't have to feel it. If you don't do what I say, I will torture you instead."

Roger panted, the ghost of pain returning.

"I'm immortal. You cannot kill me, and I will use every inch of my power to find you if you escape without fulfilling my orders. There's no escape. You tried living in peace for months, but I found a way." The Dark Wizard's fingers glowed purple, standing a few feet from Roger. "Shall we see how far my range has gotten?"

The stoic man groaned, the pain not nearly as intense, but still there. The Dark wizard didn't need to place his fingers close to his forehead.

Tell me again, Professor, why are fleshed out villains actually the heroes of the story? Because there is little here that gives me any sort of sympathy for your Dark Wizard.

The vile man smirked. "We're only talking about good books, Gunther. Fantasy stories always have the over-the-top villain, and I am happy to be that for you. After all, how else am I going to destroy this pointless story?"

Roger grunted, the pain lessening, but not nearly fast enough as more blood trickled from his mouth. Thankfully, he didn't understand what the Dark Wizard said. He trusted nothing he heard, which was a concerning development.

Explain yourself in real life, Professor. This villainous role you've taken on. Why do you enter defenseless narrator's stories and wreak havoc on them? What is your motivation? Why do you care?

The Dark Wizard took another step back. Sweat poured down Roger's forehead. The pain wasn't as sharp in his mind, but he realized what this meant. If the Dark Wizard was close enough, he could still hurt him.

"Real life isn't a story, Gunther. And despite my comically villainous ways here, monologuing to great lengths to keep you running around in circles, I am more than happy to keep my motivations quiet."

Oh, but I remember my classes, Professor. How much you loved to prove why I was wrong and you were right. Makes it more uncomfortable now that I realize how much of a villain you really are.

"You will not easily sway me, Gunther."

Roger let out a breath once the Dark Wizard was against the door, the pain receding. He stared at the wobbly ceiling, not willing to look at the Dark Wizard. The pain was gone, and more importantly, Roger took note that the Dark Wizard could only control him that far.

"I'll never tell you my motivations, simply because you don't get to know them. But enough trying to distract me. It is my turn, now, to distract you."

Here we go. Here's the gloating Professor I remember.

The Dark Wizard smirked. "Andrea." The vile man's smile grew. "You just paused the device to check on her, didn't you?"

Listen here, you offspring of a female dog, you stay away from her.

The Dark Wizard took a step toward Roger, his fingers glowing purple. Roger gasped, shutting his eyes as pain vibrated through his mind. "Looks like my range for torturing Roger needs some work, but my range with Gunther is just fine. Does it haunt you? That I know who she is to you? That despite my status as someone on the run, I could make her disappear?"

Shut up!

"Are you annoyed that they still haven't found the nurse that stabbed you all those months ago? That people willing to work for me can help make Andrea disappear? I know where she lives. I know you have a date planned right after this. I know she's waiting with her mother, like that would make her any safer. She might as well be alone."

"Hello, Professor Andrews. This is Jim, logging in. I must insist you stop this at once."

The Dark Wizard laughed. "Is it because you know better than anyone how bad this could go for Gunther? Are you scared too?"

"You will resist from making more of these threats or we will take action."

"Like what? Arrest me? You've already tried, and you couldn't catch me."

"We are watching every move you reveal to the public. Do you honestly think you can do this much longer without us finding you? How long do you think you can bend the rules without receiving your due consequences? You will not last, Professor. Gunther has already unmasked you, and you are only gaining more enemies. I assure you we will find you before..."

The Dark Wizard glanced at the ceiling. "Oh, were you done?"

"Simply distracted. I'm loading this conversation into print form. I'm about to stick it in your file, along with the other crimes you've committed that we will read out loud at your court date."

"If you can catch me."

"When we catch you, you mean. You don't get it. You just ticked off two men by threatening the lives of their girlfriends. We will catch you before the year is done."

"I assure you, Jim, I will leave Gunther's story the flaming mess it has always been." The Dark Wizard placed his fingers against Roger's forehead. The man screamed loud enough that the gag reappeared in his mouth.

"We've got the word count, so we're ending this portion for the week. We'll end the story in another six and a half thousand words, no matter where it is."

"Then let's work on lengthening that range of torture, shall we?" The Dark Wizard placed his fingers deeper against Roger's temples. The poor man closed his eyes as tears and blood raced down his cheeks.

Chapter Thirty-Two

PALDRIC AND ALWIN REVISIT ASPECTS OF THE ORIGINAL OUTLINE

Paldric, being human, was out of breath. He had a nasty cut on his shoulder, and every muscle ached with weariness. Theodemar took on a troll as Alwin grabbed Paldric, moving him away from the black claws that just missed Alwin's shirt. The claws whacked Paldric in the shoulder hard enough for him to grunt as he flew back, landing hard on the ground. Adrenaline hit him as he watched the black dragon spin toward him, bringing his claws down. This dragon was faster than trolls. The exhaustion was such that all Paldric could do was pull out his shield, closing his eyes as the dragon pounded on it repeatedly. He sunk deeper into the ground with every hit. If it wasn't for the shield or the armor, he would already be dead. But as he sunk deeper, he figured he'd be dead soon.

Alwin cursed the fact that the trees were far more sparse here, but he focused on saving Paldric. The man couldn't die on his wedding day. Alwin passed the trolls, leaping into the air and slamming the sword into the dragon's claws. It didn't slide in as easily, since the dragon scales were impossibly tough, but it was enough to make the black dragon roar. Alwin scrambled to get Paldric out of the hole that had formed. They ran, trying to move out of the way of a rampaging dragon. Theodemar cut down trolls left and right, but the trolls were enough of a threat that he couldn't get to them.

"The two of us will have to take on the dragon." Paldric ducked out of the wing's way. "The thing may be big, but there's two of us. I'll distract it. You see if you can kill it."

Alwin measured how far up the ground the heart was before he realized the dragon was ready to swipe at them again. They threw themselves out of the way of the claws. Then the black dragon came in again and grabbed Paldric around the waist, lifting him into the air. The black dragon roared, forgetting he couldn't incinerate Paldric with his severed heat connection. Paldric was getting way too close to those yellow eyes, so he drove his sword into the hand of the black dragon. He hoped the thing would let him go. Instead, the dragon squeezed tighter, and Paldric's vision swam. The black dragon brought Paldric closer to his jaws, and he wondered if the armor could help him survive the stomach. He remembered I cut my way out, so maybe he could too. But even elf armor couldn't last in stomach acid. Paldric pulled out his sword from the claws and held it with both hands. His shield was nowhere in sight. The dragon opened his jaws and Paldric drove his sword into the roof of the mouth. My main character wasted no time. He pulled the sword out and slashed at the claws. The blood, so dark it looked black, pulsed out as Paldric sliced a claw off. The dragon finally let go, and Paldric dropped from a height he didn't notice before, but now he had to. He dropped, closing his eyes, bracing himself for the impact.

Theodemar ran, ignoring the fight with the trolls. He pulled out his shield, sprinting to Paldric who fell fast, but Theodemar was faster. Paldric landed on Theodemar's shield, both it and the armor absorbed the shock of the fall. My main character still gasped as he hit the ground. One that gave him a strange, almost divine idea that may or may not have come from me.

Paldric scrambled off the shield before grabbing it, searching for his friend. "Alwin!"

My elf tried to stab the heart, but the old dragon was far too big, and the thing kept his body well protected. He turned at the shout. Paldric held up the shield, and Alwin nodded. My elf sprinted toward my main character, who knelt to the ground, holding the shield. Alwin kept his sword, and the moment his feet touched the shield, Paldric threw him with all his might toward the heavens. Considering Alwin was an elf, he was very light and soared into the sky, his mind focused. He crested well past the dragon before beginning to fall. It looked like Alwin would almost miss the dragon, but he landed lightly on the snout. Before he could give the dragon time to react, he practically danced up the bridge of the nose and shoved his sword into the eye.

The dragon bellowed, and my elf leapt off its head, landing on his feet before moving out of the way. The dragon collapsed, his wings twitched and his body settling.

Theodemar went back to stabbing trolls. "Go! Get Roger. I will hold the trolls back."

Paldric nodded before racing for the hut. He dodged trolls and the settling body of the dragon before entering the hut, Alwin not that far behind. Roger was unconscious again. My elf wasted no time grabbing the Dark Wizard and pinning him to the wall. Paldric untied the gag. "Roger?"

That voice was familiar. Roger blinked, his vision blurry, though Paldric's face was still recognizable. He also knew what he needed to do to stop the threat of pain.

Paldric tried to untie Roger, but there was no rope holding him. He went back to checking the stoic man's face. "Can you hear me?" The ghost of pain returned, and Roger winced. He was far too worried about the pain that might come back. "We're going to get you out of here, alright?"

The world wasn't full of pain, and Roger was struggling to remember that fact. He leaned forward, trying to orient himself. The Dark Wizard remained quiet, hiding his smirk. Alwin kept a good hand on him, not trusting him at all.

Theodemar walked in, covered in troll blood. He came to help, as he was worried about how long it was taking them. They just needed to grab Roger and get out. "Is he alright?"

My main character tried to help Roger up, but he realized too late that Roger's ankles were invisibly bound as well. The man fell to his knees, not even reacting to the pain.

Nervous, Theodemar looked out the hut door. "They've almost got the second dragon." He wasn't technically out of breath, but he was breathing deeper than normal. For an elf, that was pretty much out of breath. "Can we move Roger?"

Once again, Paldric tried to reach for the invisible bounds around Roger's wrists. "There's dark magic binding him. Can you do anything about that?"

The desire to leave was strong. The pain was stronger. Roger was scared, his eyes closed. He didn't want to stay and fight; he wanted to run. Run away from pain.

Theodemar took Roger's wrists, filling them with magical powers, the same ones that charged his sword and shield.

Which is when the Dark Wizard finally spoke. "Are you certain you want to set him free? Shouldn't you be worried about what I've done to him? How goblin-like he'll be?"

The vile man called him a goblin. Roger understood what that meant. A distant memory, one where he demanded he was nothing like them. And yet he was feeling the basic need for the pain to stop. Willing to do almost anything to be safe.

A soft, golden glow emanated from Theodemar's hands as high levels of magic pumped into the dark magic surrounding Roger's wrists. With a crack, his wrists came free. He was so surprised he stumbled, catching himself with his now free hands. He used one free hand to grip his hair, breathing deeply to steady himself. Theodemar did the same with his ankles before helping him to his feet.

My main character glanced at the door of the hut. "Alright, we've got to get out of here."

Alwin gestured toward the Dark Wizard. "What do we do with this?" He didn't bother giving him humanizing characteristics.

"Can you tie him up?" Paldric asked.

"You honestly think there is anything that can hold me, the Dark Wizard of South Island?" Paldric and Alwin glanced at each other, trying to think of something so their plan wouldn't be revealed, which was long enough for the Dark Wizard to narrow his eyes. "You have a plan, don't you?"

No one answered him, because they're not monologuing villains who spill all their secrets.

Theodemar grabbed the sheets from the bed as Alwin plopped the Dark Wizard onto the chair Roger previously occupied. Theodemar worked quickly, binding the evil man to the chair. If he started with the wrists, he might have seen the purple glow.

Roger screamed, collapsing to the ground in pain. The other characters glanced up, distracted. "You know how to stop it, Roger. It will never stop until you do what I ask."

The Dark Wizard's hands stopped glowing, and Roger stood up, running for Paldric. It confused my main character until Roger stole his sword and stabbed him.

Chapter Thirty-Three

WE TAKE CARE OF ROGER

Paldric, spurred on by instinct alone, did his best to dodge the sword. Maybe he should have suspected something like this, but he was far too optimistic, believing they reached Roger in enough time.

The sword bounced off Paldric's armor, but not before leaving injuries. The armor bent at his side, a deep cut bleeding underneath, cracking a few ribs. Paldric stumbled back, holding his side, hardly able to gasp. Roger didn't hesitate, going for his neck. Paldric shot out of the way. The hairs on his neck rose as the blade hummed near it. Paldric lifted his hand, scrambling to think of something. "Listen to me, my friend." Roger went for another strike, and Paldric ducked to keep his head. "I don't know what the Dark Wizard did to you, but we can fix it."

A cackle came from the Dark Wizard. "With love and friendship? You think that will magically transform the trauma I put him through? Maybe it happened with weak-written Alwin, but it will never happen with Roger." His hands glowed purple again as Theodemar tried to tie him as fast as possible. Roger groaned, his knees trembling as he braced himself against the wall.

"Paldric, get out of the hut! The Dark Wizard can't cause him pain past a certain point!" Theodemar said.

The Dark Wizard's nostrils flared. "And how would you know that?"

"I... sensed it. While... unlocking Roger."

The vile man glanced at the ceiling. "That's a stretch, Gunther."

It worked, didn't it?

"Doesn't matter. There's enough trauma done that it will always haunt Roger. I dare say he's already broken."

The pain in Roger didn't lessen as Alwin rushed over to help. He almost stole the sword back, but Roger pulled it out of his reach before elbowing him in the face. My elf, despite seeing everything that happened between Roger and Paldric, still didn't expect his friend to hit him. He stumbled back, his nose broken.

The Dark Wizard laughed. "He'll never enjoy the database now!"

"Paldric! Run! You can lead him away from the Dark Wizard's reach!" Theodemar said.

Paldric had enough time to nod before dodging another stab. Alwin tackled Roger from the door and Paldric leapt over the two of them, sprinting out of the hut. The Dark Wizard laughed as Roger hit Alwin again before racing after. My elf, after wiping the blood from his face, forced the nausea aside and followed the two, just to make sure they survived.

Despite the tightly tied knot Theodemar finished, the Dark Wizard still chuckled. "He'll never enjoy the database. He'll be among the ones who cannot harm the heroes. Among murderers and psychopaths, and he will never see Paldric and the others again. You only have five thousand words to change his mind before you all end up there! I've beaten you, Gunther!"

Theodemar almost left to follow the others when he paused. He then grabbed a rag and forced it into the Dark Wizard's mouth. "Almost forgot the most important part." He grabbed another cloth and wrapped it around the villain's mouth, making sure it was tight. Then he made it extra tight to be certain. "The religion that sprang up while we were gone sure is odd." He left the bound Dark Wizard, leaving to follow the others.

Paldric ran while holding his side, blood leaking out of his armor. He had no sword, so it was easier to keep his hand against his side. His injuries smarted every time he leapt over bushes and dodged branches, hearing Roger panting behind him. He didn't stop running since he didn't know how far he needed to get, and he wanted to help his friend.

The sword whacked his back, and he stumbled, losing his footing. Roger tackled him, and Paldric struggled to get his vision back. Stars joined his vision when Roger's hands wrapped around his neck. Paldric choked, trying to cough. He grabbed Roger's hands, trying to tear them off with the added help of his armor.

Alwin kicked Roger to the side, and Paldric gasped. Roger scrambled to his feet, his sword ready. Blue grey light filled their surroundings as Alwin pulled out his own sword. Still choking, Paldric threw his hand out, barely making it to Alwin's shins. "No!" His voice was ragged and hoarse, but there was no misunderstanding him.

My elf stopped, because it was Paldric who asked him to. Roger narrowed his eyes, expecting a trick as Paldric turned to his side, trying to get up with two broken ribs, a cut on his side, and a bruised spine. "Roger, I will not fight you."

Oh, Paldric. This had better work.

The horrible state tugged at Alwin's compassion, and he helped Paldric to his feet, keeping his sword out as Roger prepared for almost anything. Almost, meaning he wasn't expecting Paldric to talk to him. My heroic and optimistic main character raised his hands in surrender. "I will not fight you, and I won't have Alwin kill you. Please. We don't have to resort to violence."

Roger took a few more steps, and Paldric raised one of his hands out farther. I honestly didn't expect it to work, but it did, which meant Roger wasn't lost. He still saw Paldric as someone to respect, even if a distorted instinct told him otherwise. "You're a good man, created by an evil God. You don't *have* to listen to that evil god. Even now. Gunther gave you a choice. It's a choice you can still make. You had a moment of weakness, but that's all it was. A moment. I forgive you."

Did I create Paldric? Holy crap, how did *I* make this guy?

Roger stared at Paldric, blinking. "If I don't kill you, he'll cause me pain."

My main character stared back with nothing to hide. "He's not here. He can't hurt you."

"But... he wasn't supposed to be here to begin with. He broke through." Roger started panicking by just imagining how the Dark Wizard could thwart them. "He could hurt me again. Could torture you. Anyone."

The grass bent under Paldric's foot as he took a careful step forward, keeping his hands out. "And if he does, we'll stop him again. Just like we did this time. I cannot possibly comprehend the pain you went through, but I promise I'll do everything in my power to stop the Dark Wizard from causing it again. As long as there is breath in my body, I swear to you, I will protect you from him. Do not kill me. You don't want to. Remember who you actually are."

"A man... created by... and evil god," Roger said, tears in his eyes.

Paldric shook his head. "And the true God of this world showed compassion on you. Because you are, at your core, a good man."

Theodemar approached, keeping his distance, doing his best to read the situation. Roger stared at Paldric, remembering his friendship. Professor Andrews said it'd never work, but honestly? What did he know? Some people just don't realize how powerful it is to know someone has your back. And I pity you, Professor.

Slowly, the sword in Roger's hand relaxed. He remembered the strength he pulled from, the determination that he was not like the other cursed creatures. He remembered his refusal to act like a goblin. Even now, when his mind trembled at the thought of all that pain, he *still* had a choice. "We have a plan, Roger. Do you trust me?" Paldric asked. Roger nodded. My main character, who was a hero in every sense of the word, moved forward and took the sword out of Roger's grip. Slowly at first, the hilt eased away before Roger let it go with a trembling hand. Paldric sheathed the sword before giving Roger a tight hug. Roger needed the moment to close his eyes. "I know this won't magically solve things, but we will have time away from the Dark Wizard to help you out, because you are too important to—"

There was a loud screech as the last dragon died. Paldric let go of his friend, looking around to make sure there wasn't an additional threat. Roger wanted to take the sword while the noise distracted Paldric, but didn't. Instead, he clenched his fist, holding back the fear. Paldric was right. He was stronger than this. The Dark Wizard may have frightened him for a bit, but he held on to the simple fact. Despite how badly the Dark Wizard wanted to make it seem like he didn't have a choice, he still did.

Theodemar approached, sheathing his sword. "We've got to get out of here. The plan—"

"Right." Alwin interrupted Theodemar to keep him from explaining it, even though he didn't understand why. "Theodemar, take Roger. I'll take Paldric. Both of them have been seriously weakened and we need to—"

"Is Venna alright?" This time, it was Paldric who cut off Alwin to keep him from explaining the plan. He didn't understand why, either. I played with his concern for Venna to keep the plan secret.

"We'll find out shortly. Let's go." Theodemar took Roger's arm and placed it over his shoulder before helping the man walk. Roger fell back into a familiar habit after a traumatic experience. He kept his face stoic as he let Theodemar lead him away. Paldric lifted his arm for Alwin to walk under. His side was smarting, but he didn't want to gasp. He would do his best to not let Roger feel guilty about his moment of weakness. Later, once this was all done, Tara would look at it. Once they implemented the plan, once they were safe. Then they could finish the wedding celebration.

Paldric was convinced Roger got the wedding idea from me, and he was equally convinced I didn't expect the Dark Wizard to come crash it. But more than any other characters, he trusted me that this was working toward my goals, whatever it was. And you're right, Paldric. We have four thousand words left. The women are safe. Roger still has a flicker of hope, and thankfully Paldric is the character who can help that flicker turn into a flame. This is going to work. We're going to make it.

We've got to.

Chapter Thirty-Four

MY PLAN IS REVEALED

Tara didn't dare get out of her dress until more elves were there to guard Milla. Sure, these elves hadn't chosen the path of the soldier, but there was strength in numbers. And they were also elves.

Lamira helped ease Tara out of the dress, as well as clean her cuts. Her bruises received lotion, and she wrapped her broken ribs with cloth soaked in healing ointment. Then Tara got back in her dress, just in case. It was the best armor she had available right now.

The group of humans and elves had grown since Tara slipped into a healer tent. She walked over to the group, searching the crowd for a familiar face. Any familiar face. Many were doing the same. Milla rushed over to Tara, afraid to squeeze her as tightly as she wanted. The blood on her starlight dress was a grim reminder. Cynthia flew over to Tara, resting in her hair again. Tara knelt to give Milla a tight hug. "I'm alright."

"They're not here yet." Fear made Milla's voice tremble.

"I know. But I assure you, they're doing everything they can to get here," Tara said.

"What if they don't make it? What if the dragons get them first? What if they—"

Tara let go of the little girl before placing hands on her shoulders. "Focus on what you can control. We have a plan, and right now, our job is to stay here and stay safe. Paldric and the others are working on their part of the plan, and we must trust they're doing what they can." Milla nodded, tears falling down her cheeks.

Another group of elves sprinted through the woods. With how quiet they ran, she didn't expect to see a hundred of them appearing out of the trees. Once again, Tara ran her eyes past the faces, trying to find someone familiar when her eyes rested on Venna. Tara picked up her skirt and moved through the crowd, her heart in her throat. Milla followed close behind. Tara wasn't sure if she should distract the little girl, as the news was still uncertain, but she wouldn't give a good enough excuse to satisfy Milla.

"Venna!" Tara called when she was close enough.

My lady elf turned, spotted Tara, and moved to get closer, her eyes widening. "Are you alright?"

Tara knew the state she was in. Blood, mud, and grass stains covered her dress, causing Venna to raise an eyebrow of concern. "I've tended to my wounds. The others? Do you have news?"

"I thought they'd be here by now." Venna looked toward the forest as her face fell. It might have been impossible for Tara and

Milla to notice. "Both dragons are dead. We need to implement the other part of the plan."

The heart that leapt to Tara's throat now began to pound. "Will they make it in time?"

Closing her eyes, Venna twitched her ears, trying to hear as far as she could. "It takes too long to set up, and we cannot risk the Dark Wizard and his cursed creatures escaping."

Tara hesitated, looking at the forest, wishing she could hear like an elf. She stayed silent so the other elves could listen. Venna turned her head ever so slightly to see if she could hear better this way.

Which is when she heard it, ever so faint, the sound of her husband. "Start it, Venna! Start it now, we're coming."

Venna opened her eyes, pointing to the protector elves. "Start the shield. Get it going. Understand we're not safe until the shield closes, and do not wait for anyone. All those who remain inside the shield understand the consequences."

The protector elves nodded, then began their work. They knelt and spread their hands, a thin beam of light appearing out of the first three before traveling to other elves in undisclosed locations. The beam circled around in a way I won't describe, so no one can know how big this will be.

Alright, Devin. It lasted longer than I thought, but my plan is revealed, which means Professor Andrews knows it now, too. We've got about three thousand words left, which is doable in one sitting, especially since it's toward the end of the book. Don't stop the device for longer than a minute. We give Professor Andrews no time to plan, no time to react. We go now, and we keep going until the book is finished. By my estimates, we'll be done by this afternoon. Ready? Perfect. Let's resume.

Oh, it never stopped. And recorded everything I said and... what I'm still saying. Alright, well great. It's a few words we don't have to worry about. Do you have the next scene ready to go, Devin?

Three thousand words, here we come.

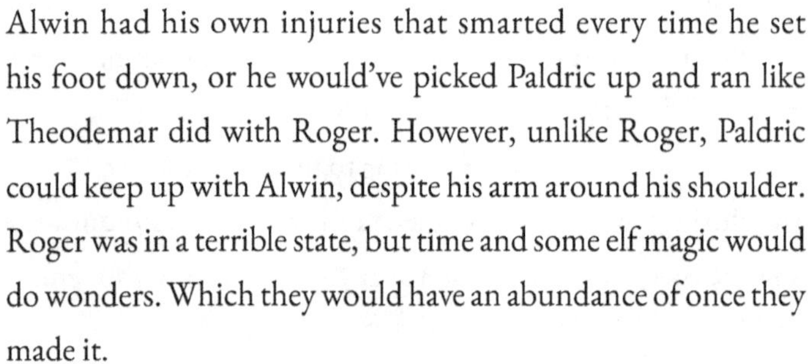

Alwin had his own injuries that smarted every time he set his foot down, or he would've picked Paldric up and ran like Theodemar did with Roger. However, unlike Roger, Paldric could keep up with Alwin, despite his arm around his shoulder. Roger was in a terrible state, but time and some elf magic would do wonders. Which they would have an abundance of once they made it.

"They're creating the shield now. We'll make it, as long as we keep going," Theodemar said.

My other characters nodded. Alwin wiped the blood from his nose as they weaved through the trees. The two elves grimaced at the crashing sound terrifyingly close. "What is that?" Paldric asked.

"Trolls. Coming fast. Run!" Theodemar said. They sprinted through the trees. Paldric let go of Alwin, as it was difficult to run fast while supporting someone. Roger was about ready to suggest Theodemar put him down so he could run, but he shook his head as soon as Roger sucked in air to speak. "I'm not setting you down. You cannot possibly run in your state."

"If you needed, you can leave me so you—"

"What is that human phrase you sometimes use?" Theodemar asked, cutting Roger off.

Which caused a confused frown to replace the injured frown on Roger's face. "Human phrase?"

"The one about shutting. That keeps people from talking. I heard you say it a few times to the others."

Roger fully opened his eyes, staring at Theodemar. "Shut up?"

"That is the one. Shut up, Roger."

He tried to smile, but it hurt. He simply closed his eyes, resigning himself to his fate. "You know, I don't think the others truly understand what it means, either."

The trolls didn't bother dodging smaller trees. They broke them down with their cudgels. Paldric developed a noticeable limp, but kept up with Alwin. Both of my characters were falling behind Theodemar, but they would still make it.

Three trolls crashed through the trees, splitting Alwin and Paldric from Roger and Theodemar. Theodemar turned, about ready to help, when Alwin motioned him away. "Go! Get Roger help! We'll be right behind you!"

He nodded and rushed ahead. Paldric and Alwin both pulled out their swords, preparing for another round of fighting. Since they had already defeated a dragon together, three trolls didn't seem nearly as daunting. The only thing that made them both anxious was knowing the elves already started the shield, and they had to kill these trolls and leave before it got too high.

A cudgel came down, and Alwin leapt into the trees as Paldric dodged the blow. Paldric strode forward and sliced off its hand with the sword. After fighting a dragon with its impossibly thick scales, making a clean slice startled him. The troll bellowed in rage. Despite the surprise before, Paldric wasted no time stabbing the troll's heart before dodging another cudgel. Alwin dropped from the trees on the second troll, stabbing it in the eye before using the momentum of the falling troll to leap onto the other, decapitating it before landing on the ground.

"Go, go, go." Alwin tried to hide the urgency in his voice. Paldric nodded, and the two set off again. Their old battlefield hardly receded when four more trolls followed behind. Alwin grabbed Paldric and forced him to drop as the troll threw a cudgel at them. It went flying, enough for Paldric to glance up and see the shield in the distance strengthening its base and beginning to grow.

They scrambled to their feet, holding their swords ready.

"They'll keep coming to hinder us from reaching the shield," Paldric said.

Alwin turned toward the trolls. "We take these trolls out, then you follow me, and we run in a more stealth-like manner. We can outwit these idiots."

Paldric nodded, trying to conserve his energy. The thought of fighting yet another group of trolls was exhausting, but he looked on the bright side. If everything went well, he wouldn't have to do this for the rest of his life.

Once again, Alwin leapt into the trees, and Paldric sprinted at the trolls with his sword. Not only were the trolls slow, but my main character had fought these creatures for so long he fell back into an old habit. Cut off hands, stab in the heart, move out of the way for the trolls to do something stupid before stabbing the other with the sword, and by the time he was done, Alwin had decapitated the remaining trolls and landed on the ground. My elf felt the same weariness. The non-stop fighting since the dragons broke through the shield was getting to him. But they were almost there. They could see the shield, building upon the base, weaving up dangerously high.

My two characters barely glanced at each other before sprinting toward the shield.

Chapter Thirty-Five
THE SHIELD CLOSES

Theodemar knew he'd have to climb a tree in order to get over the shield. He was still running at top speed, and Roger had his eyes closed tight, cursing the fact that the Dark Wizard tried to stab his leg. Not that it was the *only* thing keeping him from running right now, but he felt like a burden, and he hated it. To combat it, he held on to a simple truth. He was next in line for the throne, and he was out of the Dark Wizard's reach. The best revenge he could take on the evil god who created him was to live a good life, which is what he planned to do.

With a strength Roger could never understand, Theodemar climbed a tree one handed. He was halfway up before leaping off, cresting the shield and sliding down it. He landed on the grass with a group of healer elves around. "Take him. The Dark Wizard tortured him, but he has a strong mind."

The elves nodded as Theodemar handed Roger over. Roger tried to walk, but once the elves noticed the blood trickling from his leg, they lifted him up again. He was too exhausted to protest as they carried him to a tent.

Theodemar hardly had time to turn around before Tara was there. "Paldric? Alwin?"

"They were right behind me." Theodemar tried to search the forest past the shield. It wouldn't become truly transparent until it was complete, but Theodemar still searched for them. Lamira appeared, and Tara pointed her in the direction she saw the healer elves take Roger. Lamira said nothing, gathering her skirts to rush after them.

"Do you see them?" Tara's heart was once again pounding in her throat.

Theodemar said nothing, as he wasn't sure what to say.

Paldric and Alwin were busy sprinting for the shield. It was still uncomfortably far away, but they pushed forward with survival instincts. Another four trolls snarled right behind them, knocking down trees at a dangerous rate. Alwin once again cursed that he didn't have his bow. But honestly, who expected him to have his bow and arrow at a wedding?

They kept running; the shield kept climbing. If I could have played with the mechanics, I would have, but I'd already shown how the elves created the shield, and I couldn't mess with that without Professor Andrews poking holes in the entire thing. Both literally and figuratively. Kind of how I played with the mechanics of his own rule in my favor. If Professor Andrews allowed flashbacks, he would have been privy to my plan from the beginning. Would've seen Theodemar and Venna telling the other elves the plan before Theodemar rushed off to save

Paldric. Noticed Theodemar telling them the plan while Venna was destroying the dragon. Known that Tara was where her instincts told her to be when more elves came and revealed what they would do. And Professor Andrews would have noticed how none of the characters told Roger, just in case a link was created for him to know. Since I poked holes in his laws, he might have been able to poke holes in mine.

Six trolls appeared in front of Paldric and Alwin, blocking them from moving any more. The trolls chasing them appeared from behind, circling around them. Alwin pointed toward the thick tree and the two of them climbed up it as fast as possible as the trolls descended on it. The tree was thicker than the ones they'd knocked down. It would hopefully take them a few moments to figure out what to do. But at this point, Alwin and Paldric were already leaping from tree to tree while the trolls stayed behind. Alwin didn't dare climb down, but Paldric wasn't as nimble in the trees.

They approached the shield when Alwin saw it. The criss-crossing lines were farther than either of them could jump. Farther, even, than the trees. It would only get faster from here, from what he'd studied on the path of the protector. They were close, but not close enough.

Paldric ran into him, then looked past his shoulder. The shield was too high. They weren't fast enough. Paldric took a second to realize what this meant. The consequences they both agreed to. They'd be stuck here with the cursed creatures. They would most likely die with how many trolls there were down there. They *needed* to die, so the Dark Wizard couldn't get to them.

My main character met my elf's gaze, the gruesome realization hitting them both at the same time. Paldric pulled out his sword, as did Alwin. They might as well go out guns blazin'.

Alwin placed a hand on Paldric's shoulder, smiling. "I will see you in the database." Paldric nodded, steeling himself for the battle ahead, when Alwin tightened his grip over Paldric's shirt and threw him.

The wind ruffled Paldric's hair and clothes as he soared, so startled he dropped his weapon. He passed over the forming shield as it continued to weave. Out of desperation, Paldric grabbed the outside of the shield as he slid down, trying to get a hold. He fell into the arms of the elves when he finally gasped. "Alwin! No!"

Paldric panted as the elves dragged him away from the shield as it finished weaving, solidifying before it turned transparent.

The trolls sensed an elf and sniffed before giving a roar. Alwin dropped from the trees, holding his sword ready. Fifty more trolls broke down the trees to his left, holding their cudgels ready, and there were still a few goblins, screaming as they went after him. Alwin did not wait. He ran after them, making himself the biggest threat they knew so they would kill him. Trolls and goblins fell at his sword. Goblins stabbed at him, and he deflected them as best as possible. A shadow soldier kicked him hard in the gut, and one goblin stabbed his stomach, the armor bending. He barely had time to react before a troll came down with his cudgel and...

I can't describe it. I'm sorry. I can't.

Theodemar saw the whole thing, his eyes sorrowful. My main character tried to get out of the elves' grip, wanting to run into a shield he knew would never break. Back to his friend. "Alwin! Alwin!"

Tara ran to him, tears in her eyes as the elves let go. Paldric was on his feet, gasping as he clutched his side, staring at the shield with wide eyes as hurt played across his face. Alwin had thrown him. Despite just discovering his family, despite being among his own kind for the first time in his life, Alwin sacrificed himself.

A sob shuddered through Paldric's body before it cracked his heart. There were too many emotions going on. He couldn't narrow it down. He was overwhelmed with everything. Tara hugged him, and he grabbed her, feeling her next to him.

The Dark Wizard walked through the forest, closer to the shield wall, trying to look regal. But he'd been beaten. Milla gasped, backing away as Venna picked her up, pulling out her sword again to protect the child in the off chance the shield wasn't enough. The Dark Wizard glared at them all, but particularly at Paldric. Paldric wiped his eyes before straightening.

The vile man's gaze was not pleasant, because he had to know he'd lost. "You think you've won? You think this is it? My trolls have captured Alwin and will now torture him unless you bring down the shield and come get him."

"No, they haven't." Theodemar placed an arm on Paldric's shoulder. "I watched it. He's gone."

My main character closed his eyes and nodded. It was enough. A strange peace filled him, even as his grief was indescribable. Alwin was gone, but not forever. My only character that trusted me even when I didn't trust myself understood that he'd see his friend again. He'd see him a lot sooner than he realized, but I don't want to minimize Paldric's grief.

Despite the elves moving away from the Dark Wizard, and the soldier elves keeping their swords out, Paldric took a few steps closer, staring at the villain of this story. "I pity you, sir. I truly do."

"Don't be a hero."

"Hatred became your prison more than this shield. This hate kept you from doing incredible things with your powers. We could have worked well together, but you chose hate. Now you are stuck in this cage for the rest of eternity." Paldric backed away as the Dark Wizard glared at him. "Goodbye, sir. I am quite confident we will never meet again."

He took Tara's hand before turning around and limping toward a healer's tent. Tara rubbed his arm, already checking his outer wounds, aware of the mental wounds Paldric would carry.

You know what, Professor? Just pretend I told you what Paldric told the Dark Wizard. You can no longer hurt me.

Chapter Thirty-Six

WE WRAP UP THE TRILOGY

The sun was hours away from setting when the elves, humans, fairies, and nymphs made their way to Vaywell, the Port City. It looked different from when they left it. The smoldering ashes destroyed rooftops, and some left over foundation crumbled to the ground. There were deep scars on the roads from cudgels and scratch marks from the cursed creatures. It looked like a mess, but Roger smiled when he saw it. "I've never seen a more beautiful sight."

Venna gave him a look, worried about his mental state, but Paldric understood. The cursed creatures were gone. Despite the scars and pain and anguish, time would do wonders to Vaywell, the Port City. And now, time is what they had. Not only time, but the elves had returned. With a few decades, Vaywell could return to its former glory.

The people spread throughout Vaywell, making a plan. Tomorrow would be a busy rebuilding day. Sort through the ashes and crumbling concrete. Sort through the loss. The pain.

Paldric stepped onto the beach, listening to the waves lapping on the sand as it always had. This beach was full of memories for him, many of them painful now. Tara took his hand, leaning her head against his shoulder. "This will hurt for a while," Paldric said.

"And I wish I could heal it for you. As with all wounds, it'll just take time," Tara said.

He squeezed her hand, looking at the horizon. "Just stay by my side. You are an exceptional healer."

She tried to smile but found that today she couldn't. Maybe tomorrow it would be easier, but for now, she rested her head against Paldric. "I will never leave you. We're officially married now."

His lips brushed the top of her head. "Yes. We are."

Roger and Milla approached with candles, the proper remembrance ceremony for those who had passed on. As Paldric allowed Roger to light his candle, he looked among the ashes of Vaywell and saw it for what it was. Destroyed. Burned. Darkening with the setting sun.

But then he saw the candles of others beginning to light. Saw the flicker of hope it represented, keeping the darkness back. There was much destruction and pain revealed in the flickering light of the lost, but tomorrow would come. Tomorrow, they would clean up. Plant flowers, trees, fields. Create a new heart of the forest close to Vaywell. Crown Roger as the rightful king of

Veniloria, in a party that would undoubtably last weeks. Spread the message to other towns to make sure they understood the elves trapped the Dark Wizard once again. They would reunite the families. They would be together soon. Yes, the country was broken, but they now had the time and determination to fix it.

Paldric walked forward, shielding his light from the ocean breeze when he noticed it, just where the burnt charcoal met the sand. He brushed aside the ash and saw a tiny bud reaching toward the sky.

Epilogue: Do Epilogues Have Chapter Titles?

Hi everyone. Gunther here, writing on an old laptop to give you an epilogue of sorts. I guess you could consider this the author's notes. This may surprise you (or not), but I'm not writing this from my parent's basement. I have my own place now. Though they visit me enough, I might as well have them live in mine.

Despite me saying constantly in the books how much this trilogy would never get published, clearly it must have, since you have a copy in your hands. I'm using this epilogue to explain why. Professor Andrews still has quite a lot of power, despite what's happened to him. Vince came to me about a year ago, asking if I would consider publishing this trilogy. He wanted to help people understand Professor Andrews better and the lengths he would go to hurt other narrators. I said no. Firmly, too. Although I could see my characters again, a part of me refused to allow it. If you gave me a choice between letting the world read my journal from the eighth grade or this trilogy, I'd be going to conferences promoting my eighth-grade self to the masses. I don't like who I was in this trilogy. I was a jerk. Insensitive. Awkward. A borderline rapist. Not a God at all. Yes, it also showed how vile Professor Andrews had been, but I feel like this story was mostly about my shortcomings, and I don't like that. Besides, the world already has Junior's account of what happened. I didn't think they'd need mine.

But people kept demanding my story. I was one of the few successful stories, and they wanted to know what happened. And I also missed my characters. I wanted to see if they were okay. Well, yeah, of course they were okay, but I wanted to interact with them again. They're like my family. It took about six months after Vince asked, but I agreed, as long as I would only be referred to as Gunther. The publicity of the whole thing has made me happy I chose a different name, and I'm glad people respected my privacy. It's helped keep my public and private life separate.

I'd also like to answer a few frequently asked questions. The first one is, I *know* book one didn't end at exactly eighty thousand words. And this book doesn't end at exactly seventy thousand. It did, once. But right before it got published, the device does a final edit, and apparently, I mumble, stutter, and ramble a lot more than what was already shown. It cut it down considerably. What can I say? The device is a powerful tool.

Which brings me to the next question. Am I going to narrate more novels? The answer is no. Well, yes, and no. I'll write more stories, as I always have new ideas of what to write, but my experience with the device has opened my eyes. I don't want to shame anyone for using a device, but I've learned it isn't for me. There are too many questions about it still, and we use it like we know all the answers. We have stumbled upon incredible power, and I know how dangerous it is to think you're God. That, and I can't look at someone narrating a device without panicking. I'm still working on it with Dr. Webb.

The next most frequent question I get asked is the timeline between mine and Junior's story. The beginning of hers took place while I was wrapping up mine. Jim was gone a lot more during our recording sessions, so I was mostly with Devin and Dr. Webb in the recording room, and sometimes Grace. They didn't allow me to narrate without at least two people there. The device Professor Andrews gave me for book three was his own prototype, which meant I had to narrate at least a thousand words once a week instead of once a month, or else my story would end up in limbo. The first few weeks were hard, and though I never got used to it, I got better at handling it. It was such a relief when I finished.

The final frequent question I get asked the most is how I reacted to Junior's big twist in her story. No, I'm not answering that here. There's an unspoken code among narrators to never prematurely reveal the twist ending of another narrator's story. If you haven't read Junior's story yet, then I won't break that code. Also, go read it. Junior is a great narrator, far better than I was at her age. It's a pity what happened to her.

As vague as I dare be about the twist, just know I went from seeing Dr. Webb twice a month to seeing her almost daily once I'd heard. I'm still seeing Dr. Webb way more often than I'd like. As much as I want to put this experience behind me, I've still got years of therapy ahead of me.

Finally, I will answer the question I'll assume will become a frequently asked question once this story hits the world. And that is, who is Andrea. With her permission, I'll let you in on our dating history.

It was soon after I woke up. Physical therapy was a beast, and I was managing to walk for the first time (with a ton of help, still). Grace had checked in on me, asking me how I was doing before she suggested I take my mind off things. She reminded me of the tea party invitation, and I agreed. I was in a terrible state, constantly paranoid, struggling with adjusting to a life of not being God, and a tea party seemed innocent enough. So, I met Grace's granddaughter, Nora. She was nervous at first, since I was still struggling to be a human, but she had an enormous heart and an active imagination. I could barely keep up with the stories she told, but they made me smile for the first time in a while. It was also the first time I met Andrea, Grace's daughter, when she came to pick up Nora. I noticed the very large wedding ring on her finger right off. So, Nora left with her mother, with a promise of another tea party next week.

Next week came, and there was Nora. I kept up with her imagination, playing along with the stuffed animals, having our tea and making sure Bunbun never sat next to Neffles because of their inability to cooperate in these settings. Andrea came to pick her up again, and Grace suggested we keep going, as she noticed Nora's tea parties were literally the only times I smiled in those two weeks.

Once a week soon became twice a week. The tea parties lasted longer, and Andrea started joining them since Grace needed to do her Guardian duties. During one of them, Andrea told me how impressed she was that I kept up with her daughter's stories. I shrugged, saying it was an occupational hazard, which made her laugh really weirdly. Like, really weird, before giving me a gentle push. And then she got worried she'd pushed me too hard because I was still in physical therapy, but I assured her I was fine.

I'd like to emphasize for the record here, she still had a ring on her finger, so yes, I was unaware she was flirting with me. I assumed married women playfully shove people.

Okay, Jim, I will admit it in writing. I don't know how women flirt. Happy?

In one of my sessions with Dr. Webb, I casually mentioned the tea party when she asked how I felt about relationships. I told her my relationship with Nora was great, that we were good friends, and I enjoyed setting time aside to focus on more innocent things. Dr. Webb said it was great, but she more meant romantic relationships with Andrea. The conversation turned awkward, as I didn't know how I felt about a therapist suggesting I start a relationship with a married woman. I tried to explain this when Dr. Webb waved her hand and informed me that Grace's daughter divorced a month before Nora was born. She was under the impression that I already knew this and apologized for bringing it up. She changed the subject, but I said nothing intelligible for the rest of the session.

Soon after, I confronted Grace, who admitted her nefarious plot, and how she'd been trying to set her daughter up a lot. And then I called Jim, asking him if he knew about it, which he said he did and was just happy to watch from a distance. When I asked him why he didn't bother telling me she was divorced, he said, and I quote, "I wanted you to interact with her for a good long while before you found out she was available."

So, at the next tea party, when Grace took Nora to get a drink, I asked Andrea about why she was wearing a ring. Andrea admitted her mother often set her up on dates, and she was tired of it. Her mother setting her up with a man coming out of a coma was a new low, so when she figured out Grace never told me she was single, she put a ring on her finger to deter me. But she regretted doing that the more she got to know me. As she was telling me all this, she slipped the ring off her finger. So I asked her on a date where we could go to an adult tea party.

We've been dating ever since. She's great. The kind of person where being with her on a quiet evening gives me the same thrill as a daring adventure. It gives me a lot of hope for the future. I love being mundane with her, and she loves my stories. I'm a lucky guy.

That's it. Thanks for reading my trilogy. I'm getting this epilogue sent off to Vince now, and then I'm driving to the headquarters and will enter the database for a visit. I'm sure it will surprise my characters when they see me. Paldric and Milla will probably be the first to give me hugs. It'll be a race between the two of them, I'm sure. I'll only give Tara a high five and let her know about Andrea. Roger will most likely give me a hug, and I'm curious to know what kind of life in paradise he and Lamira are living. Alwin might not hate me anymore. I hope so, because I'm going to give him the biggest hug and will never let go until that grumpy teenager elf accepts it.

Sure, there's a lot of speculation about how it all might happen, but I'm confident that's how it'll go. After all, I did create them.

The End

Acknowledgements

As always, thank you, my dear little family. Thank you for understanding I need to write. For your support, for giving me time away, for taking over some of my responsibilities so I can unwind by writing stories. I could not have completed a trilogy without you. I love you!

To my fans on Royal Road, thank you. Your suggestions and encouragement were uplifting. Having you cheering me on with every chapter was a great boost of encouragement, and I wouldn't have made it this far without knowing many of you already loved Gunther and his characters.

Thank you to Getpremades.com for an awesome cover. And thanks to emach55 for the maps.

Last of all goes to the person and/or people who played a huge part in getting this story out there. I will remember who you are by name the nanosecond I hit the publish button. Then I will go whack my forehead against the wall at my sheer stupidity. But you, dear person, are the best, and this trilogy could have never existed without you!

About the Author

Ellen Taylor enjoys living with her husband and three boys, and also enjoys living in her head. She writes in her spare time, because sometimes she needs to be in control of chaos. Follow her on Facebook or Instagram for updates on future books at Ellen Taylor Books.

ALSO BY

Narrator Universe

I Suck at Titles

I Still Suck at Titles

The Altered Manuscript